Promoted Beyond Glory

Afterlife

Published by RFI Technical Services

http://pub.rfi.net

Copyright © Stuart Pitsligo 2016

All rights reserved. This book may not be reproduced in any form, in whole or in part, without written permission from the author.

ISBN: 9-780-9572432-9-3

Promoted Beyond Glory

Afterlife

by

Stuart Pitsligo

Chapter 1

Nathalie's car struck the ice-covered lake with a jarring crash, slamming her into the steering wheel and plunging her car deep into the frigid water. Darkness seemed to envelope her almost instantly as the headlights flickered once and then went out, leaving her trapped and alone.

Without hesitating she reached out to open the windows knowing she had to escape, but without equalising the pressure she'd never get the doors open. She hit the switch for the electric windows only to find that the power had died with her headlights and the windows remained tightly shut. She began to hit the windows with her open palm, slamming the whole force of her arm against it and trying to smash it. Again and again she hit it, screaming in anger and fear with each blow, but time and time again the glass failed to yield.

But the water found its own way in. Jets of it erupted from behind the dashboard, from under her feet, from every corner of the car, spraying her and chilling her to the bone with its icy touch. The jets hit her all over, on her legs, on her arms, even in her face. Each one that struck seemed to suck more and more life out of her, sapping her strength and her will to fight. She fought to stay focused, waiting for the creeping chill of the water to rise high enough to let her open the door and escape.

Finally, as the water reached her waist, she decided it was time to make her move. She grabbed the door handle but nothing happened, not a sound or any movement from the door. She cursed her habit of locking the doors for protection, realising that the central locking had trapped her and could now claim her life. As the water rose higher and higher, and her despair increased, the cold seemed to numb her, to slow her wits and make her think it would be easier to just relax, to accept it.

Nathalie would not give up so easily. She slammed her whole weight against the door, initially with determination, then with fear and finally with a rising sense of panic as the water rose higher.

The thud of the car hitting the bottom of the lake shook her out of her panic and she began to think more clearly. The car was pointed down, the air in the rear holding the back end up and Nathalie knew that's where her only hope lay.

Slipping out of her seatbelt she scrambled to the back seat where she tore off the parcel shelf at the back of the car. She rummaged around with her hands, trying to find something to break the glass with, but she found nothing. A creaking and snapping sound rose from somewhere behind the dashboard and the water begin to rise sharply. She knew she only had seconds left and panic returned. She began to splash around in terror, screaming for help. With her face pressed against the last pocket of air in the car, hard against the glass of the rear window, she could do nothing but take a deep breath as the last of the air left the car, leaving her freezing, drowning and alone. Within seconds everything went dark, and she was cold no longer.

When Nathalie awoke, it was an awakening like no other that she had known. A warmth seemed to surround her, wrapping her in contentment and bringing her a feeling of utter bliss. Even with her eyes still closed she could see the bright, white light that enveloped her, adding an extra layer of comforting contrast to the icy darkness she had last known.

Then awareness of her surroundings began. She was lying down, yet she felt nothing underneath her, no force supporting her of any kind. She felt as if she were floating in infinity, wrapped in this calm, soothing and warming light.

Then sounds came to her. They were initially distant, almost like an echo, but slowly they took shape and became recognisable. First it was shouts, the sound of people exclaiming loudly, their fears, their elations. Then came screams, loud and terrible and Nathalie's eyes snapped open and she sat up.

Screams in the distance gave way to laughter as she looked around her. The light had no apparent source, but she was clouded in haze, a mist that thickened around the ground, obscuring whatever it was that supported her and hiding whatever was happening in the distance.

Two men stood above her, they were clad in white robes and both smiled a bland, forced smile of false reassurance. As a doctor she recognised the smile, she'd used it a hundred times when giving patients news they'd rather not hear.

"Welcome Nathalie," one of them said.

"Where am I?" she asked as she stood up and looked around. Through the mist she saw faint outlines, people of all ages around her, waking and emerging from the haze, all with two men with them clad in the same white robes. She watched them as they were led away by their pair of robed men, each offering the same false reassurance as hers did.

"There's no easy way to say it," said one of the men.

"You're dead," said the other, seemingly finishing the first's sentence.

"Dead? What the hell do you mean dead?" barked Nathalie in response.

"Think back," said one man.

"What's the last thing you remember?" finished the other.

"I crashed my car into a lake. I was under the ice." The reality of her situation hit Nathalie as her memory returned. Could this be it? Could she be dead? As she looked around, her brain desperately searched for an answer. Hallucinations? Drugs?

"Accept it, you have passed over," said one of the men. Nathalie, struggling to find some other kind of answer to her situation, decided to accept it for the time being.

"Who are you?" she asked, not really comprehending the answers they were giving.

"Well, that's a little complicated," said one of them.

"But I suppose in your culture 'angels' would be the best word to describe us," finished the other.

"What the hell are you talking about? I'm not dead, I'm here, I'm alive."

"And where is here?" asked the angel. Nathalie looked around and realised she could give him no answer.

"So what now?" she asked.

"Follow us."

"We'll take you for processing."

"Processing? I'm not sure I like the sound of that."

"It's where we evaluate your life," an angel said.

"Don't worry, as long as you've loved your god you'll be fine."

"Bollocks..." said Nathalie, her heart sinking.

"You as well?" came a voice from behind her. Nathalie turned to see a young man standing behind her, flanked by two angels. "I think I walked in front of a car, at least that's what I assume happened."

"I crashed my car," she replied, "right into a lake."

"My name's Paul," the man said.

"You seem pretty calm for a man who just died," said Nathalie.

"So do you," he replied.

Nathalie paused for a moment and tilted her head slightly as she realised he was right. She was dead. Why wasn't she reacting? She closed her eyes and for an instant felt a flicker of apprehension before opening them again. "It's the light," she said.

"The light?"

"Close your eyes and you'll see what I mean. You'll get a brief surge of fear, then it'll dissipate. I guess it has some kind of calming effect."

"Please, follow us," an angel interrupted before Paul could respond.

"Lead the way," said Paul. The angels did as he suggested and Nathalie, Paul and the four angels walked together through the mist.

"Are you worried?" Nathalie asked.

"A little," he replied. "Are you?"

"You know, by any reasonable accounts I've lived a good life," Nathalie replied. "I mean, I'm a doctor, I work in a hospital trying to help people, but I'm not sure if that's enough here."

"You an atheist?" Paul asked.

"Yes, and you?" replied Nathalie. Paul nodded.

"I've always found religion a little sinister to be honest," he said, "usually a lot of bullshit about controlling people and taking their money."

"I've never had any time for it either," Nathalie added. "All a load of ancient myths and legends people pretend have something to do with the real world."

"Well, I don't know about you, but I'm starting to get seriously worried one of the religions might actually have been right."

"Worrying, isn't it?" Nathalie replied. "Not many gods are known to be too kind to those who reject them."

"Let's hope being a good person counts for something, regardless of what these guys told us," Paul said.

The angels led them through the haze to a clearing where people were lining up in their hundreds. Nathalie realised this must be all the people in the world that had just died. Staggered at their sheer numbers, she looked around, seeing all ages, all races of people lining up before her.

"We get about a hundred a minute," said one of the angels.

"On average that is," another continued, "we have the occasional glut, natural disasters, that kind of thing."

"A hundred a minute," Nathalie said as she contemplated the scale of death in the world. She had dealt with death every day of her career, but never had she realised what the numbers actually meant. Now she could see it all around her. Men, women and children of all colours, all creeds even all ages. The old, the young, the rich and the poor, all equal in death, taking their place in the line to be judged.

"We're running a little late just now," one of the angels said, apologetically.

"Yes, there's been a suicide bombing in Afghanistan, a big one. A few hundred arrived all at once."

"See, there's one of the bombers there." The angel pointed to a figure at the head of the queue, an Arabic man with his clothes torn to shreds.

"I'm sure he'll get in," said another angel.

"Get in where?" Paul asked.

"Why, to Heaven of course."

"Suicide bombers get to Heaven?" Nathalie yelled in astonishment.

"Well of course they do. They may not be Catholic, they're not even Christians, but their hearts are in the right place."

"Catholic?" said Nathalie in disbelief.

"Oh dear, that one wasn't baptised," said one of the angels

gesturing at the small child who stood at the front of the queue, "and his parents aren't even believers."

"He'll be going downstairs then," said an angel. Both men giggled slightly.

"WHAT!" screamed Paul. "A suicide bomber goes to heaven but a small child goes to Hell? What the fuck is wrong with you people?"

Nathalie noticed the child's clothes were in shreds, just like the suicide bomber's had been. "Wait a minute," she said, "was that child killed in the bombing?"

"Looks like it."

"And he goes to burn in hell while his killer gets into heaven?" snapped Nathalie, her nostrils flaring with anger as she was scarcely able to believe what she was hearing.

"The rules are the rules," was the only justification her companions could give her. "Muslims are a little misguided, but if they are truly devoted in their love of their Allah, then God considers that worthy. Same with the Jews and most other Christians."

"Yes," began another angel, "it's only the lapsed, or the unbeliever who has to worry."

"But what about living a good life," asked Nathalie, "being honest and decent, being..."

"Oh that stuff," interrupted one of the angels, stifling a laugh. "All very nice I suppose, but that's only being good to others. You're not being good to God with that."

"Oh shit," said Nathalie, her anger quickly turning to fear at the realisation that avoiding the fires of hell could now be a substantial challenge. All she could do was wait her turn.

Ahead of her she could hear a man having his life evaluated by another man, seemingly an angel, clad in the same robes as her companions. She heard a mention of rape, of murder, details of a brutal and savage life. But then there was a deathbed conversion, and his evaluator told him he was admitted to heaven. The murderer and rapist was gestured to walk past his evaluator and he did as he was told, vanishing into the mist. At the same time another child, possibly another bombing victim judging from his torn clothes, screamed as a flame consumed him. Five years old and unbaptised meant an eternity in hell.

"Your turn," an angel said to Paul. Nathalie grasped Paul's hand and squeezed it for a second, then released it as Paul stepped forward. He instantly felt the gaze of the evaluator on him and he waited, shaking slightly with fear of his judgement. The evaluator held the gaze for a few seconds before shaking his head with a wicked smile.

"Oh dear," said the evaluator, and Paul was consumed by a tongue of fire that emerged, wreathed in smoke from the mist around them. Nathalie heard Paul scream before it faded to silence and the fire withered to nothingness.

Now it was her turn and she braced herself for her fate.

"Now, let's see what you've been up to," said her evaluator. She waited for him to say something else, but he paused, staring long into her eyes. "Or not as the case may be," he said. "You're going back."

"Back? What do you mean back?" said Nathalie, but there was no answer. A dizziness took her, and everything went blank again.

Waking up the second time round was a slower, more painful process for Nathalie. She was aware of noises, words she was somehow familiar with but that she couldn't place. An elusive buzz of energy hung in the air around her; she could hear it, almost taste it.

A dull light overwhelmed her eyes when she first opened them. Hanging above her, surrounded by shadows, it seemed to draw her in, holding her attention. Once again she felt peaceful, encased in some protection by this mad energy that enveloped her.

"Nathalie, can you hear me?" The voice somehow seemed familiar. It came from one side, but when she tried to turn her head she found she couldn't move. Unaware of anything, she simply lay there, deciding to accept her fate, to wait and let it happen to her, rather than reach out to it.

"Nathalie, blink your eyes if you can hear me," came the voice again. She blinked several times in response. The voice seemed familiar, yet still her understanding of her environment eluded her.

"Nathalie, it's Steven here, Doctor Steven Parker, you're in hospital." That didn't make any sense to Nathalie. She was dead, why would she be in hospital in the afterlife? And why was her boss here as well?

"You've been in a car crash Nathalie, you're not badly injured, but your car went into a frozen lake and you have hypothermia."

Nathalie wasn't sure if she was happy or sad to find out she was still alive. The divide between life and death suddenly seemed to feel less important to her and in her half awake state she simply didn't care enough about the difference to warrant a reaction. Instead she lay there, waiting for whatever was to come next. Would she die again? Would she live? And which did she want? All she could do was lie back and wait.

She waited for a day drifting in and out of consciousness before she finally accepted she was alive.

"How long was I out for?" was her first question when Steven, the head of her department, came to see her.

"We're not sure how long you were in the water, but it took us over an hour to get your heart started again. Luckily someone saw your headlights as you went through the ice, otherwise you might still be down there." The details seemed inconsequential to Nathalie. She had bigger issues to discuss.

"Steven, Did anything happen?" she asked. She had no idea what answer she was looking for but she had to ask.

"Such as?" Steven asked in response.

"I don't know," she replied, "I can't explain..." Her sentence tailed off as she struggled to find the right words. "I had...something, something happened," was all she could think of. Steven looked at her quizzically.

"You mean the crash?" he asked.

"No, after that, after I died." Steven raised his eyebrows at her choice of words.

"You didn't die," he said. "Your heart stopped, you were almost frozen, but you survived, you're here, safe and well now."

"Am I?" she asked. "Am I really?" The prospect of eternal

damnation for being who she was didn't make her feel like she'd ever be safe and well again.

"You're going to be fine, just rest and get better." Steven replied, oblivious to her problems. "I'll be back to check on you later." He got up as if to leave the room. Suddenly Nathalie dreaded the thought of being left alone.

"Steven, stay, please," said Nathalie. "There's something I need to tell you."

"What?" he replied, sitting down by her bed.

"Something happened when I was dead."

"You weren't dead Nathalie, your heart stopped. You survived."

"Whatever you call it," she replied, "something happened. I went somewhere." Steven gave her a puzzled look. "Call it an out of body experience or whatever you want, but I have to tell someone about it."

"What did you see, the treatment room?" asked Steven, ready with a number of counter arguments to demonstrate to Nathalie she had merely hallucinated. He was unprepared for what followed.

"Was there a suicide bombing about the time I crashed, a big one?"

"Biggest one for years, over a hundred people. How the hell did you know that?"

"Because I saw them. I saw a bomber and the victims line up to get into Heaven or Hell." Steven stared at her wide eyed in amazement as she continued. "And the bomber got into Heaven. And a child he killed went to Hell."

"What are you talking about?"

"The afterlife, it's all true. Believe in God no matter what your faith and you go to Heaven regardless of what you do. I saw a murderer who repented as he died go to Heaven while good people went to Hell just because they didn't believe."

"Nathalie, I've been a Christian all my life and I know that God isn't like that," he replied, "he loves humanity, he wouldn't do that."

"Well think again, he's not what you've been told, but you don't have to worry, do you?"

"What happened to you, were you judged? Where were you going?" Steven asked, not sounding even slightly convinced by Nathalie's story.

"Well, I can guess where I would have gone, but I never got that far. I was about to be judged, then I heard your voice telling me I'd been in a crash." Steven eyes were a mix of scepticism and compassion. He reached out and took her hand.

"You've been working in emergency medicine long enough to know how the brain does strange stuff sometimes," he said, "and you were in a pretty bad way. You can't think it actually happened."

"Then how did I know about the suicide bombing? An angel even commented on how busy they were because of it." Steven had no answer.

"Try to get some rest" he said, deflecting the question. "We'll talk about it later."

"Yes, come back and tell me I'm crazy later," she said dismissively. Steven, uncomfortable with what she had to say, quickly left. Nathalie, alone with her thoughts, lay back and closed her eyes, hoping to drift off into a deep sleep and wake without the memory that now haunted her.

Waking brought no relief to Nathalie. Steven had spoken to the hospital chaplain, and he was there, waiting by her bed when her eyes opened. Her heart sank when she saw him, not because she didn't like him, quite the opposite, Father McIntosh had always been a good friend to all the staff. It was just she knew what was coming next. She had heard his words of religious comfort given to families a thousand times and she was in no mood for it.

"I hear you've been through some rough times," Father McIntosh said in his usual warm yet slightly detached voice.

"Where about, in this world or the next?"

He smiled at her words, but didn't say anything for a few seconds. "Oh, I don't think you'll have any problem in the next world," he said eventually. "You're a good person, you work hard helping people."

"No, that doesn't work," she said. "I have to believe in God, to worship him or I burn in Hell."

"God isn't like that."

"Don't tell me what he is or isn't like," she replied almost with a bark, "I saw it, I saw him send children to Hell. Why would he do that?"

"Nathalie," he replied, his voice sounding more and more patronising with each word, "I don't know what you saw, but I assume you..."

"No, don't assume me," she said cutting him off mid-sentence. "Just tell me this. What if I'm right? Let's just pretend I did see the gates of Heaven. What possible reason is there for what I saw?"

"If you did see Heaven, then what you say would disturb me," he replied. "But if you do believe that is what you saw, then I would counsel you to have some faith in our Lord, and not to question God's will." Nathalie could see that somewhere, deep down, Father McIntosh rather liked the idea of unbelievers being treated this way.

"So I should just shut up, and do as God tells me?"

Father McIntosh just nodded. Nathalie turned over, facing away from him. She just wanted him to go away and he took the hint.

"You know where to find me," he said as he left, "if you want to talk."

Now Nathalie was alone. She curled up into a ball, hoping in vain for sleep to take her while she contemplated her future.

It wasn't long before she was joined by Steven. Her heart seemed to sink slightly as he walked into the room.

"Feeling better?" he asked as he sat down beside her.

"No, not really," she replied.

"Still dwelling on your dream?"

"Dream? I told you, it wasn't a dream."

"You should look at this rationally," said Steven.

"What else do you think I've done?" Nathalie asked.

"Well, let's consider if it was a hallucination," he continued, ignoring her comment. "Near death experiences are common, and the human brain plays all kind of tricks when it isn't working properly."

"But how could I be right about the suicide bomb? I'd love it to be a dream or some other trick of my mind, but I just can't explain that."

"Did you have the radio on when you crashed?"

"No, I never listen to the radio, always music."

"Could you have heard a news report here before you left?"

"I might have done but I don't remember it."

"That could be it."

"But we don't know I did, so let's consider for a minute it was real."

Steven shuffled uncomfortably in his chair. "But it can't be," he said.

"Just indulge me, okay?"

Steven nodded reluctantly before she continued.

"So what was the place I went to? It was full of religious images, of angels and judgements, with dead people being sent onto their new lives."

"Nathalie, it can't have been real."

"Why not?"

"Because how many years have doctors been bringing people back from the dead? Countless years of heart operations, of drownings, of all kinds of accident victims coming back to life after their hearts have stopped and we've never heard of anything like this before. What makes you so different?"

"Maybe the memory fades really quickly, like a dream?" she said. "Even when you wake you can remember the dream, but the memory goes so quickly. The aftermath of a cardiac arrest isn't exactly the best of times for people, so maybe they forget."

"So why didn't you?"

"I don't know, maybe I was some one-in-a-million case where I somehow remembered, maybe something happened that triggered the memory, helped me keep it." Steven didn't look convinced. "I'm also young, cardiac arrests are more common in older people, maybe my brain or memory are somehow stronger."

"So out of all the cardiac arrests that have been reversed in history, you're the first to remember this amazing experience?"

"It wasn't amazing, it was horrible."

"Then it can't be Heaven you saw, Heaven isn't like that. It must have been a dream."

"That's circular logic," she snapped, "and you know better to try that with me."

"Okay, okay," he replied defensively, "so how do we resolve this?"

"How about this one?" she said. "Check the time of my arrival on my notes." Nathalie gestured at the folder by her bed.

"What does that tell us?"

"Do you have your phone?"

"Yes," Steven replied as he took it out of his pocket.

"Then pull up a news story from the web about the bombing, find the time it happened, then compare it with my notes."

"Ah, okay," he said as he began his search. A few moments passed before he found what he was looking for.

"Have you got it?"

"The website lists it as 7.17am GMT, so if we check that with your notes..." he said before pausing to check for her arrival time. His jaw dropped open when he found it.

"What was it?" she asked.

"7.16am," he replied, the shock obvious in his voice. "You were dead when it happened."

"So unless I'm a terrorist mastermind who knew all about it, then I went to the afterlife." Steven stood up and stared at Nathalie. The colour had drained from his face.

"No, no, it can't be," he said as he backed off before turning and leaving the room without another word.

A sense of inner calm came almost instantly to Nathalie. She knew now the experience was real, and for her it was just a first step. She was desperate to know more.

As she decided to go with the working theory that the memory of it fades rapidly, Nathalie found herself smiling as a realisation came to her. Here she was, perhaps not the first person to have had such an experience, but perhaps the first person to figure out what she saw and be in a position to question cardiac arrest survivors early enough to help them remember.

She slept soundly that night. The first piece of the puzzle had fallen into place.

Chapter 2

It was several weeks before she returned to work, by now the worst of winter had passed and the first hint of spring greeted Nathalie as she arrived outside the hospital. Snowdrops were already flowering in the beds by the main entrance and there was a sweetness to the air that made Nathalie feel alive once again.

Walking in through the door she encountered the familiar chaos of the department. Waiting patients, harassed staff and the grim hospital dcor instantly made her feel at home again and ready to get started. She was missing the work, the daily challenge of fighting death and pain, but with her new plans to investigate death itself, she couldn't have felt fuller of energy.

"You look pretty healthy for someone who died," came a harsh, female voice from behind her. Nathalie recognised it instantly and turned to see the source of it. There stood her good friend, the senior nurse and the person she relied on most in the department.

"Michelle Payne, you are a sight for sore eyes," said Nathalie as she hugged her friend.

"Damn good to see you back," replied Michelle. "We've missed you, without you around Steven seems to be even more of a dick than usual."

"I thought you all deserved a little break from me," laughed Nathalie.

"It's a break from Steven we need," Michelle said quietly, smiling and rolling her eyes at the same time. "Honestly, the things he knows about handling people that are still conscious you could write on the back of a postage stamp."

"That's not true," Nathalie replied, initially with a serious face before a smile broke over it. "He doesn't know anywhere near that much." Both women laughed before Nathalie continued. "Oh don't worry, I'll soon sort him out. Now, where is he?"

"He's in the cubicles with a patient, not sure where," Michelle replied.

"Oh well, I'll see him soon enough," Nathalie replied. "So what have we got today?"

"It's a quiet one so far, mostly minor injuries. We've only had one ambulance bring someone in under blue lights, a heart attack." Nathalie's ears pricked up.

"Was it a cardiac arrest?" she asked.

"Yes, he's in the usual place, we're still monitoring him. He seems to be doing alright."

"Well, let's go see him."

"Really?" asked Michelle, a little surprised at her request. "Don't you want to deal with some of the minor injuries?"

"Yes, eventually." Nathalie could see she had aroused a hint of confusion in Michelle. "Oh, don't worry I won't be long, I just want to look over the patient's notes."

"In that case I'll get the next patient ready for you," Michelle replied. Nathalie walked away, partly annoyed at Michelle's reaction, but not surprised by it. She was the consummate professional and Nathalie resolved to keep Michelle as far away as possible from everything she was planning in case she became suspicious.

Arriving at the patient's bedside she began to review the notes. She found a history of heart disease, two bypass operations, high cholesterol and borderline obesity. Nathalie looked at the body in the bed as the heart monitor beeped slowly through the silence. He wasn't long for this world, in fact she doubted he'd survive the day, but if he awoke, he'd be the first chance she'd get to test her theory.

Her heart almost skipped a beat when she heard him exhale loudly. The monitor showed a sudden jump in the heart rate and she leaned forward to see if he was wakening.

"Can you hear me?" she said in a loud voice. The man's head nodded gently. "You're in hospital," she said, this time quietly into his ear. "What's the last thing you remember?"

"I stood up," came his faint reply. Nathalie had to lean over him to hear what he said. "After I had my breakfast, then it all went black."

"Did anything else happen?" she whispered.

"No, nothing," was his almost inaudible reply.

"Are you sure?" she persisted. "Did you see any lights? Did you wake up anywhere else? Did you see anyone?"

Before he had a chance to answer, the heart monitor emitted the familiar tone that indicated his heart had stopped. Nathalie leapt into action to try and save him, but in his condition she knew it was probably too late.

"Well, that was an impressive return to work," said Steven, showing all the qualities Michelle had complained about, "killing the first patient you come to." Steven finished with a laugh, but Nathalie didn't join him. As she stared at the body on the bed before her, she felt frustration burning inside her. She felt she had come so close, that maybe a few more words would have triggered a memory, but all she had now was Steven's sense of humour. A morbid joke here and there was common in her line of work, but not now, not today. Losing a patient always hurt Nathalie, but this one seemed to gnaw at her more than others, as if a perfect opportunity had been taken from her.

She turned and stormed out the room, anger seething in her.

"Don't worry about it," came a voice from a room as she walked past. She turned to see Michelle's face looking back at her. "Despite what that arse says, you wanted to help, to look after those most in need. You always do. But you've been through the shit recently, are you sure you're ready to be back here?"

"No, but what the hell. I miss the excitement." She didn't sound like she meant it.

"Look, I'll try and keep the rough stuff away from you for now," said Michelle. "You've been in that damn resuscitation room recently as a patient so let's not send you there too many times to work until you're back into the swing of things."

"Okay," replied a reluctant Nathalie, "and thanks. You always look after me." She didn't like the idea of avoiding the resuscitation patients, but the expression of thanks was genuine.

For almost two weeks Michelle kept her promise and looked after Nathalie. In this time all Nathalie dealt with were minor injuries and non-critical medical conditions despite all her efforts to get to patients who might help her. Her professional life was a continuous stream of broken bones, bleeding and random illnesses. She barely set foot in the resuscitation room and was certainly never alone with a cardiac arrest survivor and able to test her theory. It was a source of endless frustration for her, but she bided her time, waiting for her opportunity.

A multiple car crash on the motorway finally delivered her the chance she had been waiting for. When the notification of incoming casualties arrived, she rushed to the resuscitation room, ready for what was to come. An initial report had spoken of several cardiac arrests and Nathalie saw it as a perfect opportunity.

The first sign of their arrival were the usual blue flashing lights outside the window. They cast long blue streaks through the Venetian blinds and across the wall, announcing their silent arrival to the department. Nathalie stood ready by the door as Steven ran in, anticipating her chance to test her theory.

It was three hours later, and still Nathalie waited hopefully. While three people had died in the accident, one had been revived after her heart had stopped and she now lay unconscious in the resuscitation room. It was the perfect opportunity for Nathalie, who now spent every spare moment by the patient's bedside, waiting for a result.

Nathalie was waiting by her bedside as the first indication of consciousness came from the heart monitor. After hours of a consistent pulse, it suddenly picked up its pace. Nathalie went straight to work.

"Hello, can you hear me?" said Nathalie. The patient's head nodded slightly. "What's the last thing you remember?" Nathalie waited hopefully for an answer.

"I was in a car," the patient said faintly. "I was driving."

"Anything after that?"

"There was a loud bang, I remember screams and then..." The patient's voice tailed off.

"Then what?" said Nathalie. "Did you wake up somewhere else?"

"I remember sirens, then blue lights," the patient replied.

"Nothing else?" Nathalie persisted. "No clouds, no angels, nothing like that?"

"What do you mean?" asked the patient.

"No, nothing." Nathalie felt a pang of frustration, but it only got worse for her when she heard a voice behind her.

"Nathalie, what the hell are you doing?" It's was Steven's voice, and her heart sank.

"Nothing," she replied. Steven's glaring face immediately told her to try a different answer. "I was just trying, you know to see if there was anything..."

"I know exactly what you were doing," he snapped. "My office, now." Steven turned and walked out the door with Nathalie following close behind. Unable to see his face she couldn't guess what kind of mood he was in. Was he angry? Was he concerned? The walk down the corridor seemed endless but eventually they reached his office and Steven gestured for Nathalie to take a seat.

"You're no good to me like this," said Steven. "This isn't a place for you to test your theories."

"Oh, come on, that's the first time I've..." began Nathalie, but Steven cut her off.

"Bullshit," he interrupted. "Michelle's had to work her arse off keeping you away from the cardiac cases."

"Oh," said Nathalie.

"She says every time there's one in you try to get access, and she has to re-direct you to something else." Nathalie felt betrayed. Michelle had been her friend for a long time.

"Steven, please, I need..."

"No!" he shouted, cutting her off again. "I know what you're talking about and you don't need to. You need to accept reality. You hallucinated, you're not the first, just accept it."

"I can't," she replied, "remember the suicide bomber?"

"I don't care about the suicide bomber, or about your vision of the afterlife. I care about my patients, and I won't let you harass them."

"Please Steven, I promise I won't bother them too much."

"Enough!" he shouted. "I won't have you here like this. I'm signing you off for two weeks, go away and think about things."

"No, please," she replied, but her protests were pointless.

"Go home, and think about your future. If you want a career, if you're going to be the doctor you were before the accident, then you can come back."

Nathalie walked out of the room without another word, her head held low and with her eyes full of tears.

"Nathalie!" came a voice behind her. She turned to see Michelle. "Are you okay?"

"No, I'm not," she replied, glaring at Michelle with anger burning inside her.

"What's wrong?"

"I thought you were my friend," said Nathalie.

"I am."

"So why have you been spying on me, keeping me from patients?" Michelle looked horrified at the realisation that Nathalie knew.

"I'm sorry Nathalie, but I had to."

"He's sent me home for two weeks, he's probably going to sack me now."

"Oh Nathalie," replied Michelle. She went to give Nathalie a hug but Nathalie quickly pulled back.

"Get away from me," said Nathalie, her voice almost spitting venom. Michelle lurched back in shock and Nathalie stormed past her without another word.

"I'm sorry," called Michelle towards Nathalie's back, but there was no response and Nathalie was gone.

By the time Nathalie got home her rage had turned to frustration. She felt like someone from some ancient legend, cursed to know a great secret about the world, but that no one would believe her. Like all those convinced they hold unique knowledge that must be shared with the whole world, she did the only thing she could. She turned to the internet.

Chapter 3

The dull glow of the computer monitor finally held Nathalie's attention. She had trawled internet forums and blogs for days, and she had found no answers until now, when tucked away in the corner of a story about ski deaths she found what she was looking for. The story of Angela Postl, a survivor of an avalanche in the Bavarian Alps, had something that intrigued her. She read the account again before she could be sure, of how Angela Postl had been hit by an avalanche while skiing and had been buried for over an hour before she was dug out and revived. One line seemed to hold the key to Nathalie's dilemma, Angela's description of seeing a "paradise of warmth and light, but with a darkness lurking beneath" before she woke up. It was a perfect description of her own experience.

Angela wasn't hard to track down. She had left comments about what had happened to her across social media and internet forums, leaving a trail of hints about her experience, almost all of which Nathalie could relate to. She knew Angela lived in Munich, that she ran her own marketing company, that she was single but most of all she learnt that she had been left as confused and unhappy by her experience as Nathalie had been. She had finally found someone who might understand how she felt.

Nathalie began to type a message to her, telling her how her own heart had stopped in an accident and that she had experienced something similar. She described her trip to the afterlife in detail, explaining everything that had happened to her and how she now felt. She half expected never to receive a response but within an hour Angela had sent a reply.

"I am so happy to hear from you. Please call me as soon as possible" the message read, with a phone number attached. Nathalie dialled the number without delay, her heart racing with excitement.

"Hallo," said the German accent at the other end of the line.

"Angela?"

"Yes, is that Nathalie?" said the voice, switching to perfect English.

"Yes, yes it is," replied Nathalie.

"Oh, I'm so glad you found me," said Angela, "I never thought anyone would understand."

"So it really happened to you?" said Nathalie, "you really woke up in that place, and saw the same thing I did?"

"Yes, I saw it all. I watched the innocent sent to hell, I even saw people laughing at the damned, laughing and saying they were warned as they were dragged away."

"I saw worse," said Nathalie, before relating the tale of the suicide bomber and the victim she had seen. Angela was appalled at her account.

"We need to find others like us," said Angela, "there must be others out there who feel as alone as we did."

"We should meet," replied Nathalie. "I have a few days off, I could fly over tomorrow."

"To Munich?" said Angela, surprised at Nathalie's suggestion.

"Yes, how about it? We have something in common, something no-one else has." Angela paused for a second, thinking about it.

"What do you do for a living?" Angela asked, changing the subject.

"I'm a doctor in an accident and emergency department in London," replied Nathalie.

"Just wondering," replied Angela, "but yes, come over and we can meet."

Nathalie emerged from the S-bahn station, part of the German subway system and looked at her surroundings. She had followed Angela's instructions, to get the S-bahn from the airport to Marienplatz in the city's centre and now she stood there in the open plaza, underneath the tall spire of the town hall and seeing this city for the first time.

She glanced around, looking for the gold statue on a pillar that Angela had asked to meet her beside. It stood in the centre of the square and as she approached it she saw the figure of a woman with her back to her standing by the column. The long, straight blond hair and blue business suit was just as Angela had described to her on the phone and when she looked down she could see the dark high heeled shoes Angela said she'd be wearing.

"Angela?" said Nathalie as she stood behind her. Angela turned round to face her.

"Nathalie?" replied Angela. Nathalie nodded and extended her hand to shake hers, but Angela threw her arms around Nathalie and hugged her tightly. "I'm so happy to meet you," Angela said as she stepped back. "I'm so glad I'm not alone anymore." As the embrace ended, Nathalie couldn't help but notice Angela wipe away a tear.

"Shall we get a drink, maybe something to eat?" asked Nathalie, very aware of the swarm of cafs and bars that surrounded the plaza.

"I know a nice place," replied Angela. "It's a bit of a walk, but it's not far."

"Okay," replied Nathalie, and they set off, walking through the wide, open streets of Munich.

"Have you found anyone else?" Angela asked as they moved through the crowds.

"No-one," she replied, "and I've been looking everywhere I could. Have you found anyone?"

"Not really. There was one story I read, a guy who drowned who said something about a 'terrifying vision of Heaven' but I haven't been able to find him."

"That sounds about right," replied Nathalie. "Where was he from?"

"He's Scottish. He took a tumble in the hills and fell into a lake, same story as us, he was revived and it sounds like he had a similar experience."

"We need to find him," Nathalie replied. "We need to find anyone who has had a similar experience and speak to them. We need to know more about it."

"Well, I was thinking about that," Angela replied, sounding a little nervous, "and maybe we don't need to find anyone else. You said you were a doctor, didn't you?"

"Yes, why?"

"Could you stop my heart and then revive me?" Nathalie came to a sudden halt and stared at Angela in disbelief.

"What?" she stammered. "No, no, I couldn't. Well, I could in theory, but no, it's too dangerous."

"I'm serious," said Angela, "I want to go back, I need to know more about that place. I need the truth."

"Are you mad?" asked an incredulous Nathalie.

"No, I'm desperate. Just be honest, could you do it? Not will you, but can you, with a reasonable chance of me surviving?" Nathalie paused slightly, reluctant to give the only truthful answer she could.

"I could do it, probably with a better than reasonable chance."

"But you won't?"

"No," replied Nathalie. "Besides, I've already tried this, in a way."

"Have you?"

"Yes, in the hospital. I had a theory that it's like a dream, that most people forget it a few minutes after waking up, but I've had access to a cardiac arrest patient the moment they've woken up."

"And?" asked Angela.

"Nothing, not a damn thing."

"That's okay, I understand," was Angela's reply. "This just means we need to look for others." There was an awkward silence between them for a few minutes as they continued to walk through the streets of Munich. Nathalie was already regretting not having at least explored Angela's suggestion and now wondered if Angela somehow now resented her.

"Look, I have a better idea," said Angela, breaking the silence. "Never mind eating, let's head back to my place and start trying to find someone else like us." Nathalie turned and nodded at Angela with a faint smile. She felt relieved now that Angela had broken the silence. The upbeat and positive tone to her voice reassured Nathalie that she had done the right thing in refusing her request and that maybe the two of them might achieve something without going down such a dangerous route.

"This is yours?" asked an astonished Nathalie as Angela pulled into the driveway of the three story house that stood just to the south of Munich.

"Yes, I bought it as an investment, but I liked it so much I moved in. It used to be separate apartments, but I had it redone to be one house." Nathalie looked at it in awe. Trees surrounded the ample grounds, enclosing the house and garden, shrouding it in privacy. A swimming pool lay at one side of the building, long and narrow, as if designed for swimming long lengths. At the other side of the house stood a garage, separated from the main house and wide enough for several cars. She dreaded to think how much a place like it would cost back home in London.

"What is it you said you do?" Nathalie asked.

"I'm in marketing," she replied, "I've been running my own company for almost ten years now. Another ten years at it and I can probably retire, maybe even before I hit fifty."

As the two of them walked into the house, Angela stopped to pull a newspaper from her mailbox. She glanced at it and continued to read it as she entered her house. Nathalie, following behind her, heard Angela emit what she assumed were some German profanities as she read the newspaper.

"Something wrong?" asked Nathalie.

"The bastard's killed himself, he's got away with it." was the venomous reply.

"Who?"

"This priest," she replied, pointing at the photo underneath a headline, "he's thought to be the most prolific child abuser in German history. Looks like he had thousands of victims, and at least a couple of dozen of them killed themselves. He was finally jailed a few months ago, but now he's dead. And you know what that means don't you?" Nathalie looked at her with a puzzled expression and shook her head. "He was a priest," continued Angela, "he'll get to Heaven. Can we be so sure those kids did?"

"I can't be sure of anything," Nathalie replied. "I mean, do we know what really happened to us?"

"That's why I want to go back. I want to see it again, to see if everything's the same."

"Well, I did consider one other thing," said Nathalie, "but I dismissed it, it wasn't a helpful way to think at the time."

"Oh, what?"

"Just that there may be something different about us."

"Different? How?"

"I don't know, but you and I both remember what happened to us, maybe we're some rare, one in a million occurrence."

"Is it possible we're the only ones who can remember it?"

"That's what I'm thinking," Nathalie replied. "Maybe it happens to everyone when their heart stops, but for some unknown reason we can remember."

"Does that mean you're willing to try and send me back?"

"It's dangerous," replied Nathalie, not entirely dismissing the suggestion this time.

"How dangerous?" asked Angela. "I keep pretty fit, I have a strong heart, seems like the two of us are better placed than anyone to try it."

"You could die."

"I've already died once, and I can't avoid it happening again at some point," replied Angela, "so I may as well not be scared of it." Nathalie remained silent, her mind racing with ideas she wished she wasn't having. She glanced down at the newspaper, and saw the face of the man Angela was talking about. She stared into his eyes and felt the same revulsion as Angela at the thought that he was now in Heaven.

"Is this really it?" Nathalie said, thinking aloud. "Is this really the nature of the universe? That God sits somewhere judging us depending on how much attention we give him?"

"We're the only ones who can find out," Angela said. "This could be the most important thing anyone ever does."

Nathalie again didn't answer. This time her head was thinking practically, thinking about what she'd need to try it. She just had one thing to ask before she could go ahead. "How rich are you?" she asked Angela. "Doing this won't be cheap, even getting some of the equipment won't be too easy."

"Rich enough," she replied. "My organisation has offices in six cities on three continents and it is very successful. Give me a list of what you need. I can afford it and get it, I have connections."

"You do realise what this means, don't you?" Nathalie said half hoping Angela would change her mind. "I'm going to stop your heart, then try and re-start it. I'll pump you full of drugs and use electric shocks on you. Are you really ready for this?"

"No, not really," Angela replied with a shrug. "But I need to do it. I want to know and don't try and deny you feel the same."

Nathalie sighed in resignation. "Yes, I do want to know, especially after reading about that priest."

"So we're doing this?" Angela asked.

"Yes, as soon as you get what we need we'll go for it."

"Thank you," replied Angela, who stepped forward and hugged Nathalie. As Angela held her tightly Nathalie found herself suddenly flooded by emotion and she burst into uncontrollable tears.

"It's okay," said Angela softly as Nathalie continued to cry. "You're not alone now. I know what it's like."

"I'm sorry," sobbed Nathalie as she tried to regain her composure, "It's just since the accident I've felt so..." Nathalie struggled to find the word before Angela came to her rescue.

"Alone?"

Nathalie nodded, still wiping away tears.

"Like you're the only one who knows a horrible secret and no-one will believe you?"

Nathalie nodded again.

"Yes, yes that's it," Nathalie said, relieved at hearing her feelings put into words by someone else.

"You won't be alone again," replied Angela. "We're in this together."

"It's beautiful here, isn't it?" said Angela as Nathalie stood beside her on her balcony, watching the sunset bathe the distant Alps in a warm, red light. "Alpenglow they call it, just after the sun sets and lights up the mountains like that. It only lasts a few minutes, but it's amazing."

"I wish I was here for longer," said Nathalie, "but I have to go home tomorrow, then back to work." The look on Nathalie's face made it clear to Angela just how much she was dreading her return to the hospital.

"Oh, don't worry about work," said Angela, "from what you told me, all the stress was from your colleagues stopping you from experimenting."

"Yes, that's right."

"But now you're experimenting on me, so you don't have to worry about that."

"I suppose so," replied an unconvincing Nathalie.

"Did you enjoy your job before your accident?"

"I loved it," said Nathalie, "I loved the excitement, the challenge of it all, but now all I think of is the afterlife."

"You've got me for that now," said Angela, "so try not to worry about it, instead try to find what it was you loved so much before."

"I can try, but it doesn't seem the same."

"And when you've earned their trust," said Angela, now with a sly smile on her face, "you can get to people you've revived again."

Nathalie smiled and nodded in agreement.

"Good idea," she replied.

"I'm not one for missing opportunities," said Angela, "nor am I one for giving up on the first attempt. I will keep on trying, again and again until I find answers. I want answers and I tend to get what I want."

"Then I'll march in when I get back, tell them I'm my old self, and be on my best behaviour for as long as it takes to win their trust again."

"Besides, you'll be back here soon enough," said Angela. "When do you get time off?"

"I usually work five days on three days off," replied Nathalie, "it's long hours, but the days off should give me enough time to fly over for a day or two."

"Then come back as soon as you've got your days off. And I'll start buying the things we need, so we can begin as soon as possible."

"You know, I feel pretty good right now," said Nathalie as she stood up a little straighter. "A week ago I was completely depressed, thinking everything was pointless. But since I found you I've never been so excited in my life."

"I know what you mean," said Angela. "I keep wondering if we're on the edge of something amazing, some wonderful discovery that changes the world."

"Amazing? Yes, probably," said Nathalie. "But wonderful? I don't think so."

Angela looked at her quizzically before her expression turned to realisation. "You mean what we find out isn't likely to be good news?"

"Think back to when it happened to you," said Nathalie, "and tell me if you think we'll like what we find."

"Whatever we find is the truth," said Angela, "and the truth is what I want to know."

"That's exactly how I feel," was Nathalie's reply. "Bad, good, terrifying, wonderful, no matter what it is, I'd rather know than not know."

"So you're with me in this to its natural end?"

"Natural end?" asked Nathalie, "what does that mean?"

"It means we take this as far as we can, no backing down, no turning back."

"To its natural end then," replied Nathalie. "I'm with you."

Two days later, Nathalie found herself at the door to Steven's office. She'd spent the past day going over her story in her head and now she was ready to present it to him.

She knocked on the door and waited.

"Come in," came the voice of Steven from inside. Nathalie opened the door and slowly entered.

"Nathalie, how are you?" said Steven as he stood up. "Please, take a seat." Nathalie did as she was told and sat down.

"It's been a busy two weeks for me," she said.

"Busy? What have you being doing?"

"I've been reading up on near death experiences." Nathalie was careful to keep her body language subdued and submissive, with her head slightly down and avoiding eye contact. "I even spoke to a few other people who had similar experiences."

"Oh? You mean like yours?"

"Well, a little bit. I noticed a pattern as well."

"Really?" asked Steven, getting nervous about where this was going.

"It seems people's experiences depend on what they believe. If you're religious it's all wonderful and happy, if not, it's something weird, like mine."

"So that means what?"

"It means it was in my head."

Steven breathed a sigh of relief as Nathalie continued. "I know that now. It was all just a stupid dream, a product of low oxygen levels and a hundred and one other things in my brain."

"But it was in your brain," said Steven.

"Yes, totally." Nathalie paused for a second. "Wow, I'm glad that's out," she added, her body language instantly changing, a subtle shift she had been rehearsing all morning. "I feel so stupid for the way I acted," she said as she sat up slightly straighter and looking more directly at Steven. "Can you forgive me for it?"

"Of course I can," replied Steven, "and we'll all be glad to see you back to your old self. Michelle's missing you, I think she needs you around to keep me off her back."

"Oh god, have you been micro-managing her again?" she said with mock anger, "I can see I have a lot to do."

"So you're ready to come back?"

"Absolutely"

"Then welcome back," said Steven.

Chapter 4

Nathalie inspected the equipment and supplies Angela had arranged for her. Nothing was missing from the list she had given and everything was of the highest quality.

"You must have spent a fortune on this," said Nathalie as she checked the defibrillator.

"Given that I'm trusting my life to it, I did not think it would be a good idea to cut corners," she replied.

"You certainly didn't," said Nathalie as she continued to inspect the equipment. "How the hell did you get your hands on it so quickly? I only gave you the list last week."

"I have contracts with a couple of medical suppliers," she replied, "and the manager of one of them, well let's just say he's always been an admirer of me." Angela smiled and raised her eyebrows.

"Ah, so you fluttered your eyelashes at him and he obeyed your commands?"

"Oh, I did a little more than that," Angela replied.

"You didn't..." Nathalie said, not knowing how to finish the question.

"I took him to heaven and back on the first night, then asked for the equipment on the second night. I had it all on the third, if I hadn't he knew I'd have a word with his wife." Nathalie looked shocked at Angela's admission. "I told you, I get what I want, any way I can."

"Well, you weren't short changed, that's for sure. I wish I had equipment this good back home in the hospital, our stuff is much older."

"Nothing but the best," was Angela's reply. "So, can we proceed with the first stage?"

"Yes," said Nathalie as she passed a bath robe to Angela. "If you change into this, I can start your check-up."

Angela left the room, returning after a few minutes now wearing the robe. She gestured for Angela to sit on the bed, ready for her examination.

"Now before we do anything else, I'll give you a good check up. I'll check your vital signs, then I want to hook you up to a heart monitor and give you a stress test on your treadmill. I have to be absolutely sure your heart is healthy."

"Then let's get started," said Angela as she slipped her robe off.

Two things immediately took Nathalie by surprise. Firstly, that Angela was so muscular. Secondly, she was now completely naked.

"Oh, you haven't kept your underwear on," Nathalie said, somewhat taken aback by her openness.

"Why would I?" replied Angela as she sat down on the examination table. "This is a medical examination after all."

"Yes, yes, of course" stuttered Nathalie in response.

"What would you like me to do?" asked Angela, who seemed unaware of Nathalie's surprise at her nakedness.

"Lie down," she said, "and we can get started." As Angela lay down, Nathalie was pretty sure she'd pass any test she gave her.

She had a flawless physique, with especially large and well developed abdominal muscles. Her arms were strong, with prominent biceps and her legs were as strong as any woman's she had ever seen.

Nathalie ran through the basic tests, and Angela passed each one perfectly. Her pulse, blood pressure, breathing and everything else were all those of a very fit and healthy adult. Nathalie could not find a single flaw in her health, even the heart monitor she attached to Angela produced a perfect result.

"Well, your results are perfect so far," announced Nathalie, "and all we have now is the stress test." Nathalie gestured at the treadmill in the corner. "Do you need anything?" Nathalie asked, thinking of clothes.

"No, that's okay, I can do this in my bare feet," was Angela's unperturbed reply as she strode naked over to the treadmill and switched it on.

Her energy was boundless. Nathalie kept increasing the speed on the treadmill and Angela kept matching whatever speed she was given. Sweat poured off her, but she didn't stop, she didn't even slow down. Her heart coped with it perfectly, never missing a beat and taking all the stress Nathalie threw at it.

After an hour of the punishing regime, Nathalie had seen enough.

"Your heart's perfect," she said, "and the rest of your fitness seems just as good."

"Does that mean we can go ahead?" asked Angela between gasps for breath.

"We'll do it tomorrow," Nathalie replied. "Until then, we can relax and take things easy."

"Well, it's a lovely spring day today," said Angela, "why don't we relax outside for a while, I fancy a swim."

Nathalie nodded in agreement. There was an early spring heat wave in Bavaria and to Nathalie it felt like summer and sunbathing sounded a wonderful idea. "I'll go change, and meet you outside later," Nathalie replied as she headed off to her room to find something suitable to wear.

Rummaging through her clothes, she found nothing but a t-shirt and trousers that zipped off into shorts. She briefly cursed herself for not bringing a swimming costume, but with London under eternal cloud and rain when she left it hadn't occurred to her to bring one.

She quickly changed and went out into the garden. Angela was already in the pool, swimming lengths like a professional swimmer, cutting through the water effortlessly and gracefully.

"Hello there," said Nathalie. Angela stopped swimming and waved at her before swimming to the poolside ladder. As she emerged, Nathalie was once again shocked to see Angela was naked.

"It's a beautiful day, isn't it?" said Angela.

"It's wonderful," replied Nathalie, wondering if she could find the courage to join her.

"The weather's shaping up lovely this year," said Angela as she walked to the sun loungers by the pool and laid down on one.

"Back in London it's all rain and wind," Nathalie replied, "but I see things are better here." There was an awkwardness to her voice that Angela quickly picked up on.

"Ah, yes, I suppose you British do tend to cover up, don't you?" Angela rolled onto her front as she spoke. "Please say if this makes you uncomfortable. I love the feeling of freedom being naked gives, and everyone does it around here, but I'll only do it if you're okay with it."

"No, no, it's fine," said Nathalie, "in fact, I just wish I was brave enough to join you."

"No need to do anything you're not comfortable with," Angela replied as she wrapped a towel around herself. "Besides, we need all our bravery for tomorrow."

"Yes, of course," said Nathalie with a smile as she sat on the other lounger and laid back. She suddenly felt very relaxed around Angela, and dismissed all the feelings of awkwardness she felt in an instant. Tomorrow she knew they would achieve great things together, and with that thought she smiled broadly as she soaked up the sun.

With the decision made to proceed a sense of cautious elation came to both women as the reality of the danger they faced sat at the back of both their minds. Excitement at the prospect of returning to their elusive afterlife was tempered by the unknown factors and the possibility that Angela might not survive.

It was at dinner that evening that Nathalie, ever the scientist, asked a question that had been lingering in her head, one she wanted Angela to clarify for her.

"What do you want out of this?" she asked. Angela said nothing until she had chewed and swallowed the mouthful of fried potatoes she was eating.

"I want to go back to see if it's real," Angela said.

"Is that it?" asked Nathalie. "Any other reason?"

"If it is real, we need to know about it. Like you, I'm an atheist, so as it stands, we're both going to Hell."

"Are we though?" asked Nathalie. "What if we confirm this is real? I may not have a religious belief, but I'll know there's a god, even if it's a god I don't particularly like."

"That's an interesting thought," replied Angela, her mind intrigued by Nathalie's notion. "You won't have faith, or any other religious concept, you'll just know a fact, the same way you know two plus two is four, or that the sky is blue."

"And I certainly won't love him in my heart," continued Nathalie, "or repent for any so-called sins or any of that bollocks, so what does this mean? Do I burn in hell or not?"

Angela just smiled and shook her head.

"I don't know, but it does seem like a good idea to find out. Maybe I should ask one of the angels about all this before I go to get judged."

"I wonder if you can come back once you're judged," said Nathalie, thinking out loud.

"That's exactly why I want to do it," said Angela, "we need to know these things. What are the standards we're judged by? If I get sent to Hell or Heaven before you revive me, can I come back? Can I die in this place?"

"You know, there was a time when this kind of talk would end with me dismissing someone's religious belief as an ill thought out and confused philosophy. Now it's a deciding factor in our eternal damnation." Both women laughed, but there was a

nervousness behind the laughter that neither wanted to admit to.
Then Angela raised the spectre Nathalie had been trying to ignore.
"What will you do if I die?" she asked. Nathalie turned pale at being forced to consider it.
"I don't know," was the only answer she could come up with.
"I've been thinking about it, and I have a few ideas," said Angela. "Firstly, you'll have a few days before anyone looks for me, probably my secretary will raise the alarm. She thinks I'm on a business trip abroad, so I won't be missed initially. You and I have never communicated by email, just by messages through that forum, so that'd be hard to track even if someone found it. There's nothing else that links you to me, apart from one phone call. If anyone asks, it was a wrong number and we chatted because I like to practice my English." Nathalie stared at her in disbelief.
"Angela, you're not going to die," she said, more to reassure herself. "I won't let you, I'm good at this, I promise."
"I know you'll do all you can to make sure I'm okay, but I also know there's a risk, I've accepted it." Nathalie reached out and took Angela's hand in her own.
"I'm not going to let you die," she said, "I won't let it happen." She felt Angela's hand tighten slightly and they both smiled at each other.
"I know you won't," Angela replied, leaving the subject there.
"Maybe you should try to speak to someone when you're there," said Nathalie after a brief pause in the conversation. "Another dead person I mean. It might be an interesting experiment. Try and learn their name, where they came from, how they died. Then we could look them up. That'd be absolute confirmation this is real."
"Good idea. I could even get a message back to relatives if I did that."
"Would they believe us?" replied Nathalie.
"I don't know, but consider this. We'll have both gone not just from hardened sceptics to a bizarre form of born again Christian but also we'll also have become a new kind of spiritual medium, relating messages from beyond the grave."

"This is getting too weird," replied Nathalie, shaking her head in confusion. "If your life wasn't in my hands tomorrow I'd be giving very serious thought to getting very drunk right now."

"Save it for tomorrow night," said Angela, "we can celebrate once we've done this."

"Amen to that," replied Nathalie with a laugh.

The next morning Angela sat in her bath robe, perched on the edge of the bed, nervously awaiting her controlled brush with death. She sat patiently as Nathalie began preparing her for the process, inserting a cannula in her hand to inject drugs and placing the heart monitor pads on her chest.

"Okay Angela, time for you to lie down."

The time had come and Angela did as Nathalie said, lying back on the bed and trying to get comfortable. Angela felt her stomach turn with the fear of what was to happen, but she said nothing, vowing to endure this without complaint. She was determined to see this through without flinching.

"Now, the plan is for me to stop your heart. I'll wait two minutes, then I'll restart it."

"Hopefully you'll restart it," replied Angela, showing a little fear.

Angela's body had proved less enthusiastic than her mind. Her bladder was next to useless and had sent her to the toilet for what seemed like every ten minutes for the past few hours. If she hadn't been nil by mouth for twelve hours she would have had little faith in her bowels to do as she said either. Her whole body seemed to be screaming out for her not to do this. But she would not give in.

"I'm going to give you an injection," said Nathalie, "it's a sedative and it'll make you feel sleepy. Don't fight it, just go with it."

"Then what happens?" asked Angela as she wiped away a nervous tear.

"Then you'll wake up, either here or there," replied Nathalie.

"Then let's do it."

"Are you sure?" asked Nathalie, checking one last time. "This is your last chance to back down."

"Do it. Do it now."

Nathalie took Angela's hand and injected the sedative into the cannula. Almost immediately Angela felt a tingling in her hand and arm. Seconds later she was unconscious.

The first thing Angela became aware of was a voice calling her name. It was soft and feminine, welcoming and caring. It sounded delightful, like a beacon to follow, to lead her to safety and comfort. Her eyes slowly opened as bright light seemed to flood her face. She tried to sit up but she felt weak, as if her energy had been drained and she made no attempt to move.

"Just lie there," the voice said. "It's all over now. You're safe."

Angela's heart sank. The voice was Nathalie's. It hadn't worked.

"You'll be feeling groggy from the medication I gave you, so don't do anything." Even through the haze of the drugs, Angela felt utterly depressed. Tears began to roll down her cheeks at their failure.

"Nothing...nothing happened," was all she could say.

"Well, you're safe now, don't worry about it," replied Nathalie. Angela could hear the disappointment in Nathalie's voice as she spoke. Angela somehow felt responsible for the failure, and it only made her tears flow faster.

Hours passed and the medication slowly left her system. By the time she was fit enough to sit up in bed Angela was already planning their next step with Nathalie.

"Do you remember I mentioned a man up in Scotland?" she asked.

"Yes," replied Nathalie, "he drowned, didn't he?"

"In the mountains, yes. I think I've tracked him down. I found someone on a Scottish hill climbing forum that talked about a similar accident. It could be him."

"If we can find more people, maybe we can work out what went wrong with our attempt," replied Nathalie. "I'm sure this can work, it's just we're missing something, something we might find in someone else's experience."

Angela nodded in agreement.

"I've also found a story by an ex-soldier of something similar, but I haven't managed to find him yet."

"You've been busy then," said Nathalie. "I've been looking but I've found no-one other than you."

"I didn't become a self made millionaire by giving up on the first try," Angela replied, "and now the damn drugs have worn off I won't be such a cry baby about failure." She felt stupid for her earlier emotions. Even if she was medicated, she felt she had something to prove to Nathalie, to show her that she wasn't weak.

"You need to take it easy for now," Nathalie said. "You've had your heart stopped and you've had a dose of sedatives. Eat something if you can, get a good night's sleep, then we'll try and contact the guy in Scotland."

Chapter 5

Waiting for the phone to ring was torture. It had taken them a few days and Nathalie had even returned to London for a week's work but now they had found the Scottish climber, a man called Ian Gillies, and he seemed eager to speak to them. Back with Angela in Munich, Nathalie waited with her by the phone, staring at it and willing for it to ring.

Both women snapped their heads up when it finally rang. They stared at each other, wide eyed with excitement for a few seconds before Nathalie hit the phone's speaker button.

"Hello," said Nathalie, desperately trying not to sound too keen.

"Hi, this is Ian, Ian Gillies, we exchanged messages on the climbing forum."

"Ian, it's great to hear from you, I'm Nathalie, and Angela is here as well."

"Hello Ian, this is Angela."

"Thanks for getting in touch with me," Ian said, "it's really good to know I'm not alone."

"Can you tell us what happened, what you remember?" Nathalie asked.

"The first thing I remember is waking up surrounded by cloud. It felt weird, I wasn't floating, but I wasn't actually resting on anything, if that makes sense." Angela and Nathalie both looked at each other and nodded.

"Don't worry that makes perfect sense," said Angela.

"You know what I mean then?" Ian asked.

"Yes, we both do, we woke up there as well," said Nathalie.

"Did you two meet two men in white robes?"

"Yes," Nathalie replied, "they told me I was dead and took me to wait in a line."

"Where there many people there?"

"There were a few hundred where I was," Angela said, "but it was busier for Nathalie, she had her accident just after that big suicide bomb a few months ago."

"Wow, did you see all the victims?"

"Worse than that," said Nathalie, "I saw the bombers go to Heaven while children went to Hell."

"Well, I never saw anything like that, but I did see some people who seemed to have died together in a car crash and the one who got into Heaven just shouted abuse as the others were sent to Hell. He kept saying 'I told you so' when they were in the line in front of me."

"Shit, this keeps getting worse," said Nathalie.

"Ian, how do you feel about what happened?"

"I think confused is the best word. My parents are churchgoers and although I don't really believe myself, I've always tried to be a good person, to live a decent life. Now I find out that doesn't matter and I'll burn for eternity, I mean what the hell am I supposed to do now?"

"If you could go back, have another short visit, would you?" asked Angela.

"What, you mean stop my heart?" Ian sounded incredulous at the very suggestion.

"We've tried it" said Nathalie, about a week ago. There was silence on the other end of the phone for a few seconds.

"What happened?" was Ian's eventual response.

"Nothing," Angela replied bitterly. "My heart was stopped for a couple of minutes but I saw nothing."

"Two minutes?" replied Ian. "My heart was stopped for longer than that. I was told I was under the ice for half an hour before they rescued me."

"What did you say," said a stunned Nathalie.

"I fell through the ice when I took a tumble, and my friends took ages to get me out."

"That's it, that's what we've missed," said an excited Nathalie. "I crashed my car through a frozen lake, Angela was smothered in an avalanche."

"You mean we need to be frozen?" asked Angela.

"Yes, oh it all makes sense now," said an increasingly energetic Nathalie. "The brain usually dies in a few minutes without oxygen but if it's cold it can last a lot longer, even hours in the extreme cases."

"Whoa, wait a minute," said Ian, sounding alarmed. "Are you really talking about doing this? Are you serious?"

"Nathalie's a doctor," said Angela, "if anyone can do it, she can."

"What do you think Ian?" Nathalie asked. "Want to give it a try? Or just be part of it, help us out?"

"Yes, come over Ian," said Angela. "Fly over to Munich and we can start planning it."

"This is for real, yes?" asked a still incredulous Ian.

"Ian," said Nathalie as her tone of voice changed to her best bedside manner, "we've been where you've been. And we want to go back. Do you want to come with us?" There was a pause for a few seconds before Ian answered.

"Yes, yes I do."

Nathalie felt exhausted as she stood at the arrivals gate of Munich airport. She had flown back and forth between Munich and London several times now whenever she had the spare time, but exhaustion was setting in. She felt she never had any spare time to relax, or to do anything else. All she did now was work at the hospital or travel to Munich. Now she was here in Munich again with Angela to meet Ian, but she had no energy, no will to do anything. As they waited for Ian to arrive, Angela couldn't help but notice.

"You're exhausted, aren't you?"

"I'm fine," Nathalie replied, "I've just had a few late shifts, that's all."

"It's the travelling, isn't it?" said Angela. "I know what it's like, all these flights take their toll."

"I don't have much choice, do I?" Nathalie replied. "All I have in London is a little flat, you have the big house with the space to do what we're doing."

"You could move in with me," Angela said. The very idea sounded delightful to Nathalie, but it didn't sound practical.

"I have a job back home," was her attempt at a protest.

"Quit it, get something here."

"I don't speak German."

"Neither do half my staff, we all work in English. Munich is full of international companies, lots of big pharmaceutical companies that are always hiring. You'd get something right away."

"Oh, that does sound tempting," Nathalie replied.

"There's plenty of space for you to move in. You've seen the house, you could have your own apartment."

"I'll think about it," said Nathalie, although she felt she had already decided to.

A few moments later Ian arrived. They recognised him instantly from the photo and both women approached him. He was taller than they expected, with short, dark hair and a lean physique. Nathalie thought there was a steely darkness hiding behind his eyes, a strength within waiting to be unleashed.

"Ian? Ian Gillies?" asked Nathalie as she approached him.

"Nathalie?" he replied. Nathalie extended her hand and he shook it enthusiastically.

There was no such restraint from Angela. No sooner had she introduced herself she hugged Ian tightly, exclaiming how exciting it was to meet him. Ian on the other hand had the usual quiet reserve of the Scots, a reserve that had just been beaten into submission by the enthusiastic hospitality of the Bavarians.

"It's really good to meet you both," he said once he had escaped Angela's embrace.

"It's nice to find someone else who won't think I'm crazy," said Nathalie in response. A sadness came across Ian's face as he recognised the same loneliness he felt in himself.

"I know what you mean," he replied. Nathalie smiled and gently touched his shoulder.

"Well, you're with friends now," she said as they began to walk to Angela's waiting car.

Driving to Angela's house, the conversation quickly turned to what Angela and Nathalie were working on.

"We've tried it once," explained Nathalie, "but it didn't work. Angela was only dead for a couple of minutes, the idea of freezing didn't occur to me."

"So now you want to freeze her?" asked Ian.

"Exactly," she replied, "and here's what we plan to do. We'll strap her to a board with a mask on to let her breathe. Then we'll lower her whole body into a tank of iced water."

"It'll hurt, but I'm willing to do it," Angela chipped in.

"That's an understatement," Nathalie said, "it'll be agony for several minutes until the hypothermia kicks in. Eventually you'll lose consciousness and your heart will stop. I'll monitor your heart rate and temperature until your heart stops, then give you some time, probably ten minutes first time round, then pull you out the water and start rapid re-warming so I can revive you."

"And you really think this'll work?" asked Ian. Nathalie and Angela glanced at each other nervously.

"The truth is we don't know," Nathalie replied. "But so much rests on this that we have to try it. It's a great experiment."

"Possibly the most important in history," said Ian, "to help determine the very nature of our reality."

"And that's why it's worth the risk," said Angela. "That's why we have to be prepared to die for it." Ian looked cautiously at both women. It seemed a good idea to him, but he wasn't sure he was ready to be the first to try it.

"So when do you plan on doing this?" he asked.

"We're building what we need, a big vat for the ice and a system to pull the person out quickly," replied Nathalie.

"And it's almost ready," continued Angela. "We should have it ready in a day or two."

"You mean you'll be ready to try it while I'm here?" Ian asked, surprised at the speed things were moving.

"I'll need your help," said Nathalie. "A spare pair of hands will be essential if I'm to minimise the risk to Angela."

"Okay, I'm in," he said, finding himself intrigued at the notion of a return to the afterlife.

The car turned through the gates into Angela's driveway. Getting out Ian found himself almost in familiar territory. "This feels like Perthshire, like my home," he said. "All these thick forests and clear air. You wouldn't think we were by a city."

"It's lovely here, isn't it?" said Nathalie in response. "Even from the balconies you can't see anything else man-made for miles, just trees everywhere."

"We could even bury someone here and probably get away with it," added Angela. A chill went down the other's spines at this harsh reminder of the reality they could face. Her comment brought the conversation to a dead stop, leaving an awkward silence that lingered until they were inside.

"What would I have to do," said Ian, breaking the silence as they sat down in the main lounge, "to try this as well?"

"How fit are you?" asked Nathalie. "Fitness is important, I won't do this on anyone who isn't in good shape."

"Pretty fit," said Ian, "I climb mountains for fun, so I keep active."

"How's your general health? Any medical conditions?"

"No problems of any consequence. A bit of a dodgy knee from a tumble on a mountain, but that wouldn't matter, would it?"

"No, that'd be fine," replied Nathalie with a smile. "I'll give you a fitness test later, just to check you have no underlying problems."

"And then we can try to make progress," said Angela as she entered the room with a tray laden with coffee cups. "I don't know about you Ian, but I'm very eager to go back again."

Nathalie's eyes met Angela's as they shared a knowing glance. It was clear to both women now that Angela was a driving force, pushing ever onwards while Nathalie remained the thinker, the cautious one who considered every step and took every precaution.

For this endeavour they were a perfect match.

"Do you have any plans for once you get there?" Ian asked.

"Nothing really," replied Nathalie, we just want to get another look initially."

"I'm not sure that's wise," said Ian, "we should know exactly what we want to do, even have a list of things to do."

"That's an intriguing idea," said Angela, "any suggestions?"

"There's probably a few things we should try as soon as we get there," was his reply. "Firstly, try pinching yourself, see if we feel pain."

Nathalie and Angela nodded in agreement.

"Then, once you've done that, try holding your breath, find out if we need to breathe."

Again Angela and Nathalie nodded together at his comments.

"Then try some sudden, vigorous exercise, maybe jumping up and down on the spot. See if you get tired, and check your pulse."

"So we first check our physical responses?" asked Nathalie.

"And how we interact with the environment," Ian added, "to see if it operates under the same laws of physics as ours."

"So we can tell if we still exist in this universe you mean?" asked Nathalie, now becoming intrigued by Ian's methodical approach.

"Precisely," he replied, "and to find out what our restrictions are in it. Because if we need to breathe, then are we mortal there? We know nothing about the place. Not about whatever god is up there or what the place is like. We need information, we need data about where we're going. It's a whole new environment."

"Okay, so I do a number of physical tests," said Angela, "and we can work them out over the next few days. But there are others there, other dead people and things that call themselves angels. What should I ask them?"

"We've already thought of speaking to other dead people, maybe with luck we can get some details from a few of them and confirm them back here," said Nathalie.

"Oh, I like that," said Ian, "find things like locations, cause of death. We'll know the time of death, so there's a chance we can track someone down. Then it becomes verifiable, even repeatable. We can start to demonstrate to others that it's real."

"But going back to the angels," said Nathalie, "I think the first thing to confirm is who God is. If they tell us which religion is the right one, then we have a lot more information."

"And try and find out what Heaven and Hell are like. Are they as we've been told, or something completely different?" added Angela.

"Well, that's probably more than enough for your first visit Angela," said Ian. "Once we get those answers, we can start to think what else we want to do."

"Well, we'll have the answers soon," said Nathalie. "With your help Ian, we should be ready to go in a couple of days."

"So what exactly will happen when we try it?" asked Ian.

"Okay, I'll try and explain it as simply as I can," replied Nathalie.

"Don't worry about it being complicated, I want to know," he replied.

"Well, once I've checked Angela's vital signs, I'll prepare her with a heart monitor and a thermometer," said Nathalie.

"I assume the heart monitor goes on her chest, but the thermometer?" he asked.

"It'll be a rectal one," Nathalie said. Ian raised his eyebrows. "Not the most comfortable, but the most reliable given the circumstances I'm afraid."

"Are you monitoring the temperature for the actual process on the day or to collect data?" Ian asked.

"Both," Nathalie replied. "Next she'll undress and climb on the board."

"Undress? You mean she's naked?" said Ian.

"Yes, I figured it'll be easier to handle her unconscious body without wet clothes to strip off when it comes to reviving her. Every second is vital."

"Are you okay with that?" asked Ian as he turned to Angela, "I mean if you want I can wait in another room unless I'm needed."

Angela just laughed. "Oh, it's no problem," she said. "I know you British are a little shy about these things, but round here we don't bother."

"Oh, okay," was Ian's somewhat awkward response.

Nathalie couldn't help but smile at Angela's familiar comments and Ian's familiar shock.

"Once we strap her onto the board," continued Nathalie, "we'll put a mask on her so she can breathe underwater and then lower into the ice water. It'll take a few minutes for her heart to stop and once it does, we'll wait ten minutes, then bring her out and start to revive her."

"What are we lowering her into?" asked Ian, "I mean, what's it made of?"

"It's a large plastic vat," said Angela, "about four feet deep and long enough for my head to go under the water. We've got an industrial ice maker set up beside it, working twenty four hours a day so we have enough ice ready to go whenever we need it. All we do is lift a flap on the side of the machine and the ice pours into the vat."

"Can we break the vat in a hurry?" asked Ian.

"Why would we?" Nathalie replied.

"Well, if we have any problems getting her out, we need to be able to tear the side off in a hurry. If it was glass I'd have a sledgehammer handy, but for plastic I guess we need some kind of cutting tool."

"Okay, good idea," said Angela. "We should have something suitable, so we'll keep it handy during the attempt."

Nathalie and Ian nodded in response.

"We should record the process as well, somehow," said Ian.

"You mean set up a camcorder?" said Angela.

"It's more to record anything you say when you wake up, so you can just tell us what you remember without waiting for us to record it."

"Good idea, we'll have one ready to roll for when we wake up." Angela replied.

"That's all I can think of just now," Ian said, "but we have a couple of days and if I come up with anything I'll bring it to you."

"You've given us quite a bit to think about already" said Nathalie, "I think you're going to come in very handy with us."

"I just want to help," said Ian. "I want to know as much as you do."

Chapter 6

Nathalie watched while Angela sat staring into empty space. The day had finally come to try again and this time there was a deeper sense of foreboding than either had felt on the first attempt. Now the two of them were here again, once more trying to cheat death together.

"Your vital signs are good, if a little elevated," said Nathalie.

"Not surprising, is it?" said a subdued Angela. She looked up at Nathalie. "Shall we begin?"

"Yes," she replied. "Lie down and roll over." Nathalie held up the rectal thermometer as Angela stared at it. All Angela's drive and determination seemed diminished in her, but slowly she did as she was told.

"Does it hurt?" Angela asked. Nathalie lifted up Angela's bath robe, ready to insert the thermometer.

"Does what hurt?"

"When you put it in?" There was a tremor in Angela's voice that disturbed Nathalie and she decided to switch to her best bedside manner. Sitting down on the bed beside Angela she placed a reassuring hand on Angela's hip.

"Well, let me tell you a story about that," Nathalie began. "Before I worked in emergency medicine, I spent six months performing colonoscopies, which is basically sticking cameras up people's bottoms. I saw a lot of old people, but every so often I'd get someone who wasn't so old, and the young men could be an interesting bunch. They were almost always either petrified or over compensating, full of bravado and trying to be as macho as possible."

"But there was one, he was different from the rest. For most people it's horrible, a forced intimacy, but to him it was a fascinating experience. He asked questions throughout the procedure, always wanting to know what was going on. At the end of it he told me why he was so relaxed. A few days beforehand he'd had exactly the same experience, but at the other end when he'd had a camera stuffed down his throat. He said it had been a traumatic experience, and that in comparison he hadn't expected this to be anywhere near as unpleasant, adding that it should be easy as this end didn't have a gag reflex."

Angela laughed at the comment.

"He said that although it wasn't as bad as the endoscopy, it turns out that while his backside doesn't have a gag reflex, it does have a fairly powerful clench reflex, and that one end almost felt as bad as another. Of course I then had to embarrass myself, because without thinking I rolled my eyes, laughed and said 'tell me about it'. As soon as I said it I realised he knew exactly what I meant by it."

"We're not talking about medical procedures, are we?" said Angela, now laughing along with Nathalie.

"No, we're not!" she replied.

Angela collapsed into uncontrolled laughter and knowing she would never be this relaxed again, Nathalie took her chance. Without a word of warning she slid the thermometer straight into Angela's anus. A brief high pitched yelp cut short Angela's laughter, a yelp that ended with Angela more surprised than anything else.

"Is that it? Is it in?" she asked.

"It's all the way in," Nathalie responded as she placed the straps around her legs to hold it in.

"Really? Is that it? I can barely feel it."

"You won't be saying that when you try to walk," Nathalie said, "although these modern wireless ones are nice and small and they'll feed me your temperature to a monitor that'll record everything. Now, time to go. Are you ready?" Angela nodded and stood up. The two women walked together through to the next room where Ian was waiting. He stood sombrely by the board that Angela was to be strapped to.

Angela walked towards it. She looked at the straps on it as if it was some sort of torture device or a sacrificial altar. Her stare lingered as her natural will to live fought the urge to see beyond death. It took a burst of sheer will power to overcome it.

"Let's do this," she said and threw off the bath robe. Ian caught it as it fell and he tossed it to the side of the room. Adrenalin now started to pump in Angela and excitement began to batter down her fear. She jumped onto the board and laid her hands and ankles on the straps.

"Are you sure you want to go through with this?" Ian asked.

"Yes, yes, let's go now," she said. Ian tied the straps around her wrists, ankles and waist as Nathalie attached the heart monitor to her. When everything was in place Nathalie stood by her head with the face mask.

"Last chance to back out," she said, her own voice now trembling. Nathalie's fear was also building, a fear beyond anything she felt on the first attempt. Her stomach was churning as if she was the one to risk death today.

"Time for me to die," Angela responded with a smile. Nathalie kissed her forehead and placed the mask over her face. Nathalie and Ian both took one of Angela's hands in theirs as Nathalie began a short countdown.

"I'm dropping you in five...four...three...two...one..." Nathalie hit the button to release the board and as it slid into the vat she felt a sickening twist in her stomach at Angela's scream of pain as the freezing water consumed her. She looked at Ian who had himself turned pale, shaking and sweating with the same fear as she was. She grabbed his hand and held it tightly, fighting to control her stomach and even her bladder as the screams of pain from Angela slowly began to subside.

Angela's eyes snapped open the moment she felt awake again. Immediately she felt a sensation resembling bliss, of floating freely in utter peace, but it quickly turned to a pang of elation when she realised she was enshrouded by a familiar haze, and that they had been successful. But the elation quickly gave way to a sense of urgency about her planned experiments and she leapt to her feet and looked around her. It was just like the last time, with people emerging from the haze to be greeted by pairs of angels in white robes. Her two angels approached her, smiling the same bland smile worn by all the angels.

"Hello Angela," the first one said. Angela ignored him, she was already focusing on the experiments they had discussed. She reached down to her arm to pinch it, but before she could do that she realised something unexpected.

"Oh, I'm naked," she said. The angels thought she was talking to them.

"Yes, you must have died that way," said one of them.

"Would you like a robe?" asked the other.

"No, it's okay," she replied, brushing them off. She pinched the skin on her arm and yelped slightly as she felt the pain.

"Would you come with us?" said an angel. Angela couldn't answer. She was holding her breath. She quickly found herself gasping for air. She thought about trying some exercise after this test but she could already feel her heart pounding as she breathed heavily.

She had her first set of data from the afterlife.

"Are you alright?" asked the second angel as Angela bent over while she caught her breath.

"Yes, I'm fine," she replied. The angels looked concerned.

"Oh dear, she doesn't really understand, does she?" said an angel."No, I understand," Angela replied, "I'm dead, this is the afterlife." As she spoke her eyes darted around. She needed to find someone to talk to, someone dead she could get information from. As she saw a group of people a few metres away she began to walk towards them.

Almost immediately she stopped. She felt a dull, uncomfortable ache and realised she still had the thermometer in her. She reached behind her and pulled it out. Curiously, it was an uncomfortable sensation, and it surprised Angela that it didn't feel any different to how she'd have expected it to feel while she was alive.

She made a mental note and continued to the people. She approached the first one and extended her hand.

"Hi, I'm Angela," she said. The man reached out to take her hand.

"Sorry, did you say you were an angel?" he asked, having misheard her German accent. Angela decided to lie.

"Yes I am," she replied, "can you tell me your name, and where and how you died?"

"Don't you know?" he replied.

"Yes, but it's a test, we need to make sure you have made the journey intact," was the answer she made up on the spot.

"Oh, okay then. My name is George, George Cameron."

"You seem very accepting of your death George," she replied.

"I knew it was coming. I've had cancer for years."

"Where did you die?" she continued without stopping for any small talk.

"At my home."

"And where was that?"

"I live in a town called Marathon, in Canada on the shores of Lake Superior."

"Any living relatives?"

"My wife, and two children," he replied. Tears formed in his eyes at their memory. Angela placed her hand on his shoulder.

"What were their names?" she asked.

"My wife is called Melissa, and my kids are Douglas and Peter."

"Thank you," she replied. She turned to the man's two angels who had watched the exchange with surprise and said "over to you now," before turning and walking back to her own angels.

"Are you ready to go now?" they asked her.

"Oh, I have a few questions first," she asked. "First of all, which god are we talking about her? There are so many to choose from."

"Well, strictly speaking, God is represented by the Catholic Church." said an angel.

"Although any of the Abrahamic faiths are pretty close to the mark. Judaism was right in its time and Islam follows the same god, so all of them will get in."

"Get in? You mean to Heaven, yes?"

"Yes, to Heaven."

"And what is in Heaven?" she asked.

"It is your new life, a life with God."

"And if I don't get there?"

"Then you will go to Hell."

"And what's it like in Hell?" she asked.

"Oh that I cannot say," replied an angel.

"Only the damned have been there," replied the other, "and only the damned know its tortures."

"So you haven't been there?" she asked.

"Of course not."

"So do you know anyone who has been there?" she persisted.

"Well, I meet lots of people who go there," said an angel.

"Although we've never actually met anyone who has already been there," replied the other.

"So that's a no. You don't know anything about it, not really."

"Just that it's a place of suffering," replied one angel.

"So what makes you get sent to Hell?" she asked.

"Not believing in God," replied an angel.

"And not loving him," added the second. Angela felt herself wince slightly at this revelation. She knew a god of some description existed, but she would never love him, not after what she had witnessed.

"Why should I love him?" she asked. "There's so much suffering in the world."

"It's not his fault is it?" replied an angel.

"And it's not like he can do anything about it." The last comment took Angela by surprise.

"What do you mean he can't do anything about it?" she exclaimed. "Isn't he all knowing and all powerful?" The angels both turned to look at her.

"Well, you'll find out one day, won't you?" an angel said.

"But it won't be today," said the other.

"Wait!" shouted Angela as the mist began to enshroud her, but it was too late. She was hit by a bout of dizziness and everything began to go black. She was going back.

Angela sat up violently, panting for breath. Nathalie ran to her side, holding her shoulder as Angela continued to breathe heavily.

"It's okay," said Nathalie, "you're back, you're back."

"George Cameron, George Cameron," Angela shouted between breaths.

"Who's that?" Nathalie asked.

"Write it down!" she replied.

"Relax," said Ian, "we're filming everything on the camcorder, remember? Who is he?"

"He's from Marathon in Canada, wife is Melissa, two children as well, Douglas and Peter," she replied.

"It worked then?" asked Nathalie. Angela looked at her and nodded as she smiled.

"It worked perfectly," she said. "I've been back, seen it all again."

"Did you manage the test?" asked Ian.

"All of them, and more" she replied, wide eyed with excitement.

"Okay, let's all just relax," said Nathalie, "your body's been through a lot, you need to rest."

"Yes, but I've so much to tell you," Angela said.

"We're not going anywhere," replied Nathalie, "so take it easy, rest for a few hours, then you can tell us everything."

"I can't sleep," she continued, "I'm too excited, I need to tell you all about it." Angela began to climb up from the bed, but she was immediately hit by dizziness and had to be helped back down on the bed by Nathalie.

"Okay, you can talk just now but lie down," said Nathalie. Angela nodded in defeat as she lay back on the bed. Nathalie took hold of Angela's hand as Ian took Angela's other hand. "Now, tell us about it, tell us everything."

"I woke up," Angela started, "the same as before amongst the haze. But this time I was naked."

"You were naked?" asked Ian.

"Of course," added Nathalie, "when I was there I was in the clothes I wore when I died."

"I still had the thermometer in me as well," added Angela, "and it was uncomfortable when I pulled it out."

"So we can take things with us," said Ian. "Looks like the ancient Egyptians were right then when they buried people with their possessions."

Nathalie raised her eyebrows.

"I had to breathe as well," Angela continued, "and when I breathed again after holding my breath my heart was pounding."

"So we have bodies, even a metabolism," said Nathalie.

"Can we die there?" wondered Ian.

"We'll worry about that later," said Nathalie, "now carry on Angela."

"I was told the Catholic Church is the true church, although Jews, Muslims and other Christians get into heaven."

Ian's put his face in his palm. "Oh for fuck's sake," he said, "is that bullshit really the truth?"

"Afraid so," said Nathalie, "I was told that as well."

"It's also not enough to believe in him," Angela said, "we have to love him too."

Nathalie and Ian looked at each other nervously.

"Yes, that's me screwed as well," Angela added before lying back and closing her eyes.

"You're exhausted, aren't you?" Nathalie asked. Angela nodded. "Then get some sleep and we'll talk more later." Angela never heard her. She was already asleep.

Chapter 7

The cool Bavarian evening air made the balcony the perfect place for Nathalie to contemplate everything that had happened. Standing in the soft breeze she stared out into space, her mind focused on the events of the day, of both Angela's experiences on the afterlife, and the medical effects on her body of what she had endured. She never noticed as Ian walked out to stand beside her.

"You did it," he said as Nathalie jumped slightly in surprise. "You got her back there."

"Yes, we did," she said, pride only slightly showing itself on her face.

"So when do I try it?" Ian asked.

"I need to have a close look at Angela's health, see if it's affected her first," she replied, "but after that, you can go as soon as Angela's on her feet again, probably in a couple of weeks when I have a few days off work."

"We could never have done this without you," he said, putting his hand on her shoulder.

And I can never go as well with you, she heard herself saying inside as she felt a longing to go herself, a longing she knew these two could never help her fulfil. She just nodded in response though, not wanting to diminish the accomplishment.

"We should give some thought to what she said though," she said, wanting to turn her mind to more productive thinking. "I think we've learnt a lot from her already."

"Agreed," he replied, nodding.

"We know it's a real world, with real physics," she continued. "We have bodies, we need to breathe and we have a heart. The next step from that is to find out if we need to eat or drink."

"And if we do, what do we eat and drink?" said Ian as his mind took the facts one stage further.

"And what about the toilet?" said Nathalie. "Do we need to go in the afterlife?"

"Are you suggesting I squat down and try and take a dump when I get there?" Ian asked with a laugh.

"We'll add it to the list of experiments," she replied, also with a laugh. "But it makes me wonder, is there an ecosystem in heaven? We need food for energy, the energy here comes from the sun, so where does the energy come from there?"

"Now we're talking about the laws of thermodynamics," Ian said, "so maybe we need to think about the physics over there next. Are there any basic experiments we can do?"

"That's an interesting idea," she replied. "We know we can take objects with us, so can we take something for an experiment." The thought hung in the air for a few seconds.

"Maybe a pendulum of some kind?" was Ian's first suggestion. "We could swing it and see if it slows down."

"Perpetual motion machines, of course," she replied, "a pendulum that never stops would be one."

"What about magnets?" Ian asked. "We take a couple over, see if magnetism works."

"A compass as well," Nathalie suggested.

"Even better, how about something electronic?" said Ian. "Electronics require all kinds of physical laws to work properly."

"How about a digital camera?" asked Nathalie. Ian paused, letting the idea hang in the air for a few seconds before answering.

"If we took a photo, we'd have physical evidence," he said. "We'd have something that resembled proof."

"If it works," Nathalie replied. "But I doubt it will. Angela said she removed her thermometer but it was still in her when she woke up."

"So it seems we can't affect things in this world," said Ian.

"This world?" replied Nathalie. Ian let out a laugh.

"This world, universe, dimension, whatever we call it," he replied.

"So what do we call the other place?" Nathalie asked. "It has physical laws, some of them would suggest this place is in our universe, but do we really think we're still in this universe?"

Ian shook his head. "I guess the best name for it for now would be "The Pearly Gates," he said.

"Oh stuff that," replied Nathalie, smiling, "far too damn long winded. Let's just call it 'the Gates' for now." Ian agreed with a shrug of his shoulders.

"Okay, so we have experiments to do, but what next?" said Ian.

"What do you mean?"

"Well, once we've learnt about this place, what do we do with that knowledge?"

"If we can find a way to prove it, we start telling people," Nathalie replied.

"And if not?"

"We still tell people."

"You mean start our own religion?" Ian asked. Nathalie threw her head back and laughed.

"Well, I wouldn't call it that," she replied, "but people deserve to know the truth."

"So we find out all that we can, then tell the world?"

Nathalie nodded.

It was a subdued Angela that lay along the sofa. Wearing her bathrobe she lay with her head on Ian's knee as she recovered from her experience. More than a day had passed since her return to the Gates, but despite her fitness, her recovery was slow. There was work to be done though, and she insisted on getting started as soon as possible.

"Well, I've done some checking," said Nathalie as she sat with her laptop on her knee, "and I've found George Cameron from

Marathon in Canada. His wife posted a comment online that he had died, at pretty much the same time you did."

"So it is real," Angela replied.

"It would seem so," Nathalie said.

"What worries me the most is this idea of loving God," said Ian. "And if you don't, you get sent to Hell. It's all a little more fire and brimstone than most Christians would think."

"I'm more interested in what Heaven and Hell are," said Nathalie. "And if we're there for eternity or not."

"Well, we're supposed to be," Ian replied. "I mean, I'm no theologian, but isn't the Heaven and Hell thing for eternity?"

"You know, I'm not so sure," said Nathalie. "We should forget all the scripture and treat this as something entirely new. We've all heard atheists commenting on how if God is real then he's a psychopath, or neurotic, or any of a number of things. Well, it turns out he is real, and he could well be any of those things. We only have his word for anything after all."

"God's been lying to us?" asked Angela.

"I'm starting to see him less as a creator and more as a tin pot dictator," said Nathalie, "like Stalin, or Kim Yong-il."

"He does seem to demand people love him rather than each other," said Angela, "which isn't exactly the church's official line."

"But the angels say Catholics are correct in what they believe," added Ian.

"Clearly we need more information," said Nathalie.

"Maybe we need a priest," said Angela. "It'd be interesting to tell them what we've found."

"Bad idea. I did that after my accident," said Nathalie, "and the bastard told me to love God."

"I don't know, it might be interesting to ask a few," said Ian, "see what they think. Why not tell them of our experience? We've already proven to ourselves this is real with the details of George Cameron, we could prove it to a priest as well. It is their area of expertise after all."

"You could even send him to the Gates," said Angela, "maybe he'll get some answers for us."

"This is getting insane," said Nathalie, shaking her head.

"Let's not rush things then," said Ian. "Let's just plan for my return. I have a few experiments to try and a few questions to ask, so let's just concentrate on those for now before we start to worry about anything else." Nathalie nodded. "One step at a time, and re-evaluate after each one," he continued.

"Well, it depends on Angela, but if she's up and about by then, let's aim to send you back in two weeks," said Nathalie.

Even as she said it, she felt a pang of jealousy as she watched Ian and Angela on the sofa together. It hadn't escaped her notice how much time Ian had spent with Angela since her return from the Gates. She dismissed the thought, cursing herself for thinking so childishly and tried to put such things to the back of her mind. She had more important things to think about.

Two weeks passed quickly and Ian's time to return had come. They had prepared a watertight bag to wear over his shoulder for when he reached the Gates, containing the tools he would need to perform a few basic experiments. He took a weight on the end of a piece of string to use as a pendulum. He had two magnets and a compass to test for magnetism. And he had a mobile phone, filled with applications that were set up to rapidly drain the battery to see if electronics worked at the Gates. He had a lot to think about as he waited to go.

But it didn't stop the fear. As he sat in his bathrobe as Nathalie checked his vital signs he was visibly trembling and sweat was pouring from his brow.

"You don't have to do this," she said as she watched him shaking with fear.

"I know," he stammered back, "but I have to."

"Well, it's time," she said, "your vitals are all good, you're ready to go."

"So you just have to..." he said before Nathalie cut him off.

"Insert the thermometer? Yes. Roll over on the bed." Ian did as he was told. Nathalie gently pulled up his bathrobe and began to delicately slide it in. He whimpered as it entered him, and when he rolled onto his back Nathalie was sure she saw a few tears, but she said nothing, allowing him to retain some dignity.

"Time to go," she said. He slowly stood up and began to walk to the next room. They walked through the door together and Angela was waiting by the water tank, with everything set up and ready to go. Ian leant against the table, trying to steady his nerves. He took a deep breath and threw the bathrobe off. Suddenly he felt vulnerable in his nakedness. He found himself fighting the urge to panic, to turn and run, and he focussed all his mind on going through with this.

He didn't even notice when he lost control of his bladder. Nathalie felt her heart almost break when she heard the sound of trickling water and she took him in her arms and hugged him tightly. Even when she felt his urine soak through her trouser leg she held him, not letting go until she felt he was ready. When she did, she placed a single kiss on his lips. There was no passion, no fire in the kiss, it was a kiss of friendship, speaking of the unspoken love these three shared, and it brought a little strength to Ian. Angela embraced him as well, and shared the same kiss with him before he found his strength to begin.

"I'm ready," he said as he took a deep breath.

He lay on the table, strapped down securely with Angela stroking his brow while Nathalie fitted the mask. Again his bladder failed him slightly, but no one said anything, letting it pass without comment.

"Are you ready?" Nathalie asked. Ian nodded.

"Are you sure?" asked Angela. "You don't have to."

"Do it," he said through the mask. Nathalie hit the switch and he slid into the water. His screams of pain reduced both women to tears until he was silent.

Even before he opened his eyes, Ian could feel the blissful sensation he remembered from his first visit. Opening them and sitting up, the first thing he realised was that the thermometer was no longer in him. That took him a little by surprise, as he remembered Angela's description of removing it.

Almost as soon as he realised he didn't have the thermometer, he felt an urge need to empty his bowels. The strap that held the thermometer in was probably the only thing that stopped his bowels going the way of his bladder, but now the thermometer was gone he didn't think he could hold it. He jumped to his feet and squatted, letting his bowels finally go. They emptied in seconds and once he was finished he stood up, suddenly at a loss for something to wipe himself with. After a few moments thought, he decided that given the circumstances, it wasn't worth worrying about.

"Okay, come on, focus," he said to himself as he reached into the bag. First out was the mobile phone which he switched on. Holding it he could feel it heating up in seconds as the applications sucked up the battery power. The 'no signal' warning was not unexpected and he quickly took a couple of photos with the phone's camera. Everything seemed to function as normal.

Next he took out the pendulum and began to swing it. He watched as it's slowly swung from side to side, slowing down at the same rate he would expect it to back home.

"Hello Ian," came a voice from behind him.

"Be with you in a minute," he replied as he checked the compass. There was no clear magnetic pole, but the magnets themselves affected both it and each other in the normal manner, with the like poles repulsing each other and the opposites attracting.

"Sorry, just checking something," he said as he turned to see the two angels waiting for him.

"Could you come over here please," an angel said, his face slightly screwed up at the smell Ian had produced. Ian looked down at his faeces on the ground.

"Ah, yes, sorry about that," he said.

"Oh, don't worry, it happens all the time," one angel replied.

"Was it a violent death?" asked the other, "that usually causes these things to happen." Ian just smiled and nodded, hoping he could give these angels the slip and do some exploring.

A few meters a head emerged from the mist as a person sat up. An older woman, he reckoned her to be in her fifties or sixties, stood up from the haze that surrounded them. She was clad only in a surgical gown but she was confused. He slowly walked over to her, wondering what the hell he was going to say.

"I'm dead, aren't I?" she said as he met her. "They told me the operation was risky." The woman looked down at herself and shrugged her shoulders. She was morbidly obese, and Ian assumed that was what she meant.

"You seem rather accepting of it," said Ian.

"I was expecting it to be honest."

"What's your name?" he asked.

"Yvette," she replied.

"I'm Ian. What's your second name?"

"Smith," she answered. Ian smiled, knowing he'd remember that name easily.

"Is that a Welsh accent?" he asked.

"Yes, are you Scottish?"

"Yes, from a little town near Perth. Yourself?"

"Cardiff," she replied, "I was in the hospital there..."

"Will you come with me Ian," said a curt voice from behind him. Ian turned around to face the angels that had followed him.

"Yes, of course," he said, "but can I ask you something first?"

"Of course," replied an angel.

"Am I right in thinking I have to believe in God and love him to get to Heaven?" he asked. "And that what else I've done is largely inconsequential?"

"Yes," replied an angel, "your love of your god is your salvation."

"And I have to be of an Abrahamic faith, Christian, Muslim or Jew, correct?"

"Yes, that is correct," said the other angel.

"Can you tell me where certain people are, certain famous people from history?" he asked.

"We know of everyone's judgement, so yes, ask away," the angel replied, with a slightly smug look on his face.

"Mahatma Gandhi?"

"Hell, he was a heathen."

"Julius Caesar?"

"Hell, he thought himself a god."

"Adolf Hitler?"

"Heaven of course," replied an angel.

"His men did march with 'Gott mit uns' on their belts after all," replied the other. Ian swore under his breath.

"Even though he murdered millions?" Ian asked, dreading the answer.

"How did that hurt God?" the angel asked.

"Okay, never mind," said Ian as his mind moved on to other questions, this time to a thought that had been developing at the back of his mind since he arrived. "When I arrived, I pretty much shit myself. You said that happens a lot, yes?"

"Oh, it's a regular occurrence," was the answer.

"So who cleans it up?" he asked. "And where does it go? Does it rot down, does it go into the ground, what happens to it?" Both angels looked confused.

"Where? It goes nowhere," an angel answered.

"So why isn't this place covered in shit?" he continued. Again, there was a look of confusion.

"Why would it be?" was the answer. It made no sense to Ian, but he decided not to linger on it. He took a second to check the phone before he continued. The battery charge had already dropped a few percent, just as expected.

"So where am I?" he asked.

"You're at the gates of Heaven, in the afterlife," an angel replied, seemingly happier to have had a more normal question.

"Okay, so where is this relative to where I was?" Ian asked.

"You are in the afterlife, is that not enough for you?" was the slightly irritated response.

"No it's not," replied Ian. Both angels looked slightly annoyed. "Because I'm not a disembodied spirit. I have flesh, a heartbeat, I need to breathe. I have a metabolism, and if I need to take a shit I need to eat and drink. Where does the food come from, does it grow? Is it like food on earth?"

"Please, so many questions," said an angel that now struggled to contain the annoyance in his voice. "Yet soon you will be with your lord, if you believe. Such things no longer matter."

"Am I even in the same universe?" Ian asked, not giving up, "because this place seems to have the same physical laws as where I came from. Magnets work, so do electronics. It's like I'm just somewhere else, like a different planet." The angels looked at him with confusion.

"You are here, in the afterlife. There is nothing more to say," replied an angel, now looking genuinely confused. "These magnets you talk of, they are of no consequence. You will soon face God, that is all that matters. Now please, follow me so that you can be processed."

"Sorry, no, please wait, I have more questions," said Ian, but as he said it he felt a dizziness come to him, and darkness claimed him. His time was up.

Ian's eyes slowly opened as he roused from his slumber. Angela's warm smile was the first thing that greeted him as she stood over the bed, holding his hand.

"Yvette Smith," he said weakly, "in a hospital in Cardiff."

"So it worked then?" said Angela. "You went back as well?"

"Yes, and I've got a lot to tell you," he replied. Angela hit the remote switch to start the camera.

"Tell me," she said. "What was the woman's name again?"

"Yvette I think, Yvette Smith, she was having surgery in Cardiff."

"We'll check it out," she replied.

"Ah, he's awake," said Nathalie as she entered the room.

"It worked," he said, "I was back there."

"How are you feeling?" she asked. "You've been asleep for a while, for a few hours."

"I feel like someone's parked a car on my chest," he answered, "but otherwise okay."

"That'll pass," she replied, "so just worry about getting better."

"I can talk now," he said, "I have a lot to tell you."

"Go ahead then."

"First thing, I didn't have the thermometer in me when I arrived."

"That's odd," said Nathalie, "Angela had it."

"That's what I thought," said Ian, "but as soon as I realised it was out I had to go to the toilet."

"Are you saying you had a shit at the Gates?" said Angela, laughing out loud.

"The angels said it happens all the time," he replied.

"Makes sense," Nathalie said, "death is often a traumatic experience. But what about the experiments? The phone was still switched off and there were no photos on it."

"It worked when I was there," Ian said, "everything worked as it would here, the magnets, the pendulum, even the phone."

"What about the compass?" Angela asked.

"There was no magnetic pole, but the compass followed the magnets."

"It's almost like you were still in this universe," Nathalie replied.

"Yes, I asked that," said Ian, "but again they were confused. They said I was at the gates of Heaven and that I'd soon be facing God. I asked about food and why the magnets still worked and they didn't know how to answer. I don't think it was an act, they seemed genuinely confused by my questions."

"Interesting," said Angela, "I never thought they were that smart."

"They did claim to know where everyone from the past had been sent to, famous historical figures I mean."

"Such as?" asked Nathalie.

"Well, Gandhi and Caesar went to Hell, but Hitler went to Heaven."

"Oh, for fuck's sake this is getting ridiculous now," said Nathalie, close to exploding with rage. "What kind of fucked up lunatic is sitting in Heaven, lording it over us? How can he let in Hitler?"

"Nathalie, whoever's up there, he's not the loving, forgiving God of Christianity," said Ian. "He's like the God of the Old Testament, craving attention and love, and being merciless to those who don't give it to him."

Nathalie paused and took a deep breath to contain her anger. "Anything else you need to tell us?" she asked.

"Not that I can think of, but I was wondering, what happened when you took the thermometer out of me?" Nathalie laughed before she answered him.

"As soon as I undid the straps holding it in, it shot out, followed by the contents of your bowels," she replied, "all over the blanket you were on."

"Oh, sorry," he said, feeling embarrassed. Nathalie took his hand and kissed it.

"Don't worry about it," she replied with her best beside manner. "That's nothing unusual, I've seen a lot worse."

Ian put his head back on his pillow. By now he was struggling to stay awake and Nathalie could see this. "Time for rest," she said. "We'll talk more when you've slept a bit."

Once again Nathalie found herself sitting on the top floor balcony's bench in the fading evening light, staring south towards the Alps and contemplating the day's events. It was another success, another step towards uncovering the truth, but she couldn't help the nagging sense of jealousy that lurked at the back of her mind. She desperately wanted to make the journey back herself, but she was the doctor and she had no-one to revive her.

And then there was her imminent return home to consider. Another three day break was almost over and she was facing another return to the seemingly endless banality of daily life. In twenty four hours she'd be on a plane back to London and after so much had happened, she didn't think she could bear to be separated from Ian and Angela.

"I wish you weren't leaving," said Angela's voice from behind her, seemingly echoing her on thoughts. Nathalie turned and saw Angela standing at the door. She walked in and sat down on the bench beside Nathalie.

"Should I quit my job?" she asked, "and come here and live with you?" Angela nodded and smiled.

"Yes, and I hope Ian does too," Angela replied. "The three of us should stay together. We have too much to do."

"I had pretty much already decided to," said Nathalie, "but I should look for a job first."

"Don't worry about it," said Angela. "I can support you until you get something."

"What about Ian?" Nathalie asked.

"I can give a home to anyone who is with us," she said.

"You really mean that? I can move in as soon as I can?"

"How much notice would you have to give?" asked Angela.

"Three months, and I can't just walk out on them if I want a reference," said Nathalie. The smile drained from Angela's face. "But I can probably get myself signed off sick within an hour of getting back. Given my accident and my behaviour at work, they'd probably love to be rid of me."

"You mean that?" said Angela, as a smile broke across her face.

"If it goes according to plan, I can be back by the end of the week," Nathalie replied.

"Fantastic," said Angela, "that means you can really focus on making this as safe as possible for us." Nathalie felt herself wince at Angela's use of the word 'us'. It didn't feel like that for Nathalie. Not until she could make the journey to the Gates herself.

Chapter 8

Ian looked at the grey building in front of him. Recessed from the rest of the street and just a few minutes walk from some of Edinburgh's most notorious strip clubs, this didn't feel to Ian how a Catholic church should look. It seemed almost unassuming, hidden even from the rest of the world. A sudden sense of caution came over Ian as he approached the main doors. How would they react when he told them what he had seen? Would they even believe him? He wondered if he should tell them about Nathalie and Angela and about their return trips to the Gates if they didn't.

As he stepped through the doors, the church seemed to open up and grow, as if he had stepped into a grand cathedral, not just some dull unassuming building on a side street. Wooden pews stretched to the altar at the far end and large murals, taller than a person, ringed the room, depicting the Stations of the Cross. A plaque by the door told the story of their restoration and Ian smiled and thought of Angela when he read that the paintings were originally by a Bavarian artist over a century ago.

He took a seat near the back of the church. The pews were mostly empty, but there was the occasional person sitting by themselves nearer the altar. He looked at the pulpit on the left, which was empty. He felt awkward, even clumsy as he sat there, not sure of what to do now, or where to go.

"Can I help you?" asked a voice from behind him that seemed to hauntingly echo the tone of the angels. Ian turned round and he saw what he assumed was a priest, a man with a strangely friendly face and dressed in clerical clothing. Ian stood up to greet him.

"Hello," he said, "my name's Ian." He extended his hand to the priest.

"Hello Ian," said the priest. "I'm Father Peter Harrison."

"I'm not really sure why I'm here," he said, still uncertain of how to start the conversation.

"Is something troubling you?" asked Father Peter as both men sat down.

"I'm not sure if troubled is the right word," Ian answered.

"Why don't you tell me from the start then?"

"I died recently," said Ian, which got a confused look from Father Peter.

"Died?"

"It was an accident, I fell through some ice." Father Peter nodded in understanding. "I was hill walking with friends, and I was under the ice for a long time before they got me out. So long that my heart had stopped for quite a while."

"That must have been a terrifying experience," said Father Peter.

"It was, more so than you realise," said Ian.

"How so?"

"When I died, I went somewhere," Ian said. Again Father Peter looked confused.

"You mean hospital?"

"No, I mean the afterlife."

"You mean you had a near death experience?" asked Father Peter.

"I saw the afterlife," said Ian, "with angels and judgements. I saw people sent to Hell, and some to Heaven."

"You stood at the Pearly Gates?" Father Peter hovered between scepticism and fascination. He'd heard of near death experiences from members of his church before, but no-one had ever reported anything like this to him. He decided to listen to what Ian had to say before he decided if he believed him or not.

"Yes, I saw it all."

"Tell me about it," Father Peter said.

"I woke in a haze," Ian began, "dressed as I was when I fell in the water, only dry."

"You took your clothes with you?" asked Father Peter.

"Oh, I was no disembodied spirit," said Ian, "I had aches in my muscles from the climbing I had done. I breathed, I had a pulse, I even felt hungry." Father Peter now seemed fascinated by what he was hearing. Unlike other near death experiences, there was nothing vague about this account, it had a physical reality, something lacking from other accounts. It had already opened a theological can of worms, but Father Peter wanted to hear more.

"It sounds very real," said Father Peter.

"There were other people there as well," continued Ian, "and I spoke to one of them. She told me how and where she'd died. I remembered and looked her death up. She was real, she died in surgery in a Cardiff hospital."

"You met other people there?" Father Peter found Ian's last comment somewhat disquieting. It had a feel of authenticity about it now. He had so far believed that Ian believed what he said, even if it had just been some kind of hallucination, but to meet another person and to know their name brought to Father Peter the prospect of certainty, of proof, a concept almost alien to his religion.

"They say about a hundred people die a minute, and they all go through the same process up there, they all meet in the same place. I saw lots of other people."

"You said some went to Hell," said Father Peter.

"More than some," he replied, "the unbelievers, the unbaptised, all those who don't love God are condemned. I saw children sent to Hell because they weren't baptised and murderers get into Heaven."

"No, you must be mistaken," said Father Peter, "God is forgiving, he wouldn't damn a child."

"I saw it," said Ian, "I saw it with my own eyes, children damned, and scum sent to Heaven. I even saw a few people on their way to Heaven mocking those who were going to Hell."

"You can't have seen that," said Father Peter, shaking his head. "I can't believe that."

"Think again," said Ian. "Remember the jealous, angry God of the Old Testament, who demanded sacrifice and flooded the whole world? Do you really think he's changed that much?"

"Of course he has," said Father Peter, "the Bible tells us how much he loves us."

"And he demands love in return, unconditional, unquestioning love, and he damns those who don't give it to him."

"No, God loves us, he forgives us."

"I saw it all," said Ian. It was too much for Father Peter. He stood up and began to walk away backwards, still facing Ian as he talked.

"No, you're wrong, you must be," he said as he backed away before turning and walking off at a brisk pace that was almost a run.

Ian sighed. This was no more than he expected. Even though this church had been quite specifically stated as the true church, its members clearly could not comprehend the reality of the situation.

He began the slow, despondent walk back to his car. He passed the trio of strip clubs and felt the urge to go in. He felt a terrible loneliness without Angela and Nathalie around and the idea of a private dance seemed attractive.

He walked into one of the bars, the seediest looking one he could find. It was small, little more than a bar with some space to stand by it. At the end of the bar was the stage, if you could call something so small a stage. Barely a metre across a woman stood on it as she danced nude for a baying crowd of men. He looked at her, and all he could think of were his friends. He wondered if Angela and Nathalie would think less of him for being here. As his eyes lingered on her form, he felt a sudden pang of guilt and rushed out. Part of him could see Angela wanting to jump up on the stage herself, but he knew Nathalie would be a little disappointed in him for being there.

He returned to his car and with the image of the nude dancer still in his head, decided to call Angela. It wasn't for any real reason, he just needed to hear a friend's voice especially after the conversation with the priest. Angela was delighted to hear from him and had some good news.

"Oh, I'm so glad you called," she said as he told her about his meeting with the priest, "as I have someone else for you to try."

"In Scotland?" he asked.

"I found a post online from a man who said his father had a similar experience. He lives in a place called Arbroath. Do you know it?"

"It's about an hour and a bit's drive from here," he replied.

"Fantastic!" she exclaimed. "He said his father was a fisherman who was thrown overboard in winter and was revived in hospital when the coastguard rescued him."

"Ah, another one who was frozen," replied Ian enthusiastically.

"The trouble is, he's dead, and I can't find a way to contact his son."

"Oh," said Ian.

"But this post said that he talked to the priest about it, and the priest was confused," said Angela, "so you could try the church there. Apparently it's the one in a place nearby called Montrose."

"A Catholic church?" asked Ian.

"Yes, I think so. Can you go there?"

"I can be there by lunchtime," he replied.

"Good, call me once you've been." Ian hung up and got his car started ready for the drive, his spirit and enthusiasm riding high once again.

The first thing Ian noticed when he left his car in Montrose was the wind. The warm spring Edinburgh air had been replaced by a blast of icy wind from the North Sea that seemed to suck the life from him. Grabbing his jacket for the short walk to the church he cursed the weather and headed quickly through the church gate.

The church in Montrose was a modest one compared to the grandeur of the interior of the Edinburgh church. There were no grand murals on the wall, hardly any silverware and no gold crosses, almost no opulence of any kind. Small, tasteful paintings marked the stations of the cross, and the pews stretched almost right to the altar. It was a place of simple worship for a small community and Ian hoped he might get a more honest audience than the last time.

"Can I help you?" asked a head as it popped up from between some pews. A man dressed in clerical clothing stood up, holding a hammer and a handful of nails. Despite having so much time to think about it on the long drive up, Ian still felt unsure how to open the conversation. He tried to find the words, but he struggled to say anything.

"Come in, sit down," said the man with a friendly smile. Ian walked to the pew the man was at. "Call me Father Richard," he said, holding out his hand and giving Ian a firm, friendly handshake.

"My name's Ian," he replied as he sat down.

"You look troubled," said Father Richard. Ian nodded. "Well, I find a good strong cup of tea always helps, do you want one?"

"Yes, please," replied Ian as the priest disappeared through a side door, returning with two mugs of tea.

"Do you want sugar?" Father Richard asked.

"No, thank you," replied Ian as he took a mug. Its heat felt good in his hands after the cold Montrose air.

"Now, why don't you tell me what's troubling you?" said Father Richard. Ian took a deep breath.

"Do you know what a near death experience is?" Ian asked.

"Yes, yes I do," replied Father Richard, his eyes narrowing slightly.

"Well I had one, I drowned in freezing water before I was revived."

"I'm guessing this was quite an experience," said Father Richard.

"You could say that."

"Tell me everything."

Ian began to recount his story, telling Father Richard only of his experience after his accident. Father Richard looked at Ian intensely as he talked, following every detail of the story, never interrupting. Eventually Ian reached the end of his account and Father Richard sat back in his pew, shaking his head.

"I never would have believed it," said Father Richard. "How can two people have such a similar experience?"

"Someone else had this?" asked Ian, trying not to sound like he knew the answer.

"A fisherman, years ago. I had just arrived here, I was still a young man, but he told me of an experience he had in his youth, when he was thrown out of a boat in a winter storm and fished out an hour later with his heart stopped. They managed to revive him, but he came back with a strange story of an afterlife where judgement was severe and without mercy. I dismissed it at the time, but your story is so like his."

"I've learnt since my accident that when you die in cold water like that, you can survive a long time with a stopped heart," said Ian. "Maybe that gives you the time to start to cross over."

"If your story is true, it's both wondrous and awful," said Father Richard. "I almost wish I could go and see it for myself."

Ian made a sudden decision to tell him everything. "I might be able to arrange that," he said. Father Richard looked at him with a puzzled look. "There are others who have had the same experience. We got together, through the internet. One was a doctor, someone used to reviving people with stopped hearts."

"No, surely not," said Father Richard, wide eyed with astonishment.

"Two of us have gone back. We've performed experiments, tried to figure out what kind of a place the afterlife is."

"Are you mad?"

"Probably, but if you're in good physical condition, you can go back yourself."

"You can't be serious," said Father Richard.

"Don't you want to know? To see for yourself?" Something inside Father Richard wanted to accept this insane offer, but he held back.

"No, of course not," he said, "I have my faith, that's enough."

"Really? Is it really enough? Don't you want to see for yourself?"

"What good would it do if I went?"

"We don't know what to make of it all," said Ian, "but you're a priest. No-one is more qualified to interpret what they see up there than you."

Father Richard couldn't answer that. He shrugged his shoulders, by now lost for words.

"Look, I won't push it," said Ian passing Father Richard a card, "but here's my phone number. If you change your mind, call me." Ian stood up and began to walk away before turning back. "Just think about it. You seem a decent guy, it'd be good to have you along with us." He turned and walked out the door. Father Richard was left on his own, sitting with the card and desperately fighting his own sense of curiosity and trying to think of a reason why he should not take up Ian's offer.

Ian was only a few miles down the road when his phone started ringing. He pulled over and looked at the number. He didn't recognise it, but optimistically thought it might be a local number. As he answered it, he heard a familiar voice.

"This is Father Richard," said the voice.

"Hi Father Richard, it's Ian here."

"Your offer, about going to the afterlife. Is it true? Can you actually do it?"

"Yes, we can do it," said Ian. "We've done it twice now, under very controlled circumstances, so we know it wasn't just luck."

"What does it involve?"

"We have to freeze you. You get dropped into ice cold water and it hurts like hell, but you breathe through a tube. The cold gets you in a few minutes, so it's over quickly."

"And I'll be all right afterwards?"

"You have to be in good shape to do it and I can't give you any guarantees, but we have a good doctor on the team, she knows what she's doing."

"Well, I was told in my youth that you have to be as fit as an athlete to do God's work, so I've always kept in shape."

"Does that mean you're interested?" asked Ian.

"I wouldn't go that far," he replied, "but if you want my help I'd certainly be happy to come and speak to you all to discuss it and try and help you interpret it."

"Well that's our big problem," said Ian, "we don't really know what to make of it and getting a priest to believe us isn't easy."

"Where do you do this?" Father Richard asked.

"In Munich," Ian replied, "but don't worry, we'll pay for your flight and we have a place you can stay."

"Okay, I'm in."

"We need to talk," said Nathalie as she poked her head round Steven's office door.

"Yes, of course, come in, sit down" he replied, standing up. He waited until Nathalie was seated comfortably before sitting down. "How are you?" he asked.

"To be honest, I'm struggling a little," she replied.

"How so?"

"I don't sleep well," she replied. "Every time I close my eyes I feel like I'm back inside my car, terrified, thinking I'm about to die. I have nightmares every night. I wake up screaming and sweating, sometimes several times a night."

"Oh, Nathalie, I never knew," Steven said. "I mean we've all thought you were looking tired, but we didn't think it was this bad."

"I've tried to be strong," she continued, trying desperately without success to fake some tears, "but I can only handle so much."

"How much sleep are you getting?"

"Not much, sometimes I sleep okay when I have days off, but when I'm in here and we get casualties from a traffic accident, then that's it, forget sleeping that night." She managed to force a few tears out as she spoke, something that made Steven shuffle uncomfortably in his seat. "And I just can't go on," she continued, "I just feel so alone and helpless." As she finished, she thought about Angela and Ian, how close they seemed to be getting, and of how she saw no way back to the Gates and she had no problem crying. The tears now flowed freely.

"How can we help you?" said Steven, who was by now feeling overwhelmingly uncomfortable at having such an emotional staff member to deal with.

"I don't know," she replied between sobs, "I don't know how I can take it anymore, it's all too much for me."

"What can we do to help you?" Steven asked.

"I can't handle it here," she said, now appearing to cry uncontrollably.

"Do you want counselling?" Steven asked.

"It might help," said Nathalie, "but it's this place, coming here that makes it all worse."

"You mean the memories of the accident?" said Steven, "you associate them with this place?"

"Yes," she said, now getting her tears under control before she went in for the kill. "Every moment I'm in here reminds me of my accident." She paused for a second before continuing. "I can't come here anymore."

"Are you resigning?" Steven asked.

"I don't want to," she replied, "but what else can I do? I feel terrible, letting you all down like this."

"Nathalie, it's okay," he said. "I hate to lose you but I understand. If you need to go, you need to go. I'll give you a good reference of course and help you find something if you want."

"How long do I need to stay for?" she asked, forcing out a last few tears.

"You don't," he replied. "You're a wreck. I'll sign you off with post traumatic stress right now until I can sort out the paperwork for your resignation."

"Thank you," she replied.

"I'll need something in writing from you," Steven continued, "just something to confirm you're resigning. Don't worry about the date, just say it's with immediate effect or something." Nathalie nodded submissively, saying nothing. "Just make sure you stay in touch," he continued, "you have friends here after all."

"Yes, of course."

"Will you try to find something right away?" he asked.

"No," she replied, "I think a few weeks to myself, maybe get away somewhere, somewhere far from here."

"That sounds a very good idea," said Steven.

"Thank you for this," said Nathalie, trying to hide her excitement, "it's definitely all okay?"

"Well, it leaves us a bit stretched, but I'll get cover easily enough," he replied, "but don't worry about it, your health is the main thing here."

"I'm sorry," she said.

"We just want to see you get better," said Steven. "Now, I take it you want to avoid saying goodbye to everyone?"

"Yes, I'd rather just slip away quietly for now."

"Then go," he replied, "I'll explain to everyone and we can all get together for a proper goodbye later, okay?"

"Thank you," said Nathalie and stood up. Steven stood up and reached out to shake her hand.

"It's been a pleasure working with you," he said as they shook hands.

"You too," said Nathalie. A painful silence followed for a few seconds.

"I'll see you around then," said Steven. Nathalie smiled weakly and nodded before she turned towards the door.

"Goodbye," she said.

"Goodbye," he replied.

Nathalie quickly headed to reception and out of the main door without being stopped by any of the staff. As she walked out into the rain she felt a terrible weight fall from her shoulders. She was free to move to Munich.

Chapter 9

"Call me Richard," said the group's latest recruit as Ian introduced him to Nathalie and Angela in the grounds of Angela's house. Now stripped of the clerical clothing and wearing what he would call 'civvies' Richard seemed less like the kindly priest Ian had met in Montrose and more like an army officer. He may have been in his late fifties, but Richard was lean and fit, with the appearance of a man ten years younger and he held himself with pride and dignity.

He was an immediate hit with both women who warmed to his friendly smile and kind demeanour almost instantly.

"Hello Richard," said Nathalie, shaking his hand. Angela too greeted him with a handshake, deciding that a hug and a kiss might not be as welcome to Richard as it had been on her first meeting with both the others.

"So, Nathalie, you're the doctor, yes?" asked Richard. Nathalie nodded.

"Yes I am, I take it you have a few questions."

"Well, not so much questions, I just want to know what happens."

"Ian, why don't you take his bags to his room," said Nathalie before turning back to Richard, "and I'll take you inside and show you where it happens." Richard followed Nathalie into the house, through the corridor that led to the room they had set up for their work. Richard looked at the water tank, now filled with ice and water, with the board someone would be strapped to inside it and the rest of the equipment with a sense of excited dread.

"So this is it?" he asked.

"Yes, we call it the departure lounge, although there's a room next door as well where we prepare whoever is going," answered Nathalie.

"Prepare?" asked Richard.

"Yes, has Ian explained any of it to you?"

"Not really, he mentioned icy water and a lot of pain, but not much else."

"Be warned, some if it you might not be too comfortable with."

"Such as?" asked Richard.

"Well, firstly, we do this naked," said Nathalie, waiting to see how he reacted.

"Naked, why naked?" asked Richard, more confused than shocked.

"The first thing we do when we treat a hypothermia victim is to remove their clothes, especially if they're wet. I'd rather not have to waste time removing them, especially as I don't have any trained nurses with me."

"Oh, okay," said Richard, "so it's a safety issue?"

"I like to reduce risk," answered Nathalie.

"Anything else?"

"Just the agonising pain of being plunged into freezing cold water," she replied. Richard nodded, seemingly unphased by it. "Oh, and the rectal thermometer," added Nathalie.

Richard briefly gave her a suspicious look, wondering what kind of people he'd gotten himself involved with, but a few seconds of consideration made him realise it made sense. "I guess it's the best way to monitor body temperature," he said.

"I'm sending Angela back tonight," Nathalie said, "we want you to be there, to see what it's like at this end in case you ever choose to go yourself."

"I'm not planning it," he replied, "but I probably should, shouldn't I?"

"Well, I want you to know what's going on and that you know exactly what we're doing here," replied Nathalie.

"And if I did want to try it myself?" Richard asked.

"Then I give you a fitness test," she replied, "and if you pass you can do it the next day."

As he paced up and down by the water tank, the biggest thing Richard feared was seeing Angela naked. He had never even seen a naked woman before and there was no denying Angela was an attractive woman.

"You look nervous," said Ian, who had a pretty good idea of what the cause of it was, "almost like a teenager going on his first date."

Richard laughed nervously. "Oh, tell me Angela's really fat under her clothes, or she has hideous tattoos, or something," Richard replied, trying to break his nervousness with a joke.

"Sorry mate," replied Ian, "she's got one hell of a body so I suggest you make a lot of eye contact." Both men laughed, but Richard's laugher died when the door opened and the two women walked in.

"We're ready to go," said Nathalie, "everyone okay here?" She looked directly at Richard, trying to gauge his feelings but all she could read in him was apprehension. "Well, let's do it then."

"Here you are," said Angela as she dropped her robe and handed it to Ian. Richard tried to avert his gaze, but he couldn't help himself. His eyes turned to Angela's body, but he didn't linger on her curves, instead he looked at the straps around the tops of her thighs.

"It keeps the thermometer in," said Nathalie as she noticed where he was looking. Richard's head immediately snapped up and away from Angela who was by now jumping up onto the bed. As she sat on the board, she turned round to look at him.

"Don't be embarrassed," she said to Richard. "What we're doing here is something special, something that could be quite wonderful, and now you're here, we're friends."

"Yes, yes, sorry..." he mumbled, feeling both awkward and embarrassed.

"Come here," said Angela, holding out her hand to him. He stepped towards her, taking her hand. He felt his heart pounding like crazy inside himself. "Don't be shy," Angela continued, "don't feel awkward, or nervous or anything else you need to apologise for. "We're friends, and we have nothing to hide from each other." She placed her other hand on his cheek. "So just relax. Step back and watch without worrying, okay?" Richard nodded, his nerves somehow soothed by Angela's words. She kissed his hand and let it go.

"It's time to begin," Nathalie said. Angela lay down on the board and Ian did up the straps while Nathalie connected her to the heart monitor. As Ian began to place the mask on her face, she turned away from it and looked at Richard. She decided to do one more thing for him, to do something that might make him feel comfortable.

"Richard, will you hold my hand for me?" she said. "The next few minutes will be difficult, and I need your help."

"Yes, of course," he said, stepping forward and holding her hand. "I'm here for you," he said, offering her whatever comfort he could.

"Please don't let go, not until I've gone," she said. She felt his hand tighten around hers. Ian and Nathalie shared a knowing glance as Nathalie realised Angela had found a way for Richard to act like a priest, by offering her comfort in her hour of need.

Damn, she's good with people, Nathalie thought to herself as she watched Richard relax into his new role within the group. Even as the mask was fitted to her she maintained eye contact with him, holding his gaze.

"Ready?" said Nathalie. Angela nodded. "Right then, begin in three, two, one, drop!" Nathalie hit the switch and the board slid into the water. Richard never let go of Angela's hand, holding it tightly until it finally went limp.

Angela jumped to her feet as soon as she knew that she had arrived. The familiar floating sensation, delightful as it was the last time, was now an old experience and she wanted something new. But what was also familiar was the uncomfortable feeling she had from the thermometer.

"Oh, what?" she said out loud. "Ian doesn't have it but I do? What the hell's that about?" She began to undo the straps but she paused, thinking about why she had it this time and deciding to leave it in for now.

"Welcome Angela," said the now familiar voice from the approaching angels, in its now familiar bland tone, "please come with us."

"Yes, yes, in a minute," she replied before turning away from them. She opened the bag around her neck and began her experiments for this trip.

"Angela, do you know where you are?" asked one of the angels.

"Yes, I'm dead, I'll be with you in a minute," she replied.

She removed a pair of scissors from the bag and after taking a deep breath she stabbed them into her arm, cutting through the skin. She tried not to make any noise, but the pain as she drew it down her skin, superficially cutting open the flesh for the length of her forearm made her squeal just a little bit. Blood dripped down from her arm but she steeled herself to the pain.

To the right of her, she saw a figure emerge from the mist. It was a man, he looked young, to Angela he looked about in his thirties. Dropping the scissors, she ran over to join him.

"Hello," she said. The man looked at her and muttered something in a language she didn't understand. She thought it might be Russian.

"Do you speak English?" she asked. The man nodded.

"You are English?"

"No, I'm German, but I speak English. What did you say first?"

"Ah, I said I'd died and gone to Heaven."

"Well, yes, I'm afraid you have. What killed you?" The man look shocked, but his eyes were fixed on Angela's naked body. "Come on, answer me, how did you die?"

"A car accident I think. I remember driving, then this car came round the corner at high speed." He seemed dazed, but Angela tried to keep his mind focused so she could get her information.

"What's your name?" she asked.

"Nestor, Nestor Malakhov."

"Where was your accident?"

"Just outside Omsk." Angela smiled and touched his arm with her hand.

"Good luck," she said, and turned round to face her angels.

"Will you please come with us?" said an angel, now beginning to show a hint of impatience. Angela decided it was time to question them.

"So, this is the place we get judged, yes?" she asked.

"Yes, I believe you know it as the Pearly Gates," an angel replied.

"So, this is the biblical god then, not any of the others like Zeus or Baal?"

"Yes, quite right," was the reply.

"Forgive me for asking," Angela continued, despite the angels' obvious annoyance at her lingering around and not following their instructions, "but what's the whole theological system here? Is this the god of the Old Testament, the fire and brimstone guy?"

"Yes, that is our god," came the reply as the angels seemed to relax, now seeming quite pleased to be on this subject.

"He was a bit crazy back then, wasn't he?"

"Well, those were different times, it was a harsher world. He realised his mistakes, so he sent his son, Jesus Christ to..."

"What do you mean mistakes?" she asked. "I thought God was infallible?" The angels looked at each other, hoping the other had an answer. After a few seconds, their expressions changed first to relief, then back to one of bland friendliness.

"That's not for you to worry about," said one of them.

"You're going back," finished the other.

"No, no, it's too soon!" exclaimed Angela, but she felt the familiar dizziness begin to take her and everything went blank.

Richard's face was the first she saw when she woke up. His kindly smile was somehow reassuring to her, his warm and friendly expression the complete opposite of the angels.

"Welcome back," he said. "How are you feeling?"

"Tired," she replied, "have I been asleep?"

"Solidly for about six hours."

"Oh," replied Angela, "I woke up quickly last time. I had to pass on a name, I have one again."

"Nestor Malakhov?" said Richard. "You muttered his name when you first came round, we assumed you met him while you were gone."

"It was a car crash, in Russia, I can't remember the place." Angela cursed in German as she tried to remember the location she had been told.

"Omsk?"

"Yes, that was it," she replied.

"You said it in your sleep a few times. There's no news yet, but we'll keep checking online."

"It seemed shorter this time," said Angela, thinking about the whole experience now for the first time.

"Tell me about it."

Angela took a second to think back to her experience, and then burst out laughing.

"When I ran up to that man he said he'd thought he'd died and gone to Heaven," she said. "I guess he wasn't used to seeing naked women running up to him."

"What else did you see?" asked Richard. Discussing her nakedness was something he'd rather avoid, and he was keen to change the subject.

He neednt have worried. Nathalie had been in the next room reviewing her medical notes on Angela and having heard her voice decided to join them.

"So you're back then?" said Nathalie as she walked into the room. Angela sat up in the bed, letting the bedclothes fall to the side as soon as she heard Nathalie's voice. She threw her arms open and Nathalie embraced her while Richard turned his head away to avoid looking at her naked body.

81

"I've got more to tell you," said Angela as she sat back in the bed.

"Well, put some clothes on and stop embarrassing Richard," replied Nathalie, half seriously, but half teasing, "and if you're strong enough, come and join us upstairs."

"Yes, okay," replied Angela as she pulled her bathrobe on. Nathalie helped her to her feet and the three of them proceeded slowly up the stairs to the first level, where they joined Ian on the balcony.

"Ah, you're awake," said Ian, "and I have some news for you."

"About the name I gave?" asked Angela.

"Well, there's no name, but there is a report of a man in his thirties dying in a car crash in the city you mentioned, in a head on collision."

"You did it again Nathalie," said Angela. Nathalie smiled back at her but she felt the slight taste of jealousy again, and a longing to make the journey herself.

"So what else happened?" asked Ian.

"I found something interesting," Angela said. "The thermometer, the one that Ian didn't have when he went, well I had it in me again."

"It came back?" asked Ian.

"It seems to have. I left it behind last time, so maybe if we leave things behind they take some time to return, or whatever the equivalent is of it there takes time to return back here."

"Okay, I think I know what you mean," said Nathalie. "If we assume everything has an equivalent version of itself at the Gates, then if we leave something there, it'd be lying on the ground somewhere for a while before it returns to this world."

"But the thermometer never left here," said Ian. "Angela had it when she came back the first time."

"Nothing leaves here, but there's a duplicate of some kind of us and everything we take with us up there," said Richard. "So if we remove it from ourselves, the duplicate of it must stay up there for a while when we return."

"So that's why you had no thermometer," said Angela.

"Exactly," Ian replied. "The duplicate of it was somewhere up there."

"And remember you said the angels were confused about who cleans up shit?" said Nathalie. "I guess nobody has to clean it up if it just disappears."

"That would mean anything we take with us will eventually disappear, even if we stay dead," said Richard.

"A few days, a week or two at most seems the sort of time scales we're talking about," said Nathalie.

"Of course it does," said Richard, "it'd have to otherwise this wouldn't work."

"Why?" asked Ian.

"Because whatever goes up there with you stays here," replied Richard, "and if it stays down here it'll change. Take your clothes for example. Over time they'll decay, get worn down and eventually end up in landfill somewhere. Insects might eat them, animals might eat the insects and eventually somewhere up the food chain another human eats some of the atoms from the clothes you took to the Gates."

"So nothing stays up there, not for any length of time?" asked Nathalie.

"They can't," replied Richard. "Not even our bodies. All of us will end up as parts of other people eventually. It's a cycle that's being going on for thousands of years."

"I cut myself as well," said Angela. "It was painful, and there was a lot of blood."

"Like the real world?" asked Nathalie.

"Yes, exactly," was the reply.

"You're like astronauts on the moon," said Richard.

"How do you mean?" asked Ian.

"Well, when they landed on the moon, they knew nothing about it, not really," explained Richard. "They didn't know if they'd be buried under dust, if they could they walk in the low gravity, that kind of thing. So they checked everything in stages. One of the first things they did on that first moon walk was to try different ways to walk. Everything was little baby steps."

"Cool, we think like astronauts," said Ian.

"I remember being fascinated by it as a kid," said Richard. "I used to read up everything about the moon missions, and I'm starting to think you guys have a lot in common with them."

"We've treated this scientifically," said Nathalie, "we realised this was an entirely new environment, so we've been testing the laws of physics over there, learning as much as we can."

"We've confirmed it's a lot like this universe, same laws of thermodynamics, electromagnetism, that kind of thing," added Ian. "It could even be a part of this universe."

"Or we could be part of that universe," said Richard.

"Like fish in an aquarium?" asked Ian.

"They'd have a pretty narrow view of the universe," Richard replied, "maybe we do as well, maybe we're only able to see a small part of the wider reality.

"Guys," said Nathalie in a whispered voice. Both men turned to look at her. She was pointing to the sleeping form of Angela, who was now slumped in the chair. "I think she needs her bed."

"I'll get her," said Ian who gently scooped her up in his arms and carried her out of the room. She nuzzled into his chest slightly as he carried her, occasionally muttering something he couldn't understand as he carried her through to her bedroom. As he laid her on the bed she opened her eyes, half in a daze and smiled at him.

"Don't go," she said dreamily.

"I'm here," he whispered, leaning forward so she could hear him.

Suddenly, their eyes met, and the stare lingered for a few seconds. Angela lifted her head towards him and the two shared a lingering kiss before Angela seemed to drift back into a half asleep state. She reached out clumsily and took his hand, while a dozy smile formed across her face.

"Stay with me," she said dreamily. "Always here with me," before sleep took her again and her head slumped against the pillow. Ian leaned forward and kissed her cheek.

"I would stay in a heartbeat," he whispered before sitting down in the chair by the bed. As he watched her sleep he could hear the faint voices from the balcony as Nathalie and Richard continued their discussion.

"Why are you here?" he heard Nathalie ask Richard.

"How do you mean?" he replied.

"Well, you believe in God, you have faith, what answers do you need?"

"I may have faith," replied Richard, "but my faith is in what God has taught us. And ever since I first heard the story from the fisherman who almost drowned it's made me wonder. Who is God? Where does he come from? The Bible tells us nothing beyond the Heavens and the Earth, and most assume that's all there is. And I wonder if that's all God thinks we need to know for now, but that's no longer enough for me."

"So you believe there could be other gods, other heavens?"

"Belief," said Richard, lingering on the word. "Belief dies in the face of evidence, one way or the other. And like all evidence, it usually asks more questions than it answers. I choose the search for the truth over belief any day."

"That's the history of science," said Nathalie. "Answer one question, ask ten more."

"Exactly, so when we prove that there is a Heaven of some sorts, and you people have clearly done this, then we ask questions about it. Your friends have performed experiments and gathered facts about this place."

"And you, I guess you have your own thoughts, maybe your own ideas for experiments," said Nathalie.

"I'm starting to think the Bible is more notable for what it doesn't tell us than what it does. Creation is never put in context. Even God himself is an elusive figure, described more in metaphors than actual detail."

"So you're looking for context?" asked Nathalie.

"I believe God loves us. But I want to know what God is. He's never told us, and he's our only source on what he is. I can't dismiss the possibility of a wider theological reality."

"In that case, I guess you just invented theological field science," said Nathalie. Both laughed at the concept.

"Have you ever heard of a man called James Clerk Maxwell?" Richard asked. Nathalie shook her head.

"No, never," she replied.

"He's often given grand titles like the man who changed everything, or the inventor of the modern world. He was a scientist in the nineteenth century, born in Edinburgh, who did something no one else did."

"What was that?"

"He explained something beyond our physical comprehension, namely electromagnetism. He showed that space itself could have properties. Take a magnetic field. We can't see it, smell it, or sense it in any way. But it's there, it's a part of the universe."

"So how did he change everything?" asked Nathalie.

"He gave us electricity, radio waves, even the beginnings of Quantum Theory and Relativity. Einstein was his natural successor, who gave space and time physical properties as well, again things we can't sense ourselves."

"Physics isn't my strong point, but I think I understand you," said Nathalie. "You're saying there could be things around us we can't sense, aren't you?"

"Something must tie us to this other place," said Richard, "both us physically and the objects you've been taking with you. I've been wondering if there isn't some physics going on here we don't understand."

"You're not going to say it's just God's divine power, or something like that?" asked Nathalie.

"Divine power." Richard paused, thinking about the phrase. "What does that mean? If God interacts with the world, be it killing first born children or parting the Red Sea, all he's doing is manipulating matter and energy. There must be some laws governing how he does that, some mechanism responsible for it."

"So it's not magic," said Nathalie.

"What is magic?" asked Richard. "You can summon the power of an orchestra with a click of a mouse button. To people a thousand years ago that would be magic."

"So magic is what we call things we don't understand," was Nathalie's response.

"I'd say it's more things we don't think we can explain," replied Richard.

"And you think we can explain divine intervention?"

"I think there will be some kind of mechanism behind it," Richard said, "something explainable, even something we can model mathematically. But it's something beyond our comprehension for now."

"You seem pretty scientifically literate for a priest," said Nathalie.

"Oh, we don't all have our heads in the sand," he replied, smiling. "I find that understanding the universe and how it works brings me closer to God. To study science is to study his mind."

"So how does your faith stand now?" asked Nathalie.

"My faith has always been about love," he replied. "I've never been one to rant and rave from the pulpit and I've never forced guilt on anyone, or damned anyone for disagreeing with the church's teachings. I believe God loves us, I just don't believe he exists in isolation. I never have. Why would we have the first commandment if he did?"

"Which one's that?" asked Nathalie.

"You shall have no other gods but me," Richard replied. "Kind of pointless if he was the only god don't you think?" Nathalie shrugged her shoulders.

"Not my area really," she said. "But I'm glad you're here. We need you, we need your knowledge."

"If I can help you in any way, I will," he replied, "but I wonder if there's more I can do."

"Such as?" she asked.

"I think you should give me that fitness test," he said.

"You mean you want to go?" she asked. "Really?"

"How can I not?" he replied. "People talk about faith all the time, but we all want to see the truth, to know it for sure. I'm not going to let that chance pass me by."

"You sure about this? There's still a risk."

"When I said I read about the moon missions," he said, "I always envied the astronauts, exploring this whole new world. That's where the excitement is, in going to the new world, not sitting in mission control or building the rocket."

Nathalie felt a twitch of anger within her at his mission control metaphor. Now she had another person to be jealous of.

"So yes, I want to do it," he continued. "And do it as soon as possible."

Chapter 10

"This is about as uncomfortable as I've ever felt in my life," said Richard with a nervous laugh as he sat naked on the bed.

"Oh, don't worry," said Nathalie as she applied the pads for the heart monitor to his chest, "I'm a doctor so I've seen it all before. Besides, for a man of your age, you're in damn good shape, so it's not like you've anything to be embarrassed about."

"Oh," said Richard, starting to blush.

"Sorry," said Nathalie, giving Richard a warm smile, "I keep forgetting you're a priest. I shouldn't really say these things, should I?"

"That's okay," he replied, "I'm not embarrassed, I know you're a doctor, it's all just so strange. I can't get over the fact you're about to kill me."

"And save you," replied Nathalie, "but I know what you mean. Just between you and me, Ian wet himself with fear when he did it."

"I'm not scared," he replied, "but I'm about to test my faith in ways no one's faith has ever been tested."

"You'll be fine," she said, "you can do this, I have faith in you."

"You have faith?" Richard asked. Both of them laughed.

"Well, that's us all done," she said as she finished attaching the last pad. "Just one last thing to do and we're ready."

"The thermometer?" he asked nervously.

"Roll onto your side for me," she said. Richard did as he was told and braced himself.

"Now, close your eyes and say twenty hail Marys," she said. Richard let out a snort of laughter and the thermometer slid straight in. Richard yelped with fright at the cold sensation of it.

"That was...interesting," he said in a voice about half an octave higher than normal.

"Always make them laugh," she said. "It makes you relax your clench reflex."

Richard considered laughing, but the sensation of the thermometer was remarkably distracting and he found it was all he could focus on. He felt it would be a struggle to move but Nathalie put her hand on his hip and rolled him onto his back.

"Let's get it secured before it pops out, shall we?" she said. She began to do up the straps around his legs and Richard, now feeling even more awkward, just lay there.

Once the straps were done he knew it was time to go. He pulled the bathrobe on and stood up, walking one awkward step at a time.

"Are you alright?" Nathalie asked.

"I'd be lying if I said I wasn't getting a bit scared now," he said. Nathalie noticed his breathing was beginning to speed up and that the fear was rising in him.

"I don't care if you are a priest," she said as she leaned forward and kissed him gently on the lips, like she had with Ian before. "You're one of us now, so that makes you my friend, and I love my friends."

"Thank you," he said, partly shocked by the kiss, but also touched by her words.

She watched as his breathing came under control almost immediately. She took his hand and held it in hers. "Ready?" she asked.

He nodded and together, hand in hand, they went through to the main room.

Ian was waiting for them as they went through but Angela was nowhere to be seen.

"No Angela?" asked Nathalie.

"She's asleep, she seems a bit rough after yesterday," Ian replied.

"I'll check on her later, we can manage ourselves though," Nathalie replied. She turned back to Richard. "Whenever you're ready," she said.

He calmly took off his bath robe and climbed onto the board. Nathalie strapped him in and when she put the mask on him the time had finally come. She took his hand and held it tightly.

"Are you ready?" she asked. Richard nodded. "Then in three,

two, one, go!" Nathalie hit the button and Richard slid into the water. Much to their surprise, Richard never made a single noise, not a scream or any obvious sign of pain. Only the tightness of his hand around Nathalie's revealed the pain he was in, a tightness that slowly faded as his hand went limp.

The sensation of floating was the first thing Richard felt as he lay, suspended in the haze, as if he was opening his eyes into some kind of waking dream. He felt that he could lie there forever, enveloped in this bliss, and he lingered a moment while he enjoyed the feeling.

"Hello Richard," said a voice. Richard instantly sat up to greet whoever it was, but he winced when he felt the thermometer still inside him. He quickly undid the straps and slid it out, grateful to be finally free of it.

"Hi," said Richard as he stood up and turned to see the two angels who greeted him.

"Do you know where you are?" asked an angel.

"I'm dead," he replied.

"And how do you feel about that?" asked the other angel.

"Well, I'm a priest for the Catholic Church, so finding myself here is not entirely unexpected," he said with a laugh of joy. He felt delighted to be there, about to bask in the glory and love of his god and had difficulty in hiding his feelings.

"Oh, in that case we can beat the queues," an angel said, "so just come with me."

"With you, yes," replied Richard as they began to move through the mist that surrounded them.

They emerged into a clearing where dozens of people waited in lines. Richard looked at them with fascination, trying to observe as much as he could. Some were in tears, others were clearly happy. Most seemed to be in a state of shock.

"Are these all the other recent deaths?" he asked.

"Yes," answered an angel, "it's quite quiet just now though."

"How many do you get?" Richard asked.

"About a hundred a minute," an angel replied, "on average. But like I say this is quiet."

Richard continued to observe the people. There were a few in military uniforms, a lot were in their bed clothes. Only one other person was naked like him, a young woman who was at the front of her line, and she was desperately trying to cover herself up as tears poured down her cheeks. He ran over to her, hoping to offer her some comfort, but two angels beside her stood in his way. When he reached her side he noticed she had a pair of trousers on that were around her ankles.

"Can I help you?" the angel asked.

"It's not me, it's this poor woman that needs help," he said. The angel looked at her in disgust.

"She deserves no help, her kind never do," said the angel. Richard, shocked by the harshness of the angel, pushed him aside and ran to the woman's side.

"Help me, please," she said in a thick Australian accent, tears streaming down her cheeks.

"Do you know where you are?" Richard asked. The woman glanced around and a look of terrified understanding seemed to engulf her face. She screamed and dropped to her knees. Richard knelt down beside her.

"Am I dead?" she asked through the tears.

"Yes, I'm afraid so," Richard replied. "How did you die?"

"He grabbed me as I was walking home," she sobbed, "he dragged me to a field."

"Who did?" asked Richard.

"He tore my clothes off, he wouldn't stop hitting me," she said, still sobbing.

"Did he..." said Richard, not wanting to say the word.

"Rape me?" she said and nodded. "Then he started hitting me, punching my face, oh it hurt so much," she said, collapsing into tears again. Richard sprang to his feet and turned to the angels.

"Can't you help her?" asked Richard.

"Help her?" said the angel, "why would we help her. She isn't a believer."

"But she's in pain, she needs help!"

"She's about to burn in hell," said the angel with a snigger, "that'll make her forget her pain."

"Why?" exclaimed Richard. "What's she done to deserve

damnation?"

"She doesn't love God," the angel replied. "We don't need an evaluator for this one, it's so obvious in her heart even I can tell that."

"That can't be enough," he shouted, "doesn't God love his children, and forgive them?" The angel laughed.

"Forgive? Not her kind," said the angel. "If you don't believe, you are damned." The angel stepped forward to grab her but Richard pushed him and jumped between the angel and the woman.

"I won't let them hurt you," he said to her over his shoulder. She just stared at him in disbelief, her mind unwilling to accept anything about her situation.

"Step aside," said the angel as he moved forward. Richard threw a punch, hitting the angel square on the jaw. He felt bone in the angel's face crack under his knuckles as a mist of blood exploded from the nose and the angel fell to the ground. The other angel just laughed.

"Do you really think you can stop us?" he asked. "Look, she's already going." Richard turned as he heard the woman scream. He watched as flames began to surround her and started to drag her down, pulling her into the mist. As the last lick of flame enveloped her head she went silent and the flame snuffed out. She was gone.

"Is that how it is?" snarled Richard, snorting each word in seething anger. "What about mercy? What about love?"

"Where was her love for God?" asked the angel. "God has no mercy for those who reject him, only vengeance." Before he could ask anything else, the angel seemed to disappear, vanishing into the haze.

"Are you finished?" Richard turned round and saw the angels that met him when he arrived. They were smiling the same bland smiles as when he arrived.

"Is this real?" he asked, "or is it some test?"

"Test?" replied the angel. "No, this is no test. Now come, it is time to be judged."

"But that woman, that poor woman," he said.

"Oh, you mean the atheist?"

"She was a child of God," said Richard, clenching his fists and shaking with rage. "She may have strayed, but I'm sure she was a good person."

"Good person?" asked an angel. "Why would God care about them being a good person if they don't love God?"

"Oh no," said Richard, burying his head in his hands and realising the truth of the situation, "this can't be true."

"Well it is true," said the angel, "but don't worry, you're going back."

Before he could say anything, a wave of dizziness hit Richard and everything went black.

Nathalie's smiling face was a sight too painful for Richard to bear when he woke up. Sitting by the bed and holding his hand, her warmth was too much and he immediately burst into tears. Without a word Nathalie climbed onto the bed and cradled him in her arms.

"It was horrible," he said between sobs, "they're all cruel, evil bastards."

"What did you see?"

"A woman. She was screaming and crying and nobody cared. She'd just been raped and murdered but the angels didn't care about her, they just left her to suffer. And because she was an atheist, they sent her to Hell. It was horrible!"

"Oh, I'm sorry," Nathalie said as she continued to hold him, "I wish we'd been wrong, but we've all seen this kind of thing."

"I didn't believe you," he said, "not in my heart. I thought you must be mistaken."

"Did you find out anything about the woman?"

"She was young, probably still a teenager. She was Australian I think."

"Okay, we'll check it out," she said.

"It was almost as if they enjoyed tormenting her," he said, the disbelief evident in his voice. "I just can't believe this is the god of the Bible."

"Did you tell the angels you were a Catholic priest?" she asked.

"Yes, and they seemed to be ready to hurry me through when I did."

"I guess that confirms it," Nathalie replied. "They've told us before the Catholic Church was the true church."

"But it can't be," said Richard between sobs, "it just can't be. Where was the love, or the forgiveness?"

"I think we can assume there's a difference between what God says and what the truth is," said Nathalie, hoping to give him some answer. "Clearly he needs us to love him, and to do that he comes across as loving and forgiving."

"It's as if Jesus never came to earth," said Richard, "and that the vengeful god of the Old Testament still exists."

"Well, it's funny you should say that, but Angela said something interesting while you were asleep."

"Oh, what?" asked Richard.

"She said to one of the angels that God seemed like the one from the Old Testament, and the angel said that God had realised his mistakes and sent Jesus to fix them."

"Mistakes?" asked Richard.

"That was our reaction and Angela's as well. When she pointed out God was supposed to be infallible, they struggled to answer."

"Did they give any answer?"

"No," said Nathalie, shaking her head and looking disappointed. "She returned before they had a chance to give one."

"That's a shame. I'd like to hear them explain that one."

"Are you okay?" asked Nathalie. She released her embrace and he sat up, now with his tears under control.

"Not really," he replied. "You've just turned everything I've ever believed upside down."

"We've shown you the truth," Nathalie replied. "I wish it could have made you happy, but it didn't, and I am sorry about that."

"No, I'm glad I know the truth now," he replied. "It means that I can help more people reach Heaven if I know the truth. I'll have to lie and tell them God loves you and will forgive you, but as long as they believe it then I can save them."

"Will you be going straight back home?" asked Nathalie.

"I think I should," said Richard.

"You should stay for a couple of days, just to make sure you're okay," said Nathalie, "but after that there's no medical reason for you to stay."

"Thanks for taking care of me," he said.

"I wish you'd stay though," she added, "at least a little longer." She turned and kissed his forehead before climbing off the bed.

"Well, let's see how I feel," Richard replied, before yawning.

"Are you hungry?" asked Nathalie. "Is there anything you need?"

"No, I'm just a bit sleepy," he replied.

"Then rest," Nathalie said, "and I'll speak to you later."

Chapter 11

Richard woke with a jolt, his mind a spinning frenzy of thoughts within seconds of opening his eyes. He stared out of the window, trying to find some focus for his musings and his eyes lingered on the peaks of the Alps to the south, their snow now receding in the warming of the Bavarian spring. All he could think of was the anger he felt and his determination to resolve the conflict in his heart.

His head turned slowly at a knock on the door.

"Come in," he said. The door opened and Nathalie walked in. "Good morning," he said.

"Afternoon actually, you've been asleep a long time," she replied. "How are you feeling?"

"Physically? Apart from a sore chest I feel fine," he replied. "I also have a lot to think about."

"Well, about that," Nathalie replied, "if you're feeling up to it, we're about to sit down and go over everything we've learnt, and we could use your insight."

"Okay, I'll be down in a few minutes," he replied. Nathalie nodded and left, leaving him alone to reflect on his experience. His eyes turned to the Alps again, their distant peaks holding his gaze as his mind struggled to accept the new reality he had found himself in. He had a series of thoughts, dark, disturbing ideas about God, but he dismissed them all, sending them to the back of his mind where they lingered, hanging there unresolved.

He turned and headed out the door, his mind still in turmoil. Arriving in Angela's lounge he met the rest of the group, who sat round the dining table. He took a seat and listened as Angela began to speak.

"Well, we've made a few trips to the Gates now," she said, "and Nathalie and I thought it was time we reviewed everything. A lot has happened, and we need to think about what we want to do next." Ian and Nathalie nodded. Richard didn't react.

"Let's start with the medical side of things," said Nathalie. "Angela, I've stopped your heart three times now. Each time it's re-started without a problem, but the daily checkups I've been giving you show a definite weakening of your heart. It's probably temporary, but I don't want to send you back again anytime soon." Angela nodded, agreeing reluctantly.

"Ian, you've been back once," she continued, "and your heart seems to be doing fine. You can make another trip back soon, but I want to monitor you after that." Ian nodded as well.

"Richard, you're as strong as a bloody ox," she said, "you have the fitness of a man half your age, by far the fittest person here and unless I find any problems today, you can make a trip back at some time in the next few weeks." Richard nodded as well, but with less enthusiasm than Ian.

"So depending on what we decide here, I think we need to consider finding more people," said Nathalie. "Each person can only make the trip a few times before it starts to become a bigger risk, so I think we need to minimise that."

"Okay," said Angela, "we'll give that some thought. Now, let's discuss what we've learnt."

"Well," began Ian, "the afterlife is clearly a physical world. Many of the laws of physics that apply here also apply there. The laws of thermodynamics and electromagnetism seem unchanged, although we should do some tests on the laws of chemistry next time, maybe start a fire, that kind of thing."

"And given the disappearing and reappearing thermometer," said Nathalie, "it seems like anything we leave behind stays there for a while, then returns the same way we do."

"Biologically we seem to be the same," said Angela, "we have a heart and lungs, we need the toilet and we can bleed."

"Next time we could try eating," said Nathalie, "see if it satisfies hunger."

"We could maybe gorge on something like chocolate," added Ian, "see if it makes us feel sick."

"I volunteer for that task," said Nathalie, generating laughter around the table from everyone but Richard.

"Seriously though, we should be careful," said Ian, "if we bleed, it may mean that we're mortal."

"Agreed, we shouldn't try anything that would be physically dangerous," said Nathalie.

"Is there anything else we haven't explored about biology?" asked Angela.

"We haven't tried anything regarding sex and reproduction," said Ian.

"We could test arousal in some way," said Nathalie, "But unless you want to take along a microscope and examine your semen, we'd probably have to leave it at that." Everyone looked at Ian, wondering what his response would be.

"I suppose I could," he replied awkwardly. "I could take a sample with me and quickly examine it."

"That would just be your sperm from this world, not that one," said Nathalie.

"Oh," said Ian, realising what she meant. "You mean I'd have to...to produce it there?" he asked.

"Don't worry," replied Nathalie as she tried not to laugh, "we're not quite at the stage of getting you to masturbate at the gates of Heaven, at least not yet."

"Don't laugh," Ian said to Angela as he heard her stifle a snigger, "or I'll take you along to give me a hand." Nathalie's eyes narrowed slightly as she saw Angela laugh along with Ian at the joke.

"Back to serious matters," Nathalie said, almost with a snap in her voice, "because all these are just minor details, and we have one big question to answer, one more important than anything else." She turned to Richard. "Who is God, and what does he want from us? That should be our main focus now."

"If you want a straight answer, I can't give you one," said Richard.
"For now, we just need your insight," said Nathalie.
"Okay," said Richard, gathering his thought. "This is clearly not the God of the Catholic Church, regardless of what the angels say. This God has no interest in people being good and kind and loving their neighbour. He seems like the wrathful, paranoid God of the Old Testament."
"I'm not too well read when it comes to the Bible," said Ian, "can you explain that a bit more?"
"The major moral compass of the Old Testament is the Ten Commandments," said Richard, "how many can you name?"
"Let's see, there's don't steal, don't kill, honour thy father and mother," said Ian, struggling to remember any further ones.
"Those are the later ones," said Richard, "but the first four, the most important laws, are one, I am the Lord God almighty, you shall have no other gods but me, two, that you shall not make for yourself an idol, three, do not take God's name in vain and four, honour the Sabbath. Those are all about him, and they kind of show you his priorities."
"So what we're finding is far more consistent with ancient Jewish texts than anything in the New Testament or modern church teachings," said Nathalie.
"Exactly," said Richard. "A vengeful, jealous God, with little interest in how people treat each other is what we have. A God that would destroy the world with a flood just to make a point, or turn a woman into a pillar of salt for the slightest moment of doubt."
"So we're dealing with a maniac?" asked Nathalie.
"Not just a maniac, but a manipulative, insecure and paranoid maniac. Someone who would demand a man sacrifice his son just to test his faith. A god who will threaten you with eternal damnation if you don't love him unconditionally or give you an endless list of minor offences for which you get stoned to death for committing." Richard sat back in his seat and took a deep breath before adding his final verdict.
"This is not someone you want to make an enemy of."
As usual, Nathalie found herself alone on the balcony at the end

of the night. Her thoughts lingered on Richard's words and how they could investigate further, but her mind kept returning to Ian and Angela. She felt bitterly jealous, both at their return visits to the Gates and the relationship that had developed between them and now she found herself fighting the urge to leave them.

She stood and walked to the edge of the balcony. The warm evening air of late spring seemed to sooth her mood and the gentle breeze that felt as if it flowed through her summer dress acted like a drug, calming her thoughts yet strangely invigorating her at the same time.

Her mood was instantly shattered by the sounds of lovemaking coming from the window below her. It was the unmistakeable voices of Ian and Angela that she heard, turning her stomach with feelings of betrayal and jealousy. Her fingers tightly gripped the balcony's handrail as she raged inside, wanting everything they had that she did not.

She stormed out the room, shaking with anger. She needed to get away from them, to not hear the damn noise they were making, but the sounds from below filled her flat. She ran out the door, down the stairs and out into the garden, only stopping when she reached the trees by the swimming pool and dropping to her knees. She began to cry, the tears flowing without control or inhibition, the feeling of isolation now overwhelming her.

"What's wrong Nathalie?" came the voice from behind her. She turned round to see Richard sitting by the pool, illuminated only by the gentle moonlight.

"What do you think?" she asked as Richard came over and sat beside her.

"Those two finally together?" he asked. Nathalie nodded.

"What are you out here for?" she asked.

"I needed to think, this seemed a nice place to do it," he replied.

"About what we said today?" she asked.

"Yes."

"I'm sorry we did this to you," she replied as she stood up.

"Forget it," he said, "I told you before, I'm not."

"But your faith, your belief," she said.

"It means nothing when you know it's a lie," he replied. "I was out here wondering if I would stay a priest."

"You could stay here, with us," she replied.

"There's nothing here for me, not really," he said, shaking his head.

"There could be, if you weren't a priest."

"What do you mean?" he asked. Nathalie leaned forward, inviting Richard to kiss her, but he didn't respond.

"Don't you see, it's perfect? Those two are a couple now, and we would be as well. The four of us could carry on with this, together."

"Nathalie, no," he said, leaning back away from her slightly.

"Give up being a priest," she said, "and you can stay here with me."

"Nathalie, I took a vow."

"Break it with me, right here, right now," she replied.

"No, I can't," he said, reaching behind him and taking her arms away from around his neck. "I owe it to my community."

"Are you sure?" she said, beginning to feel awkward.

"Yes, I'm sure," he said. She turned round and sat on the poolside bench and wiped away a tear.

"I'm sorry," she said.

"Look, I'm very flattered," he said, "and if I didn't have responsibilities, I'm not sure I'd be able to resist." He sat down beside her. "But it's time I left."

"Must you?" she said.

"I really should."

"Not even one night?" she said. "No-one would know."

"I would know," he replied. Nathalie, realising it wasn't going to happen, turned away from Richard.

"Do you want to go now?" she replied. "There's a late night flight you can catch."

"I think it's for the best," he said. "I'm all packed ready to go."

"Will you say good bye to the others?"

"No," he replied, "I'd rather just leave."

"Get your bags, I'll get the car key," she said.

The journey to the airport was silent. Both had regrets about his leaving, but both knew he had his reasons and there was no discussion of it.

"Just drop me at the door," he said as they approached the airport terminal, "no need to come in."

"Are you sure?" asked Nathalie.

"Yes," he replied, "long goodbyes are the worst."

The car pulled up to the airport entrance. With few cars around, Nathalie felt she could linger for a few minutes, hoping for a last few seconds to talk. She climbed out the car to open the boot and as Richard retrieved his suitcase, she made one final effort.

"If you want to come back, I'll be here," she said.

"No you won't," said Richard. "I know you're feeling lonely. I know you hate the fact you don't get to go back to the afterlife yourself. But it'll pass. You'll get other people involved."

"Was it that obvious?" she asked.

"About you not being able to go back? To me maybe, but then understanding people is what I do."

"Do you think Ian and Angela know?" she asked.

"I doubt it. Maybe you should tell them." Nathalie looked at him as they both shared a smile.

"Thank you," she said, "for everything."

"Thank you too," he replied.

"Can I ask one last thing of you?" she said.

"What's that?"

"Don't be a priest, just for ten seconds." She put her hand on his cheek. Her touch felt electric against his skin and for one brief moment he couldn't resist her.

"Okay," he said. Without waiting a second longer she leaned forward and kissed him. He took her in his arms and kissed her back, giving in to his passion. For one brief moment he thought about returning with her, but as the kiss ended, the thought died with it, and his will to return to Scotland reasserted itself.

"Now go," she said, and without a word from either, he turned and began to walk away.

Nathalie returned to the house heartbroken and alone. Getting out of the car she stared up at the window by Angela's bedroom. The light was still on. Unable to face going in and hearing them, she turned from the house and walked towards the swimming pool. Sitting on the bench she closed her eyes and thought back to her only trip to the afterlife and remembered the tranquil sensation that greeted her when she woke up. She found her mind lingering on Angela's description of that blissful feeling as her eyes became transfixed by the moonlight glistening on the pool. Her head began to dream of what it was like for them, knowing where they were, and arriving there naked, free of anything, just drifting into this other world.

She stood up and stepped towards the edge of the pool. Kicking off her shoes she pulled her dress over her head and pulled down her underwear, kicking it to the side. She began to step down into the pool, its cold water enveloping her naked body one step at a time. When it was up to her waist she lay back, stretching out her hands and staring at the sky.

"Floating in infinity," she said as she drifted slowly across the pool, gently driven by soft, wind borne waves. It felt almost blissful to her as she lay there, with only the gentle sound of the water in her ears to distract her.

But it was not enough. She knew that as things stood, there was no way for her to return to the afterlife. It was almost all she could think about and it was the one thing she desired more than anything, anything that is except for what was in the house and in that bedroom with the light.

She leaned forward and put her feet down on the floor of the pool. The past few days with Richard had only been a distraction from her true heart's desire, she could see that now, and she decided it was time to risk all, to be upfront, honest and to hold nothing back.

She stepped out of the pool and looked at her clothes on the ground. She bent down to pick them up, but something made her stop. She didn't want the clothes, she didn't want to hide behind anything and so without collecting them she straightened up and walked naked into the house.

She headed slowly up the steps and turned towards Angela's bedroom. She could hear their voices as they talked and Nathalie paused at the door for a second before knocking.

"Come in," said Angela's voice. Nathalie opened the door and walked in.

"I need to speak to you both," she said. Both Ian and Angela were speechless for a moment to see her standing there naked, and neither responded. Instead Nathalie just climbed onto the bottom of the bed, kneeling between their feet.

"Is Richard gone?" asked Angela, "I heard the car, did you take him to the airport?"

"Yes," Nathalie replied, "I think it was too painful for him to stay."

"Are you okay?" asked Ian.

"I'm fine, never better," she replied.

"What is it?" asked Angela, sensing an issue between them.

"I need to be honest with you, with both of you," she said. They both nodded earnestly. "When I had my accident, I felt alone, so lonely I couldn't handle it. Then I found you." She gestured at Angela, who smiled slightly. "We met and I suddenly had a friend."

"And I had one too," Angela replied, "a friend who finally understood."

"But you were more than a friend," Nathalie continued. "You were the driving force behind all we would go on to achieve. You convinced me to do it, you funded it, you even volunteered both times we first went to try it."

"I trusted you," Angela said. "And I always will." Nathalie moved slightly up the bed and took Angela's hand.

"And then there was you," she said, turning to Ian. "You brought focus to me, a scientific approach to our exploration. Without you we would never have made the discoveries we have, or have found Richard. We would be stumbling blind without facts or theology to guide us." Nathalie reached down and held his hand.

"But you made it all possible," Ian said. "Without you we wouldn't even have started this."

"We're a team, the three of us," said Nathalie. "And we should stay a team, always."

"Is there something you want?" asked Angela as she sat up in the bed.

"I want to go to the Gates," she replied as she began to cry, "I want to go where both of you go, but I can't, not without another doctor."

"If we can go, you can go," said Ian.

"We'll find a way," said Angela as she wiped away Nathalie's tears, "and we'll start working on it tomorrow."

"You mean it, really?" said Nathalie through her tears.

"If it means this much to you, of course," she replied.

"It does," Nathalie replied. "I want what both of you have."

"Have we made you feel left out?" asked Angela.

"Yes, a little," Nathalie replied.

"I once said that you never had to feel lonely again," said Angela, "and I meant it. Come here." Angela lay back and opened her arms. Nathalie lay down beside her and draped her arm and leg across Angela, cuddling up to her side as Ian embraced her from behind.

"When I heard you two together, it really hurt," said Nathalie, "and it made me feel alone again. I threw myself at Richard, I think I scared him away."

"Just lie here with us," Ian whispered into her ear. "You don't have to feel like that ever again."

Nathalie closed her eyes and smiled as she lay, sandwiched between them and entwined in their arms. Everything felt perfect.

Nathalie was woken in the early hours by the soft morning sun that filtered through the window. Rousing from a deep slumber, she felt Ian's arms around her and smiled. The memories of last night came flooding back and she lingered a few seconds in his arms, relishing the moment. She turned to see where Angela was, but as the bed was otherwise empty, she decided to find her. Slowly moving Ian's hands away from her she sneaked out of the bedroom, making as little noise as she could.

As she stepped out the doorway, she stepped straight into Angela's shadow. Turning to the door at the end of the corridor she saw Angela standing on the balcony, silhouetted by the rising sun, with her back to Nathalie. As she got closer, Nathalie was delighted to see that Angela was also naked, and she slid her arms around her waist, holding her body to Angela's.

"Good morning," Nathalie said as she placed her chin onto Angela's shoulder.

"Mmm...it is, isn't it?" Angela replied.

"Last night was incredible," Nathalie said. "I didn't really expect that to happen. All I wanted to do was to be held, to lie in your arms, but what you two did was amazing."

"You've sent Ian and me to Heaven and back a few times," Angela said, "I guess we thought it was time we returned the favour." Both women giggled.

"I've never been with a woman before," Nathalie replied, "at least not before last night."

"Neither had I," said Angela, "but I never met a woman like you before."

"Are we together then?" asked Nathalie. "Together in every way?"

"Yes, we are," Angela replied. "My bed is yours now, yours and Ian's."

"That sounds perfect."

Now that you're here permanently, maybe I should offer Ian a job," said Angela. "That way the three of us can stay together and move forward with this."

"That would be very nice," said Nathalie.

"I had another thought as well," said Angela. "I think you shouldn't look for a job here."

"Why not?" asked Nathalie.

"You should stay here," said Angela, "and devote yourself full time to this."

"You'd support me?" asked a surprised Nathalie.

"I've been thinking," said Angela, "about how to take this forward. We need more people, with different skills. There's more like us, and if you devote yourself to this, I know you can find them, bring them here and do what you've done for us."

"I could do that," said Nathalie.

"But before all that," said Angela, who turned to face Nathalie, "we need to find another doctor, to send you back."

"It'll be tough," she replied, "we'd almost certainly need someone who had been to the afterlife, the same way we had. Most doctors would run in terror from trying something like this."

"It's our first priority," she replied, "and we need to do it as soon as possible."

"Oh, I couldn't wish for anything better," said Nathalie as she hugged Angela tightly.

"You work on this, I'll earn the money and Ian helps out both of us," said Angela. "And together we'll take this as far as we can and learn whatever there is to learn."

"He's been invaluable with this," Nathalie said, "he really helped us focus on investigating this, rather than just going there and having a look." Nathalie turned and walked to the edge of the balcony, staring at the Alps in the far distance. "And there is still so much to learn. It's a whole other world." She turned round to face Angela. "We need more people. As many as we can find."

"We will," said Angela as she sat on the bench. Her gaze hung on Nathalie for a few seconds. "You know, I don't think I ever realised how beautiful you are," she said. Nathalie blushed and smiled.

"Thank you," she responded as she sat down beside Angela, leaning her head on her shoulder. "You've given me so much strength," Nathalie replied. "I'd be lost without you."

"We're all together now," said Angela, "and we're staying that way."

"Ian goes home tomorrow, doesn't he?" said Nathalie with a soft sadness to her voice.

"Yes, but he'll be back, hopefully to stay."

"I hope so," she replied, "we should be together, the three of us."

"We will be," said Angela. "And we know that not even death can separate us."

Chapter 12

Nathalie stepped out onto the back porch of the house and took a deep breath, inhaling all the beautiful smells of the late Bavarian spring. This place was like paradise to her, isolated from the rest of the world and with warm sun, still air and little rain. It was now three days since Ian had left, but Nathalie had settled comfortably into her new routine of staying at Angela's house and looking for more people to recruit. With no full time work to exhaust her she had even, for the first time in her life, started to exercise regularly, making full use of Angela's gym equipment.

Now she lay, face down on a sun lounger, a parasol shielding her from the sun as she worked at her laptop, searching for any mention of near death experiences.

Her first lead proved elusive, but she stuck with it. On an internet forum dedicated to sustainability she found a reference by a user to a near death experience. They didn't elaborate publicly, instead they mentioned something about a 'member's area' and said they'd give the details there. A little more investigation revealed that access to the member's area required that you sign up and make a certain number of posts.

Nathalie had now spent several days posting on a subject she didn't really know much about, but by early afternoon she had finally been granted access to the member's area. She quickly found the entry, by a user calling themselves 'clean marine' and she realised she had struck gold.

As she read the posting, she found everything she was familiar with. This 'clean marine' was an ex-U. S. Marine who had almost died on an exercise in the North Atlantic when the helicopter he was in ditched in the sea. He had been the only survivor, being pulled from the freezing water after more than thirty minutes and revived. But he had gone to the afterlife, had been to the Gates and witnessed everything they had. As soon as he mentioned the bland, emotionless angels and the judging, Nathalie knew she had to contact him. To her excitement, the online icon was active by his profile, meaning she could contact him immediately. She clicked the chat button.

"Hello, I read about your near death experience," she typed. She waited for a few seconds before a response appeared.

"It's all true," came the reply.

"I believe you," she typed back. She waited for a few seconds and there was nothing. She decided to type something a little more enticing.

"When you woke up, were you in a haze and wearing the clothes you died in?" she typed.
"How did you know that?" came the almost instant reply.
"Did your two angels seem to talk as one person, each taking it in turns to say a sentence?"
"Yes, how do you know?"
"I crashed my car through ice on a lake. I went there too."
"Did you see people getting judged?" Nathalie smiled. She knew for sure she had a real one.
"Yes, we've seen children sent to hell," she typed.
"What do you mean we? Are there more of you?"
"I'm a doctor," Nathalie typed, "I've sent three people back by stopping their hearts."
"Shit! Really?"
"We've learnt so much. Want to join us?"
"Where are you? I live in Texas."
"We're in Munich, in Germany."
"I can't afford to fly that far."
"We'll pay," she typed, hoping it would persuade him to come over.
"You're serious about this?"
"Did you feel dizzy and black out when it ended?"
"Shit, yes, you've really been there, haven't you?"
"My name's Nathalie, what's yours?"
"Daryl."
"Hello Daryl, welcome to our team."

The conversation continued for a few minutes, as they exchanged a few details. They agreed Daryl would try and fly over for a week as soon as possible, and he promised to get back in touch within a day.

With excitement at the new recruit flowing through her, she picked up the phone and dialled Ian. He answered almost immediately.

"Nathalie, hi," he said. "How are you?"
"We've got another one!" she squealed down the phone.
"Who, tell me everything," Ian replied excitedly.
"He's American, an ex-marine who had an accident at sea."

"Did he drown in cold water?" Ian asked.

"Exactly," she replied, "and he had the same story we did about what he saw."

"That's fantastic news, is he coming to Munich?"

"Yes, not sure when, but soon," she answered.

"Oh, you're brilliant," he said, "I miss you so much over here."

"I miss you too," she said.

"I spoke to my boss today, and I resigned," he said.

"How long till you're finished?" Nathalie asked with excitement.

"I'll be finished in three weeks," he replied, "then I'll be over."

"Angela really misses you too," Nathalie said. "She spent half of last night telling me how much she loves you." Ian laughed.

"And the other half?"

"Telling her how much she loves me," Nathalie replied, laughing along with Ian.

"Anyway, I have to go, I'm at work."

"Yes, that's okay, see you soon," she replied, and hung up.

She turned back to the internet, enthused by her success and eager for more. As she began to trawl through social media for more leads, she began to realise that she might just be going about it the wrong way. An idea grew in her head and a new plan began to form.

Angela returned home at her usual early evening time, sounding the car horn to let Nathalie know that she was coming. Even before Angela was out the car Nathalie came running from the door to greet her, throwing her arms around Angela and kissing her.

"Someone's had a good day, haven't they?" said Angela. Nathalie nodded enthusiastically.

"Come on, let me show you," she replied, taking Angela by the hand and leading her inside.

"Did you find that one you told me about last night, what was his name, clean marine?" Angela asked.

"Yes," Nathalie replied, "he's an ex-marine, he had an accident at sea and he'll be coming over soon."

"Oh, good work," replied Angela.

"But there's more," said Nathalie.

"More? Someone else?"

"No," Nathalie replied, "I had an idea. I thought it might be an idea to advertise."

"Advertise?" asked a confused Angela, "like on TV?"

"Online," said Nathalie as they entered the lounge. Nathalie opened the laptop and showed Angela the fruits of her afternoon's labour.

"Ah, a website," said Angela.

"Tailored to exactly our experience rather than other near death experiences, but with essential things missing."

"Such as?"

"That we arrive wearing our clothes, about the angels talking in turns, that kind of thing."

"So it stops bullshitters from getting through," said Angela.

"Effectively, yes. We can screen out anyone who hasn't really been there."

"Hmm..." said Angela as she considered the concept. "I have a few marketing tools from work we can use, search engine manipulation, that kind of thing, it should help people find us."

"There has to be more out there, and they don't exactly shout about it," said Nathalie. "Maybe this is what we need."

"Okay, let's do it."

Almost two weeks had passed and now Angela and Nathalie once again stood in the arrivals lounge of Munich Airport. Their eyes were fixed on the arrivals board, waiting for the flights that would bring both Ian and Daryl to them on this Friday evening.

Ian arrived first and both women swamped him with hugs and kisses. Their time apart had been torture and their reunion was a sweet moment for all three.

Daryl arrived around an hour later. Nathalie immediately recognised him from a photo he had sent her, and he strode over to meet them when Nathalie called his name.

He was shorter than she expected, but still stood almost six feet tall. He had short, tightly cropped blond hair and his muscles seemed ready to burst out of the red shirt he wore.

"Hi guys," he said in a thick Texan accent, "I'm Daryl Shannon."

The other three introduced themselves, shaking hands each time.

"Thanks for coming, our car's this way," said Angela as she turned and led them out the door.

"So what happened when you had your near death experience, I mean once you died," Ian asked as they climbed into the car.

"The helicopter I was in crashed into the ocean," Daryl began, "and I was plunged underwater. After a few moments everything went black, then I woke up in that place."

"We call it 'the Gates' usually," said Nathalie.

"As in Pearly?" Daryl asked. Nathalie nodded. "Well I was met by two of those angel people, they had bland smiles, like they were on drugs or something. They talked funny too, like they were the same person, each one finishing the other's lines. They took me to a place where he said we'd be processed, and I assumed that was judged, you know like by Saint Peter, to see if we get into Heaven. I joined a queue and I saw some sights there that made me feel real bad about things."

"Such as?" asked Ian.

"You have to understand, I was raised in a small town in Texas. Everyone went to church, everyone prayed to the lord and I was one of them. I was a good Christian boy, even joined up to help fight the wars after 9/11. I went to Afghanistan proud to be fighting for my country and my god. Hell, I even swallowed the bullshit they told us about Iraq and Saddam and I was there too, killing strangers I never knew, just so soccer mums could fill their big damn SUVs up with cheap gas."

"The point I'm trying to make, is I believed in God, and I lived like the Bible told me. Then I wake up in this hell hole they pretend is Heaven and what do I see? Some of my own buddies who died with me in the chopper getting sent to hell just for not believing. These guys were heroes, guys who had risked their lives to free people in Afghanistan, and God's so full of himself he can't let good people like that in just cos they don't believe in him? And one of those damn angels even laughed as one of my buddies was carried down. I wanted to hit the little bastard, but I was sent back to Earth before I got the chance."

"So what happened to your faith?" asked Angela.

"My faith? What faith? I know God exists, and I know he's a son of a bitch. But I was always alone, I never knew anyone else that had been through it. I spoke to my preacher, but he told me I must be mistaken. Bullshit I was mistaken and you folks are proof of that. I gave my life to God, I even didn't do the things I wanted to because he said not to, and then I find out what he's really like."

"So do you want to make another trip there?" asked Ian.

"Yes, yes I do. A few minutes is hardly enough time for an experience so important and I want to speak to those people, find out more."

"We give everyone who wants to go a fitness test before we send them," said Nathalie.

"I'll pass that," said Daryl, "I used to run marathons in full kit, and I still keep myself in damn fine shape."

"Now that I don't doubt," said Nathalie. "I'll give you the test in the morning, and then we can take the next step."

"You mean you send me back?"

"First we'll discuss what you'll do there," Nathalie said, "we usually do a few experiments, but if you want to just explore your first time, that's fine."

"What sort of experiments?" Daryl asked.

"We're testing the laws of physics," said Ian. "We've taken things like magnets and pendulums to do our experiments."

"Sounds cool, what have you tried?"

"We've looked at electronics, magnetism and energy, all are the same there as here," Ian replied.

"What about gravity?" Daryl asked. "Why don't you get me a big rock and one of those scales you get in grocery stores so I can weigh it?"

"I have some weights from a diving belt," said Angela, "they'll fit in your palm but they're pretty heavy. I have scales as well that you can use."

"Well, that's me all sorted," said Daryl, "but I'll try and think of something else."

"Don't worry about it your first time," said Nathalie. "Just explore, speak to people, find out anything you can. Just leave the rest to us."

Daryl had passed his physical with flying colours and now he lay naked on the board, strapped down and ready to go. Around his neck on a length of rope was Angela's diving weight and a small but heavy duty suspended weighing scale, ready for Daryl to use when he arrived at the Gates.

"You ready for this?" Nathalie said as she was ready to place the mask over his face.

"Bring it," said Daryl. "Let's do this." Nathalie put the mask over his face and hit the switch and Daryl plunged into the freezing cold water.

There was no lingering in the mist, no floating in infinity for Daryl. Instead he leapt to his feet as soon as he arrived, tearing the weight and scales from his neck. He quickly did the weight experiment, it was two kilograms, just like it was back on Earth, but then he discarded the scales, keeping hold of the diving weight.

"Hello Daryl," said an angel as two robed figures approached him.

"Where do I go to be judged?" Daryl asked as he pulled out the thermometer.

"Over here," replied the second angel, who gestured to the area behind Daryl. He turned and ran, quickly finding himself surrounded by others who were joining the queues.

"Step forward boy," he heard one of the angels who were evaluating the dead say. He turned to see a child, a boy no more than ten years old look up to the angel. The boy wore a surgical gown and look terrified, but he stepped forward as he was told, encouraged by the two angels who stood astride him.

"Yes sir," he said in a meek voice. Daryl watched with a burning anger as he saw the boy's angels smile at each other malevolently behind his back.

"You don't go to church do you?" asked the evaluator.

"No sir," the boy replied.

"You weren't even baptised, were you?"

"No sir," the boy replied again, with tears in his eyes.

"Do you even believe in God?" asked the evaluator. The boy just stared at him, shaking with fear.

"Please, I've been good," the boy finally said, but the evaluator had seen enough.

"To Hell with you boy," he said, and the child was consumed by fire.

Daryl screamed with rage and ran forward, knocking the boy's angels to the side and heading straight for the evaluator. He smashed the diving weight into the evaluator's face and with a satisfying crunch, the evaluator staggered back before falling to the ground, his eyes wide open in shock. He turned to the two angels who stared at Daryl in terror as he lunged forward, striking one down with the weight. The other turned and fled but Daryl pursued him and knocked him to the ground. He jumped on top of the angel before it could recover and smashed the weight down on its head. Dead people all around him screamed and ran as he rained blow after blow down on the angel's head, crushing the skull and dashing its brains out across the ground.

"Help me," he heard a weak voice whimper from behind him. He turned and saw the first angel start to get up, but Daryl knocked him to the ground, grasping his throat with both hands and squeezing tightly. The angel writhed underneath him as he closed his fingers ever tighter around his neck until the angel finally lay still.

The people around him were terrified at the sight of this naked maniac, smeared and splattered as he was with the blood of angels. Now scattered through the haze, they tried to hide the best they could, but they neednt have bothered. Daryl had no interest in them.

He turned and walked back to the evaluator, who lay bleeding and moaning in pain. Daryl put his foot down on the evaluator's neck and slowly pushed his weight down on it.

"This is what I do to bastard bullies like you," he said as he felt the evaluator's neck crunch under his foot. He crushed down harder and harder, enjoying the look of terror in the evaluator's eyes. His attention was so focused on the eyes he didn't see what came at him from behind.

A middle aged woman, clad in a nightgown had picked up the diving weight and was taking slow, measured steps towards him.

As she crept up behind him she noticed he seemed to stagger, as if he was dizzy and she took her chance. She leapt forward, bringing the weight down with all the force she could muster against his head.

But she was too late. Daryl winked out of existence and the weight passed through the empty space he had been standing in. He had returned to the Earth.

Daryl's face wore a broad smile as he awoke. He felt an overwhelming sense of satisfaction in what he had done, but he had already decided to conceal it from the others.

"Did it work?" asked Nathalie as he emerged from unconsciousness.

"It worked," he replied. "It was amazing."

"How do you feel?" she asked.

"All right," he replied, "a bit of pain in my chest but otherwise fine."

"Well, electric shocks will do that to you, you'll be fine in a few days."

"Will I be able to return then?" he asked.

"No, your heart needs more time to recover," she said. "Go back home and come back in a month or so, then we'll send you back."

"A month," he asked, "that long?"

"Yes, I may have rushed sending Angela back and her heart's taking time to recover. I don't want to send anyone else back without a long wait in between." She saw a look of sadness on Daryl's face. "But don't worry, we will send you back, that's a promise."

"So what happened?" came a voice from beside the bed. Daryl turned and saw Angela sitting in the corner.

"I woke up and did the experiment, it weighed the same two kilograms there as it did here."

"So gravity's the same," said Nathalie.

"Carry on," Angela said to Daryl.

"I was alone initially," he began, "for a few minutes, then the angels came. They were as bland and false as before, and they led me to the processing area, where I joined the queue."

"You went to get judged?" Angela asked.

"I wasn't judged, I didn't have the time, but I was curious to see where I'd be sent," he said, "I know God is real and I used to love him, but that's changed. I wondered if my past would be enough."

"Interesting idea," said Nathalie, "maybe next time you should try and be judged, see what happens. You've been a good Christian most of your life, maybe you'll get a glimpse of Heaven."

"Or of Hell," added Angela.

"Either one would be interesting to have a look at," replied Nathalie.

"Do you want me to get judged next time?" he asked.

"Possibly, we'll discuss it further and see what Ian thinks," Nathalie said, "but it sounds like a good idea to me."

"So what happened?" asked Angela.

"I waited in line, I mainly talked to the angels," he replied, now just making it up as he went along. "They're not the most talkative of folks, but they said all the usual stuff, about how you need to love God and that those who don't go to Hell, even the good folks."

"Anything else?" asked Angela.

"Well, I felt a bit dizzy and everything all went black, and that was it, I was back here."

"You've been asleep for a while," said Nathalie, "so any time you're ready, you can get up and move around."

"I think I might just lie here a little bit longer," he replied. "It's all taken a heck of a lot out of me." Angela and Nathalie left the room and headed upstairs, but once they had reached the top of the stairs Angela paused and gave Nathalie a worried look.

"Something's wrong," she said.

"What do you mean?" Nathalie asked.

"He was a little light on detail, wasn't he? He told us the result of the experiment right away, and then gave an account that offered nothing new."

"I see what you mean," Nathalie said, "he just seems to have stood around and done nothing."

"So what's he hiding," Angela asked, "what did he actually do up there? He had one hell of a smile on his face when he woke up."

"Maybe he asked about a relative, found out if they were in Heaven or not," said Nathalie, saying the first thing that came into her head.

"I suppose it could be that simple," said Angela.

"But you're not convinced, are you?"

"No," was Angela's stern reply. "He came across as pretty aggressive and bitter about his past as a church goer, and he was a marine, he's a trained killer."

"Oh, come on, why would you think that?"

"He said it himself, he wanted to hit the angel."

"Look, let's just trust him for now," said Nathalie. "We need more people, and so far he's the only one."

"Okay, but let's be careful around him," Angela replied, "and maybe not tell him quite everything we learn."

"If you want, we can get Ian to try something and not tell Daryl, that way if we ask Daryl to do it, he won't know the result." Angela nodded in agreement.

"But now that Daryl's awake and you can leave him," said Angela, "Ian has something to show you." Both women walked into the lounge where Ian sat at a laptop.

"Ah, Nathalie, there you are," he said as they walked in, "I found a rather curious post online that might interest you."

"Oh, what is it?" Nathalie asked.

"It's on a medical discussion forum. I decided to have a look at hypothermia and near death experiences on the off chance that someone else has figured this out and I found a comment from a cardiologist in New Zealand that might be of interest."

"What did they say?"

"They were asking if any doctors had heard of near death experiences from hypothermia victims that were different to the common, what she calls 'light at the end of the tunnel' experiences."

"Shit, they must know too," said Nathalie.

"I've sent them a message, saying that we have one we can share, I'm still waiting for a reply."

The reply was not long in coming. Within an hour, a message popped up on the screen.

"Hello. This is Doctor Susan Bathgate. I've received your message." Nathalie quickly typed a reply.

"This is Doctor Nathalie Lamont, you said you were looking for unusual near death experiences," was Nathalie's instant response.

"Yes, I had a patient with a very strange story," came the reply.

"A visit to Heaven?" typed Nathalie. "Waking in a haze and an encounter with a pair of angels?"

"That sounds exactly like it," was Susan's answer.

"And lines of people, hundreds of them waiting to be judged?"

"You had a hypothermia patient tell you this?" was Susan's response.

"Not a patient. It was me. I crashed my car through an ice covered lake. Did your patient see people being judged harshly, many being sent to hell?"

"My God, you've been there?"

"Not just me," replied Nathalie, "there's a group of us that have all been there."

"This is incredible, but I have to tell you something else. The patient was my husband. He's tried to make sense of it since the day it happened and he's desperate to speak to others who have been there. How many are you?"

"Five of us have been," typed Nathalie.

"Ask her if he wants to go back," said Angela, who along with Ian was reading this over her shoulder.

"Would he like to go back?" typed Nathalie, who turned and smiled at Angela and Ian.

"What do you mean?" came the response.

"I can send people back. I've done it with four people now. It's worked every time. We're learning a lot about that place." There was no response. Nathalie typed her phone number in, inviting Susan to call.

The phone rang seconds later. Nathalie snatched it up before the second ring.

"Susan?"

"Nathalie?" said the voice at the end of the phone.

"Yes."

"How the hell did you manage it?" asked Susan, bypassing any formalities.

"Freezing cold water," said Nathalie. "I strap them to a board and plunge them into it."

"You drown them?"

"No, they have a mask with a breathing tube. Secondary drowning's something I'd rather avoid."

"So their brains freeze as well as their hearts?"

"Yes," said Nathalie. "It's not pleasant, but it works every time."

"You said you'd discovered things about that place."

"We found we could take things with us, our clothes, anything round our necks, that sort of thing, so we've been doing experiments."

"Experiments, what kind of experiments?"

"We've done experiments to test things like physics, with magnets and that kind of thing. Simple medical tests as well like exercise."

"That's amazing," said an excited Susan. "What have you found out?"

"That it's like this universe. We have a body, we breathe, have a metabolism, we even go to the toilet over there."

"You're kidding."

"No, and the laws of physics seem the same, electronics work, as do magnets. We've even spoken to people, gotten a few names and places of death and checked them out."

"And these are real people that died?" asked Susan.

"Absolutely," replied Nathalie.

"That's proof then, independent confirmation," replied Susan. "This is incredible."

"Does your husband want to go back?" asked Nathalie. There was silence for a few seconds.

"He might," she replied. "He's certainly said he wants to go back and see it, but I'd have to see what it is you do. Where are you?"

"We're in Germany, in Munich," Nathalie replied, "I realise that's a hell of a distance to come."

"We'll come, it might be a few weeks before we make it, but

we're coming."

"That's fantastic," replied Nathalie, "and if I show you how to do it, then maybe you can do the same for me?"

"Oh yes, of course," replied Susan.

"You're a cardiologist, aren't you?" Nathalie asked.

"Yes, here in Auckland," she replied.

"Then I'll be in good hands," Nathalie replied.

"Yes, yes, whatever you want," Susan responded, "but I'll need to go, I need to speak to David about it."

"Call me back when you're ready to come over," Nathalie said, "and we can take things from there."

"Yes, okay, bye!" The phone clicked as the line went dead.

"You're going back," said Angela, leaning forward and hugging Nathalie."I told you we'd find a way." She planted a kiss on Nathalie's cheek.

"Would we be able to send back two people at once?" said Ian.

"We'd need a whole other set up like the one we have here, but with that many people available to help, yes," said Nathalie.

Even as Nathalie spoke, a plan began to form in Angela's head, a plan to test Daryl's true motives.

At the airport they said goodbye to Daryl and Ian. While Daryl would return in a month, Ian would be back for good in a week, and that night, lying in each other's arms in bed, Angela discussed her plan with Nathalie.

"I don't trust Daryl," said Angela, "so I was thinking about what you said about sending two people back."

"We should be able to do it," said Nathalie. "One doctor and at least one helper is all we really need, so we have enough."

"I don't think we should tell Daryl we can send two people back," said Angela, "or even let him meet Susan and David initially."

"We'll piss him off if we're not honest," said Nathalie.

"I know, but we can explain it as an experiment," she replied. "We send him in, then in a different part of the house we send David in. We'll show him a photo of Daryl and see if he can find him."

"So how do we explain not telling him?"

"Independent confirmation of someone's experience," replied Angela.

"Ah, like a double blind experiment," Nathalie said, nodding.
"Double blind?"
"It's a way of testing medication," Nathalie explained. "You give a group of patients a medication and a similar group a placebo. But no patient knows if they've got the actual medication or not. That's a blind test."
"And a double blind test?"
"When the doctors administering them as well don't know who gets the actual medication."
"Ah, makes sense," said Angela, "so we can say that we wanted to observe someone as a way of measuring the accuracy of their memory."
"That'll work. If he's being honest he'll probably understand."
"But if he's not," said Angela, "we'll know." Nathalie sat up in the bed, wrapping her arms around her knees.
"I sometimes wonder where this is going," said Nathalie, suddenly seeming uncomfortable.
"Are you okay?" Angela asked as she sat up and placed her hand on Nathalie's shoulder.
"Does this scare you?" Nathalie asked.
"What we're doing? No, it doesn't."
"I used to think that when we died we just died, that was it," Nathalie continued. "But now I know there's something else, and that something really doesn't look good."
"I'm not scared," replied Angela as she draped her arm around Nathalie, "because I know what we're doing will help us."
"How do you know that?" Nathalie replied.
"What's the first thing that God commands in the Bible?" Angela asked.
"Have no other gods, isn't it," answered Nathalie.
"That's the first commandment," Angela replied, "but his first command, to Adam and Eve, was to not eat the fruit that gives knowledge."
"Yes, of course," Nathalie replied.
"God fears people with knowledge," Angela replied. "Now in a nebulous world, where people don't ask questions, God can get away with suppressing the truth. But we're investigating his

world and finding out how it works. For the first time people can go to their deaths with knowledge of what comes next, and that knowledge could be power."

"We need to know the nature of God himself, and of Heaven and Hell," said Nathalie. "We need to know everything."

"And I'm willing to bet that if we have bodies in the afterlife rather than being just spirits then God isn't the all powerful old man with a white beard either." Nathalie nodded in agreement. "God doesn't want us to have knowledge," Angela continued. "There must be a reason for that, so we need to learn as much as we can."

"It's possible he's trying to protect us," Nathalie said.

"If he's looking after us, he wouldn't be throwing all of us who don't love him into Hell," Angela replied, "and those damn angels wouldn't be enjoying it so much." Nathalie lay back on the bed, stretching her arms above her head.

"Oh, I wish Ian was here," she said. "He always seems to bring everything into focus."

"Me too," said Angela as she lay down beside Nathalie. "I feel like there's a piece of us missing when he's not here."

"I don't think straight when he's not around."

"Well that's just called being in love," said Angela, "and it suits you. I've never seen you this happy."

"And you make me just as happy," Nathalie replied as she rolled onto her side, draping an arm across Angela and kissing her. "The three of us are pretty good, aren't we?"

"We're the best," Angela replied, "we're unstoppable".

"Not even God can stop us."

"And amen to that," answered Angela with a laugh as she turned the light off.

Chapter 13

Ian arrived in Munich late on the Sunday afternoon. He had been driving for two days almost without a stop and he was tired and sore, longing for a good meal and a rest. All his worldly goods were packed into his car, and he emerged from it slowly, his aching back refusing to straighten quickly.

In any other circumstances, the sight of two beautiful women coming running towards him with outstretched arms would have been delightful, but right here, right now he was so exhausted it was slightly scary. He hugged and kissed both of them, his joy at seeing them overwhelming his exhaustion and he forgot within seconds his aches and pains.

"Come inside," said Nathalie, taking his hand, "we've missed you." Ian couldn't help notice with delight the fire in her eyes.

"Wait a minute, I have something," he said, reaching onto the passenger seat of his car. He emerged with a small package.

"What's this," said Angela seductively, hoping it might be something for the bedroom.

"Oh, it's just a little toy I thought we could use," he replied, not realising what she was thinking off.

"Well, then let's get upstairs and open it," she replied.

"What? Oh no, that's not what I meant," he said. "It's for an experiment." Both women's frivolity ended suddenly and immediately turned to more important matters.

"What is it?" Nathalie asked.

"It's a tracker," Ian replied, opening the box to reveal a small black electronic device, "it records your movement."

"It records where we walk or move?" said Nathalie.

"Yes, without needing GPS," he replied.

"So we can use it over there to map the place, get an idea of its size," Nathalie replied. "Damn, that's a good idea."

"Show me how it works," said Angela, now intrigued by the device. "Can it measure the shape of the garden?"

"Yes, you can start walking and it measures the route you cover, and then gives you all kinds of stats such as speed, distance, area enclosed, that kind of thing."

"How does it work?" asked Nathalie.

"It measures changes in momentum and the time between the changes," he replied.

"Let's go for a walk then," she said. "We can measure the area from the tree line to the pool." The three of them set off around the garden, with Nathalie and Angela intrigued by the device.

"It's pretty accurate," Ian explained as they set off, "especially if you hit the button that tells it you've stopped when you come to a halt. I had it on in the car for a while, it worked well over long and short distances."

"Looks like someone's going for a run in the afterlife," said Nathalie.

"That'll be me then I take it?" Ian said.

"Once you've had a rest from the drive you can go," said Nathalie, "tomorrow if you're ready."

"Sounds good," he said as they approached the pool. "And that pool looks good as well, I'm not used to this heat." Nathalie and Angela smiled at each other and quickly stripped off to dive in. Ian put down the tracker and joined them. Both women swam to him and Nathalie reached him first, embracing him and kissing him.

"Welcome home," she said.

As the sun set on the warm Bavarian day, Nathalie, Angela and Ian lay on the grass by the pool, their bodies intertwined. Passion had given way to exhaustion, but now minds were turning to more practical matters.

"We've been talking about Daryl," said Nathalie, "and Angela and I are a little unsure about him."

"I know what you mean," said Ian, "not exactly forthcoming about his trip back, was he?"

"So we have a little plan for when he comes back," continued Nathalie. "And it means you have to build a rig to send another person back."

"We're sending two people back at once?" asked Ian.

"When Susan and David come, we'll send you back so I can show her how it's done," said Nathalie, "but then when Daryl comes, we'll send him back straight away, but you'll help Susan to send David back, and he'll observe what he does."

"Daryl won't have met him, so he won't know who he is."

"Exactly," said Angela.

"I can stick it in the basement," said Ian. "It's well out the way, so he won't see it."

"Sounds good," said Nathalie.

"Then never mind my trip to the Gates, I'll start work on the rig tomorrow," Ian replied.

"And once it's done we can test it by sending you back," said Nathalie.

"You can try out the tracker," Angela said.

"I have something else for another experiment as well," Ian replied as he leapt to his feet and started walking back to his car. Both women rolled onto their fronts and watched him intently, curious to see what he had.

He returned with two boxes, one large and one small. He knelt down in front of the women and opened the large box, removing what appeared to be some kind of metal tube with a handle and a digital display. He switched it on and it began to click every few seconds. With every click the number on the digital read out increased.

"It's a Geiger counter," said Nathalie. Ian nodded.

"So what's in the other box?" asked Angela.

"Radiation source?" asked Nathalie.

"Several, of both alpha and beta, so we can test radioactive decay and properties of radioactivity."

"So we can determine if half life is consistent," Nathalie said, "or if decay products are largely the same."

"Okay, you've lost me," said Angela with a blank look on her face. "What are you talking about?"

"Radioactivity is energy released by a decaying atom," said Nathalie, sitting up and crossing her legs. "Some atoms are more unstable than others and may decay over a given time. We talk about half life when we describe how fast that decay occurs. Basically it means the time it takes for any given amount of a radioactive element to decay to something else."

"You've still lost me," said Angela.

"Okay, let's try an example," said Nathalie. "There's a type of uranium called uranium 238. It has a half life of about four and a half billion years. That's pretty much the age of the Earth, so there is about half the remaining uranium 238 today as there was when the Earth formed."

"And in another four and a half billion years?" asked Angela.

"There'll be a quarter left."

"Ah, I understand now," said Angela. "I think so anyway."

"Now, when something decays, it releases radiation," Ian said. "We'll be measuring two kinds, alpha and beta. I won't go into details, but alpha particles are heavy and slow moving, so they don't travel far, a few centimetres in air before they're absorbed. Beta travels faster and further, their penetrating power is about a hundred times that of alpha."

"So if you move the Geiger counter towards and away from the source the count changes?" asked Angela.

"Precisely," said Ian. "I'll calibrate it beforehand and compare it to the results we get at the Gates."

"Sounds complicated," said Nathalie, "maybe we should devote an entire visit to it."

"Probably," replied Ian, "but I have a few other ideas beyond this, and they get more and more complicated. Having two people at once may be essential for them."

"Tomorrow we all get back to work," said Angela. "But tonight's for each other." The three of them looked at each other and smiled, knowing that now they were finally all together for good.

"Life's become rather pleasant for me," said Nathalie as she lay on the sun lounger under the parasol on Angela's patio.

"Nothing to do," replied Ian, "except plough through papers on hypothermia and cardiac arrest while you lounge in the sun, eh?"

"And the garden is my office," she replied with a smile. "And with you around now I can watch you while you work." Nathalie gestured towards the tools and materials Ian had outside for building the second rig.

"Well, that works out nicely for both of us, especially now you've picked up Angela's habit of sunbathing naked." Nathalie watched with delight as he cast his eyes over her body.

"When in Munich, as they say," said Nathalie.

"I completely approve," added Ian, "who says the British don't integrate abroad." Both burst out laughing.

"You know, I've been thinking," Nathalie said, becoming more serious, "I think we need to consider some chemistry experiments."

"What, you mean blow things up?" asked Ian.

"Perhaps, but other things as well."

"Such as?"

"Will a helium balloon rise?" she asked, "and how high will it go?"

"Good one," he said, nodding, "although I'm starting to wonder the point of it all."

"What do you mean?" asked Nathalie, shocked by his response. "Do you think we should stop doing this?"

"Oh no, not that," he replied. "It's just the experiments all say the same thing, that the laws of physics are the same."

"Ah, I see what you mean," she replied.

"I mean, do we really think that a helium balloon won't rise? I'd be more interested in seeing how high it rose, maybe even with a camera stuck on it so we can see where it goes."

"You're talking about exploring the environment?"

"Yes," replied Ian, "and not just things like its physical size. I want to learn more about God and about Heaven and Hell."

"Yes, the radiation test is the decider for me," said Nathalie, "if that's normal we should move onto other things, leave the physical experiments behind."

"Mapping the area's the first thing to try, I can do that next time I go using the tracker."

"What about the radiation experiment?"

"I can do that in a few seconds," Ian replied.

"Well, it should be easier for you next time," said Nathalie, "I've found a few research papers on drugs at low temperatures, so I can safely sedate you next time." Ian breathed a sigh of relief.

"Good, that was horrible last time," Ian replied, "freezing to death like that is a nasty way to go, I'd rather not be awake if I have to die that way a third time." Nathalie started to respond, but she paused for a second. She had an issue she wanted to raise, but wasn't entirely sure how to say it.

"What did you think of Richard?" she asked tentatively.

"He's a good man," Ian replied. "Honest, devoted, I can't fault him."

"And Daryl?"

"Nothing like Richard. Richard makes me feel comfortable. Daryl doesn't."

"Is Richard one of us?" she asked.

"Us?" said Ian, narrowing his brow. "I trust him in a way I wouldn't trust Daryl, and if he stayed, we'd be stronger, that's for sure."

"You know, before I met you guys," Nathalie said, reaching out and holding Ian's hand, "I never thought about being with a woman. But with Angela it's different. I fell in love with her through what we're doing, same as how I fell in love with you. We're alone in the world with this."

"Do you love Richard as well?" Ian asked.

"I can't say I don't," she replied. "It's not normal love, it's like we're the only people in the world. We share this love because there's no one else."

"Is there something you're trying to ask me?" said Ian.

Nathalie nodded. "If he came back, how would you feel?"

"You mean would I be happy to share the bed?" said Ian. "I'm not sure, at least I'm not sure I'd say no."

"Oh, have you...?"

"Been with a man?" Ian replied. "I've never done it, but there was always that thought in the back of my head, just a hint of curiosity."

"So why did you never act on it?"

"Why do you think?" he asked. "I'm not exactly from the most liberal of areas."

"Where you came from, what did people think of gays?" she asked.

"They don't have them in the highlands," he snorted, "no one ever spoke of it, except to have a go at them."

"Let me guess, men were called gay, or a poof or something like that as an insult."

"All the time," he replied, "although mostly by men who didn't get on with their wives and spent all their spare time playing contact sports with other men." He laughed as he said it, but it wasn't a sincere laugh.

"Did you ever think you were bisexual?" she asked.

"I'm not sure that matters anymore," he replied "Like you and Angela, we all share something. And I'm not sure things like sexuality matter so much when we share an experience like this."

"So you understand why Angela and I feel the way we do?"

"We belong together," he replied, "we're all in this as one. Don't ask me to say any more than that for now."

Nathalie smiled and leaned forward to kiss him. "You've said more than enough."

Ian lay strapped to the board of the new rig he had built. For the first time he was wearing clothes, in this case a pair of shorts and running shoes. Around his neck hung the tracker and the Geiger counter and radioactive source were strapped to his chest along with a tape measure. His veins now filled with Nathalie's cocktail of drugs to sedate him and he slowly drifted off, never to feel the terror and agony of this death.

Like before, he woke in a haze. He quickly undid the Geiger counter's strap and began to measure the radiation dose. With the tape measure he moved it backwards and forwards, quickly determining that the decay rate was the same as on Earth.

"Hello Ian," said the familiar voice.

"Goodbye you," replied Ian as he dropped the Geiger counter, hit the start button on the tracker and took off running in a random direction. He glanced down occasionally as he ran through the haze, watching the numbers slowly increase.

But the numbers suddenly stopped. He was still running, but there was no increase in the numbers. For a moment he felt as if he was running on a treadmill, as if the ground was moving but he wasn't. He began to change his direction, and the numbers increased. The directional indicator seemed to indicate he had reached some kind of barrier and was now running alongside it.

A few minutes later he saw that the numbers were no longer changing. He stopped, looking around himself. He was still surrounded by haze, but there was no-one around here.

"Ian, please, come back," shouted a voice from the distance. He turned to see the two angels running towards him. To his surprise they seemed out of breath and when they caught up with him they were struggling to breathe.

He took one by the arm and began to search for a pulse. The angel was too out of breath to respond and Ian found the pulse. It was racing, as a human's would if a human as fat as this angel tried to run after Ian.

But that was another question for another time, and he started running again, changing his direction until the numbers increased. He was now moving at a right angle to his previous direction and in a few minutes he found he had stopped again. With the angel's voices trailing in the distance he turned again, running until he again found the edge.

Ian looked at the data on the tracker. He had mapped out three sides, the last two of which were the same length. He set off running again, turning one more corner before finding himself back at the first wall. He had mapped out a square, with each side a little over nine hundred metres long.

As final confirmation, he followed the tracker's path back to where he started. The Geiger counter was still there, in the mist. He now turned and headed for the centre of this large room.

The mist cleared as he walked and he stared out across the evaluation area. Hundreds of people were gathered, forming their queues, all guided there by angels.

"Oh, at last," said a strained, wheezing voice. Ian turned to see his angels stagger up to him, looking as exhausted as he had ever seen anyone look in his life.

"What are you?" Ian asked. The angels took a few seconds to get their breath back before answering.

"We are what you might know as angels," one said.

"Bollocks to that," Ian replied, "how can an angel be struggling for breath after a little run, or have a pulse that feels like his heart is about to explode?"

"You must trust us," said the other angel, gesturing between laboured breaths to the evaluation area.

"You're a flesh and blood man, just like me," said Ian.

"Like you were," replied an angel, "now your soul is in the afterlife, perhaps even to enter Heaven."

"Souls don't breathe, or even need the toilet," said Ian. "Now tell me..." Ian suddenly felt dizzy and staggered back a step, never finishing his question.

"Oh thank fuck," said an angel, "he's going back."

"This could be our most productive trip yet," said Nathalie as she sat on the balcony. Angela, sitting opposite nodded in agreement.

"Now we know the Gates are just a big room, and that those people that call themselves angels are as human as me and you," said Angela

"They certainly seem human," added Nathalie, "but I'd have to dissect one to be absolutely sure." Angela looked at her with surprise until they saw a smile break over her face. "Only joking!" she said, "although I would like to get a closer look at them myself. When I go I might take a stethoscope and a sphygmomanometer."

"A what?" asked Angela.

"Those things a doctor wraps round your arm for measuring blood pressure," Nathalie replied.

"You want to find out for sure if they're human?" Angela asked.

"A few measurements of their vital stats should pretty much confirm it one way or the other," she replied. "But even if they're not, they seem to be flesh and blood like us."

"We need to start talking to them," said Angela. "How soon until I can return?"

"Not soon, a few months possibly," said Nathalie before her face softened to a smile. "But I know you're the best person to speak to them. If anyone can charm the secrets of the universe out of them, it's you." Angela stood up and walked to the balcony's handrail, holding it and staring out towards the mountains.

"Every time we send someone back it becomes clearer to me. We've uncovered something big, something that changes everything. We need to be ready to take a few more risks."

Nathalie stood up and placed her arms around Angela, hugging her tightly from behind. "I love you too much to lose you," she whispered into Angela's ear, "but I understand. I'll let Susan examine you as well, see what she says, she's more qualified than me anyway."

Angela turned round and put her arms around Nathalie's neck. "I love you too, more than anything, but this is bigger than any of us," she said. "Besides, death isn't the threat it was. I'm not scared of anything now."

"Not even of Hell?" asked Nathalie?

"I'm going to Hell anyway," Angela replied. "So what do we have to lose?"

Chapter 14

Munich airport felt almost overwhelming to Nathalie after spending several weeks in the peaceful setting of Angela's home and garden. The wide open space and sense of isolation had been replaced by the bustle of people in their hundreds, seemingly a world away from her recent life. Ian stood beside her, holding her hand and waiting for their newest recruits.

Although they recognised them from photographs they had exchanged, Susan and David were not what they expected. David stood more than six and a half feet tall and well built, like some kind of human tank. As the crowds thinned they spotted Susan trotting along beside him, barely five feet tall and seemingly full of boundless energy coming straight towards them.

"Hello, hello" she said as she greeted them, shaking their hands vigorously. "Glad to meet you, it's been a bugger of a long journey." Ian smiled as he turned to look up to David.

"David, good to meet you," he said. David smiled and shook his hand slowly but firmly.

"You too," he replied.

"Well, let's go," said Susan, "we've lots to talk about, lots to discuss."

"This way," said Nathalie, leading them to the car parked close by.

"So, tell me more about what you've done," said Susan as they climbed into the car.

"From this side of things, we've now got two rigs for sending people back," Nathalie said.

"Ah, you mean the tanks of freezing water," said Susan. "I had some thoughts on some drugs to help with that."

"I use a general anaesthetic now to reduce stress," said Nathalie, "I've used it once, but with no ill effects."

"Yes, there's probably a few we can use," Susan replied, "but some might allow us to extend the time of cardiac arrest, and improve recovery time."

"You've been doing some homework then," Nathalie said.

"Absolutely," Susan replied, "if this works as well as you say, I'd be fascinated to learn more, and to help out in any way I can. Now, what I really want to know is how much you have learnt about the afterlife."

"Lots," said Ian, "we can be pretty sure we exist in the same universe, the laws of physics all seem the same. We've mapped the place we arrive in, it's one big room, a little under a kilometre across on each side."

"Is it always the same place?" asked David.

"So far we've assumed so," said Ian, "but that's one of the advantages of being able to send two people back at the same time, we can see if they end up in the same place."

"I'm willing to bet it's the same place though," added Nathalie. "A quick calculation of the world's death rate seems consistent with the numbers we've seen there."

"Not exactly what we expected was it?" said Susan. "You know, I was raised a good Protestant girl, but I never really believed. It always just seemed so silly. I never dreamed it would be true, and certainly not like this."

"We've been told more than once the Catholic Church is the true church, but the god behind it seems to be more like God from the Old Testament, always angry and demanding obedience and worship," Nathalie said. "There's certainly no benefit to being a good person in the afterlife."

"Have you tried asking about it outright?" Susan said.

"You mean tell the angels what we're doing?" Nathalie answered. "No, we think it's best we don't tell them that."

"Oh, I wouldn't say we're gathering information, God hates people learning, he makes that clear enough," said Susan, "but if I go, I'll have a whole bunch of questions to ask."

The conversation continued for the short time it took to drive to Angela's house. Susan wasted no time, immediately wanting to see the equipment they used. Nathalie led her to the room, while Ian and David took their luggage to their room.

"Ah, so this is where you kill people," said Susan as she paced around the tank. Nathalie couldn't help but smile at Susan's energy and manner.

"Yes, I've killed a few people here, some of them more than once," she replied.

"Treat 'em mean, keep them keen, eh?" Susan responded. Both women laughed in response, but when Susan started speaking again, her tone had changed.

"So you want to go there as well do you?" she said. Nathalie's head snapped up in response.

"Yes, to see the others going and leaving me behind has been tough to say the least."

"When can we send David back?" Susan asked. "I've given him every test imaginable on his heart, he's fit and good to go."

"In twenty-four hours then, we'll give him time to recover from the flight," Nathalie replied.

"As soon as you've shown me what to do, I can send you as well," Susan said.

"Thank you," said Nathalie. "I can't say how much this means to me."

"Oh, I know," she replied, "David's pretty keen to go again as well. Together we'll send you both back."

With his huge frame only just fitting onto the board, David now lay strapped down and ready to return. Susan stood by his side holding his hand while Nathalie fitted an intravenous line for his anaesthetic.

"You ready for this?" Nathalie asked. David just nodded. She injected the drugs and everything went black for a second before it began to clear again.

He sat up, surrounded by mist, while a glowing white light seemed to fill everything around him. Remembering what he'd been told, he immediately reached round to remove the thermometer, easily sliding it out. Around his neck hung the experiment they gave him, and he quickly deployed it as he'd been told.

He pulled the cord and threw it to the ground. The helium canister discharged instantly, filling the balloon and sending it straight up. David watched as the string it was attached to followed it up, uncoiling on the ground as it got higher and higher. He read the distance marked on the string as it continued to rise, quickly heading beyond three hundred metres.

"Hello David," a voice said from behind him. David turned round to see two angels face him.

"How did you know my name?" he asked.

"You are dead, my friend," said an angel.

"Yes, I know that, but how did you know it? Do you know everything about me?"

"Not until you are judged," one replied.

"So you take time to download my memories," countered David, hoping to catch them off guard.

"Yes, you could say that," replied an angel, slightly awkwardly.

"And you get simple things first, like my name, where I come from, that kind of thing, yes?"

"You have many questions," an angel replied.

"Yes, I'm new here and I like to learn," he quickly replied. "Now, who are you?"

"We are what you would call angels," one replied.

"Yes, but what's an angel? You look human to me, were you once a mortal man like myself? How old are you?"

"Please, hold your questions..." and angel began, but David cut him off.

"I'm going to assume you were once men, unless you say otherwise," he continued, "which means you were believers in God, yes?"

"Of course, we all honour our God," came the reply.

"Well thanks for admitting you were once men," David replied. The angels looked at each other, slightly aghast. "So, we go to be judged, yes? By another angel?"

"Yes, this way, please," was the response, eager to move David along.

"So why can't you judge me?" David asked. "You can read the basics from my mind, but do these angels have better psychic powers?" As he finished, David noticed the string on the balloon had stopped rising, measuring a height of around nine hundred and fifty metres.

"Please, all will become clear..." David quickly cut the angel off again.

"So you were once human, but now you're psychic, just not as psychic as the angels that judge us, yes?" Again the angels exchanged worried glances. "Which means God has ex-humans guarding the gates of Heaven and doing his work, yes? Is he the only divine being?"

"Please, ask us no more," said an angel, a look of panic now across his face.

"Are you scared?" asked David. "Are you worried you'll reveal something you're not supposed to? Why do you still need to keep secrets if I'm in the afterlife? What is there to hide?" Panic now turned to a flash of aggression in the eyes of the angels.

"I am sorry," said an angel.

"But you should not have asked these questions," finished the other. They both reached into their tunics, but before anything could happen David was hit by dizziness and everything went black.

"What did you say you did for a living?" asked Ian as David finished his account of his visit to the Gates.

"I'm a lawyer," he replied rather smugly. Nathalie and Angela looked at each other and laughed.

"And to think I was going to use all my people skills to charm the information from the angels," said Angela, "and then you come along and just confuse the hell out of them."

"It wasn't much of a challenge," David said, "in fact they didn't seem too smart."

"Those who follow blindly tend not to be," Nathalie said, "and from what you said they seemed ready to attack you, and for not much reason."

"Well, we don't know that," David said, "but they did seem to change their mood. I was glad to leave when I did."

"They could be dangerous," said Nathalie. "We know from Angela's experiments we can be injured, so maybe we should tread a little more carefully."

"Well, it's not like we can die, is it?" said Susan, "I mean, we're already dead."

"Even so, let's be careful," Ian added, "there's still much we don't know."

"We need to go over all that was said in detail, figure out what else we can try and ask," said Nathalie.

"We have a week until Daryl gets here," said Angela, "and then we try again."

The following morning Nathalie lay at the end of the garden, sunbathing while she reviewed her now considerable library of research. Susan had provided additional research material for her, and her reading was bringing considerable new insight. She was so involved in it she didn't see Susan approach her until the last second.

"Well, good morning," Susan said as her shadow passed across Nathalie's reading material. Nathalie jumped up in surprise, desperately reaching around for some clothes to cover her naked body.

"Sorry, sorry," stammered Nathalie as grabbed the summer dress that lay beside her and held it against herself.

"Oh, don't worry about that," said Susan, waving her hand dismissively, "we're both doctors, aren't we?"

"Okay, thanks" said Nathalie, who continued to hold her dress over herself. Susan sat down beside her.

"I was just wondering when you wanted to go on a little trip to the afterlife." Susan asked.

"Do you think you're ready to try performing the procedure?" asked Nathalie.

"Well, I'll be doing it anyway to David when Daryl gets here, so as far as I'm concerned, we should try it as soon as possible." Nathalie tried to contain her excitement. She wanted to make the journey as soon as possible, but she wanted to make sure she came back in one piece.

"Let's try it after Daryl and David go," she replied. "Once the

137

two come back I can try it any time."

"Are you sure?" asked Susan. "I'm ready to try it now." Nathalie resisted the urge to accept.

"No, not until we've done the joint trip," Nathalie said. "I want to be fit for it and a trip to the afterlife and back doesn't exactly make you feel on top of the world."

"Okay, that's probably for the best," Susan said. "Besides, Daryl's here in a few days, so we may as well wait."

"But once that's done, just try and stop me," said Nathalie.

"You have a good tried and tested method here," said Susan. "I'm looking forward to administering it to you."

"And yourself," asked Nathalie, "have you thought about it?"

"How can I not want to go, especially now I've seen it works?" Susan answered. "This is the greatest experiment in history."

"Irresistible, isn't it?" Nathalie replied.

"When do we start telling people?" Susan asked. Nathalie paused before answering, gathering her thoughts.

"I've thought about that for a long time," she replied, "and I can't find an answer. Do we tell people slowly? I sure as hell can't publish a paper in a journal about it. How do we do it?"

"Maybe this is the right way," said Susan. "Gather people slowly but surely and spread the word."

"That sounds a lot like a religion," Nathalie replied.

"Maybe that's what we need to do," said Susan. "But also, think about the wider implications of this, if everyone knows. What becomes of religion then?"

"I hadn't really thought that far ahead," said Nathalie.

"It's time we did," said Susan. "If God requires faith and devotion to get to Heaven, what happens if everyone knows he exists, and that he's harsh and brutal? Will people love him? I doubt it."

"So are you saying it might be better to not tell people?"

"On one level, yes, but in my heart, no," Susan said. "I want to know the truth, I can't turn away from it."

"There is a danger though," Nathalie replied, "God has always tried to hold back knowledge."

"What are you willing to do?" Susan asked. "Risk Hell? Risk damnation?"

"I'm facing it already," was Nathalie's reply. "I hate whatever god treats people the way he does."

"Well that is a problem," said Susan. "How do you intend to avoid Hell?"

"I don't know," Nathalie replied. "But if there's a way, we'll only find it with more trips back."

"You mean find a way to fight?"

"I never thought of it like that before."

"How else would you think about it?" Susan asked.

"We need more information," said Nathalie, repeating her usual stance to avoid the question. Silence hung in the air for a few seconds.

"Oh, there was one other thing I had a thought about," Susan said.

"Yes?"

"This whole business of always sending people back naked, it may be helpful from a clinical point of view but I'm not sure it's a good idea. From what you say it sounds like there aren't too many naked people at the Gates, so perhaps we should avoid attention?"

"I'm not sure," Nathalie replied. "I don't like the thought of having to undress someone when their clothes are wet, it wastes time."

"Then we make clothes that are easy to remove, seams with Velcro, so we can tear them off in a second, that kind of thing."

"Interesting idea," said Nathalie, "and if we have a set ready for David's trip with Daryl, then it gives David a little extra anonymity. Good idea, I'll get to work on it."

"Well, I need to get back to work as well," said Susan. "You have lots of results for me to look over." And with that she stood up and walked back to the house.

Daryl's imminent arrival had set everyone on edge. Ian collected him from the airport alone while the rest of the group prepared for his arrival, preparing both rigs and David for a return to the Gates. Susan and David were locked away in the basement, hidden and out of sight, under orders to stay quiet. Everything was arranged so that Daryl would make his trip back to the afterlife the moment he arrived. Everyone was nervous and no one was comfortable with the idea of the deceit.

"Hi there ladies," said Daryl in his usual rich Texan accent as he walked through the door. "It sure is good to be back here amongst you guys."

"Good to see you too Daryl," said Nathalie and she shook his hand. "How are you feeling? It's probably best we go for it as soon as possible, you're only here for four days and I want to give you plenty of time to recover."

"That sounds mighty good to me," he replied. "I also brought a little something I thought I might take with me. It's a little glass thermometer, I thought we might take the temperature again, just to be sure."

"Sounds all right," said Ian, "and it's with a different instrument, so it's more data."

"Well, let's get started," Daryl replied. Nathalie gestured for him to follow her and she led Daryl to the treatment room.

"Is it get naked time again?" he asked.

"Yes, once again," she said. Daryl stripped off his clothes and stood naked in the middle of the room, completely relaxed about his state of undress.

"Sit on the bed," she said, "and we can get you ready."

Nathalie prepared Daryl in the usual way, setting up the heart monitor and the thermometer. Within a few minutes he was ready to go. He walked through to the main room where Ian waited for him.

"Here are your experiments," said Ian passing him a plastic bag on a rope. "Wear it round your neck and it'll be there again when you arrive." Daryl took the bag and nodded, hanging it round his neck.

"If you climb on, we'll get started," Nathalie said. Daryl did as he was told and he was quickly strapped to the board.

"Ready when you are," he said.

"Here it comes," said Nathalie as she injected him with the anaesthetic. He was unconscious in seconds and Nathalie hit the switch, sending him into the freezing water.

David arrived in the afterlife before Daryl. His slightly weaker constitution and age meant his heart had stopped before Daryl's and now he woke in the usual haze.

David, who was fully dressed in a set of Velcro lined clothes that Nathalie had created for him, immediately jumped to his feet and reached into his pocket, pulling out a small tracking device he had been given. He looked at the readout, but there was nothing. He wondered if there was a problem, if the transmitter they had hidden in Daryl's experiment bag had somehow stopped working.

Even as he considered it, he heard it begin to beep. He looked at the monitor and turned round to face the direction it read. Daryl was less than forty metres away and David turned to walk towards him.

He saw Daryl within a few seconds. He stopped to observe him, maintaining a discrete distance to avoid arousing any suspicion. He watched as Daryl removed the glass thermometer, holding it up to read it. Daryl was so far ignoring his angels who had greeted him in the usual way, his attention instead focused on his thermometer.

Daryl took a long look at the thermometer then lowered it. He turned to smile at his angels, but as they returned his smile Daryl smashed the thermometer across an angel's face. David was frozen in shock as the angel dropped to his feet, blood pouring from his face. But Daryl had only just started. He plunged the broken end of the glass into the throat of the other angel, pulling it out amidst a gush of blood. The angel staggered back slightly before falling dead to the ground.

Daryl then turned to the angel who knelt on the ground, blood streaming from his face. He kicked the angel in the face, sending him spinning and collapsing to the ground before he jumped on the twitching body of the angel, stabbing it in the face time and time again with the broken glass of the thermometer.

David's own angels who were about to greet him turned and ran towards Daryl, each pulling a knife from their robes, but Daryl was ready for them. A punch floored the first one and a slash across the face brought the second to a halt, leaving them both vulnerable to Daryl's savage attacks. He pulled a knife from the hand of one of the shaking, screaming angels and prepared himself for the next attack.

"What are you doing!" shouted David as he approached Daryl.

"Who the fuck are you?" asked Daryl.

"I'm a friend of Nathalie, part of these experiments," he replied.

"What? They never mentioned you."

"It's the first time they've tried two at once. They wanted me to observe you to see if we experienced it the same way," David said.

"Then grab a knife and help me," he replied, "these bastards are evil."

"No, no, this has to stop," said David.

"Why?" asked Daryl. "These bastards bleed and they die. I want to kill them before they send me to Hell."

"Daryl, please, stop this," he replied. "You could ruin everything."

"I don't give a fuck," was Daryl's reply as he threw the knife at an approaching angel, hitting him in the face and killing him. David knew he had to act. He ran to Daryl's side and grabbed his shoulders.

"Please, stop, I beg you," said David. Daryl turned to face him and tried to shrug him off, but David held his shoulders.

"Let me go," Daryl snarled, but David had been a distraction for too long, and neither had seen the angel who had crawled up to them through the mist. He rose up, emerging from the mist and drove his knife straight into Daryl's back.

David jumped back, horrified as Daryl slumped to his knees. The angel pulled the knife out then drove it straight into the back of Daryl's skull. Blood gushed like a waterfall from the wound and Daryl crumpled like a rag doll to the floor. The angel glanced up at David, his eyes narrowing as if the angel was trying to understand him and who he was, but David staggered slightly as dizziness hit him. The angel continued to stare, and the cold, hard eyes were the last thing David saw before he blacked out.

Nathalie stared at Daryl's cold and lifeless corpse as it lay on the bed. Her hands gripping the bed rail exposed her anger as her white knuckles trembled with rage. Angela and Ian could only stand by and watch as she raged inside, furious at herself for somehow letting him die.

"Nathalie," said Angela softly, placing one hand on her shoulder, "we knew this could happen."

"To hell with that," she replied, brushing Angela's hand away. Angela stifled a tear at Nathalie's rejection. "This should never have happened. I had everything I needed, I must have done something wrong."

"You can't blame yourself," said Ian.

"Yes I fucking can," she growled at him. "He was my patient, now he's dead!" Nathalie almost screamed the last word at Ian, making him step back in surprise.

"Nathalie," said Ian, trying again to soothe her, but it was no use. She paid no attention to him and all he could do was watch as the tears trickle silently down her red cheeks, her body shaking with rage, her breathing heavy and deep.

All heads except Nathalie's turned as the door opened. David walked in, wrapped in a blanket and helped by Susan.

"He's dead, isn't he?" said David.

"How the hell can you know that?" asked Ian as Nathalie's head snapped up.

"They killed him," David replied.

"Who?"

"The angels," David replied. "He attacked them and they killed him. We're still mortal there." Ian and Angela looked at each other in shock before turning to Nathalie, who remained motionless, her eyes fixed on Daryl's corpse.

"I've waited long enough," said Nathalie after a few more moments of silence. She began to undress, keeping her gaze fixed on the lifeless body of Daryl. Everyone stared at her in surprise as she stripped naked, discarding her clothes on the floor. She turned and walked towards the door, taking Susan by the hand and leading her to the basement.

"Let's do this, now," Nathalie said as she began to search the pile of wet clothes in the corner for the tracker. She quickly found what she was looking for and hung it around her neck by the strap.

"Nathalie, what the hell are you doing?" Ian asked as he followed them into the room. "We haven't prepared anything."

"I have everything I need," replied Nathalie as she climbed onto the board, ready to be strapped down.

"This is crazy," said Ian.

"I need to see what's going on, and I want to have a look at Daryl's corpse," she replied. "We can't waste this opportunity."

"Are you sure?" asked Susan.

"Do it," Nathalie replied. Susan turned to prepare the anaesthetic, but Nathalie had other ideas. "We don't have time," she said, "just strap me down and bloody well freeze me."

Ian quickly secured her to the board and stood back. Nathalie nodded to him and he fitted her with the mask.

Susan hit the button and Nathalie screamed with pain as she was engulfed by the freezing water.

"Floating in eternity," Nathalie said to herself when she arrived. It was as she remembered, peaceful, relaxing, almost trance like. She felt she could become addicted to this sensation, that maybe she could just linger here, staying wrapped in this heavenly light, suspended in this haze.

Then reality snapped back to her. She jumped to her feet and began to look around. She could see shapes through the haze, people moving, almost as if there was some commotion somewhere. She switched the tracker on and quickly got a reading. Daryl was just a few metres away.

The haze quickly cleared and she found herself one of several dozen people who stood looking at the bodies of both Daryl and the angels. Some of the bystanders seemed in shock, having just died themselves and waking into this chaos, but there were angels as well and they looked on gravely.

Nathalie moved forward to Daryl's body and knelt beside it. She looked up but no one said anything or did anything to stop her. The knife that killed Daryl was still partly embedded in his skull and she grabbed the hilt and twisted it with all her strength. She heard the cracking of bone and she rocked the knife, trying to open the wound as wide as possible. When she slid the knife out, she had a big enough hole to see into the brain. It looked to her like a normal human brain, the same kind she had seen after numerous head traumas were brought before her when she worked at the hospital.

"Can we help you?" said a voice. Nathalie turned to see an angel behind her.

"Just give me a couple of minutes, will you," Nathalie said as she laid Daryl's body flat on its back. She took the knife and plunged it into his chest, dragging it all the way down to the abdomen, cutting him open. With a few more slices she opened his whole chest and abdomen, as if she was performing an autopsy.

"Please, there is no need," said the angel, sounding both confused and a little scared. Nathalie continued to work on Daryl's body, and now she began to examine the internal organs.

"Okay, the liver seems normal, as do the intestines," said Nathalie, thinking out loud as she removed the organs one at a time, slicing them out with the knife. "Although the liver looks a bit rough, did he drink too much? Heart seems okay though, as do the lungs."

"Nathalie, please come with us," said the angel. She stopped what she was doing and stood up. Her appearance, naked and smothered with Daryl's blood drew gasps of horror from the onlookers, and the thudding sound of a body hitting the ground made Nathalie turn round.

"Oh my god, she fainted," said a man.

Nathalie rushed to the body of the woman and sat beside her. "Can you hear me, hello," she said as she shook the woman's shoulders. The woman's eyes opened and she tried to sit up, but she immediately saw Nathalie's blood covered body and vomited.

"Welcome to Heaven," said Nathalie, turning to the crowd and smiling. All the anger over Daryl's death and the wonder and fear of her first return to the afterlife fell by the wayside as she had a patient to look after. Her medical training and instincts returned in an instant as she held the woman and she felt completely relaxed and at home in this role, even in these circumstances.

"Is she okay?" asked the man who had seen her faint.

"Do you know her?" asked Nathalie.

"She's my wife," he replied. "I think we just died in a car crash."

"Well, she's fine," replied Nathalie. "Just sit with her and she'll be fine." The man, shell shocked by the last five minutes of his life and death, dutifully did as she told him without questioning it.

"Nathalie, please," said the voice of an angel. Nathalie stood up and walked to him. She looked down at herself, noticing for the first time just how much of Daryl's blood she had on her. Her torso and thighs were almost completely covered with it and as she stood there, naked and covered with blood she had never felt so empowered in her life. Everyone was looking at her and everyone feared her. She folded her arms across her chest and stood tall and proud, facing the angel.

"That was the body of a human, wasn't it?" she asked. The angel looked at her nervously, trying to work out if he should answer or risk reaching for his dagger. "So we retain our human form in the afterlife," she continued, "and God retains oblivion as the ultimate sanction for those he deems truly unworthy." The angel breathed a sigh of relief. Nathalie had handed him an answer he could agree with.

"Yes, that is correct. We must obey God's will," the angel replied.

"I notice there's a couple of people like yourself lying dead there too," she said, "what will happen if I look at their bodies the same way I did his?"

"I would rather you did not do that," he replied. Nathalie stepped back, walking backwards to the nearest angel corpse.

"It bleeds like a human," she said as she looked down at the corpse, "but no matter, time we were moving on."

"This way," gestured the angel, again sighing with relief. They walked together in the direction he indicated.

"So who else does God save the ultimate sanction for?" asked Nathalie. "Mass murderers? War criminals?"

"Oh, none of these things matter here," said the angel, "and God is forgiving of all earthly sin." Nathalie came to a halt and turned to face the angel.

"So it's for crimes beyond the earthly God has you killed for," said Nathalie. The angel looked nervous again. "So what is it? Not believing in him? Hating him? What?"

"These merely condemn you to Hell," said the angel.

"So what gets you killed?" asked Nathalie. A look of disgust came across the angel's face.

"Being one of them," he said, pointing to a man in a white shirt and black tie that was staring around him, smiling with delight.

Without thinking she ran over to him but he recoiled in fear at the sight of her naked and blood splattered body.

"Oh, sorry," she said, covering herself with her hands.

"Who are you?" he asked, looking away from her.

"My name's Nathalie, sorry about the blood, I had a little accident," she replied.

"Am I dead?" he asked.

"Yes, are you religious?"

"Oh, yes," he replied, "I love the Lord with all my heart. I know he'll greet me with loving kindness."

"Is that your Bible?" Nathalie asked, pointing to the book in his hand and noticing how he seemed to cradle it in his hands.

"Yes, it was in my pocket, it seems to have come here with me."

"So what religion are you?" Nathalie asked. The man was about to answer, but before he could get a word out two angels appeared from nowhere and grabbed him by his arms. Nathalie turned to see the angel she had been talking to walking towards her holding a knife. Her eyes bulged in horror as she jumped out of his way as he approached and turned with horror to see him plunge the knife into the chest of the man she had just met. The angel stabbed him repeatedly, over and over again, almost in a frenzy until the man was lifeless and the other angels dropped him on the ground. Nathalie stared at his corpse, stunned into silence by the senseless brutality of the attack.

"His kind we kill, they are the most evil creature on earth," said the angel as he returned his knife to his tunic.

"What the hell was he?" asked Nathalie, her whole body shaking with a mixture of terrible anger and shock.

"Scum," replied the angel. "The worst kind." Nathalie, still filled with anger at what seemed like a pointless slaughter, was about to pursue the matter, but she felt a dizzy turn and knew her time was almost up. With seconds to spare she knelt down beside the man's dead body and picked up the book he had carried. The last thing she saw before returning to life was its title.

It said 'The Book of Mormon.'

Chapter 15

Angela, Susan and Ian stared at the bed containing Daryl's body. It lay there, slumped on its side, as the three of them contemplated their next action.

"How long do you think we have?" asked Ian.

"Until what?" said Angela.

"Until it starts to smell," he replied.

"It won't be long," said Susan, "especially in this hot weather."

"Do we go to the police?" said Ian.

"And tell them what?" asked Angela. "That we drowned him and he died unexpectedly?"

"We could say he drowned in the swimming pool and we didn't notice for a while," said Ian.

"Only he didn't drown," said Susan. "He died of hypothermia, I'm not sure how we can explain that in the middle of summer."

"They'd be able to tell it was hypothermia?" asked Angela.

"No question, an autopsy would reveal we were lying."

"Then we have to get rid of the body ourselves," said Ian.

"Of course," replied Angela, "but Nathalie and David are still recovering, so it'd be down to us three."

"Us four." Every head turned to see the shuffling, blanket wrapped form of Nathalie walk through the door.

"What the hell are you doing up," said Susan, "I told you to rest."

"I couldn't sleep," she replied.

"Doesn't matter," replied Susan, "you need to rest. Honestly, doctors make the worst patients sometimes." Nathalie nodded in submission and sat down by the bed.

"Any answers?" she asked. All three shook their heads.

"We haven't really decided anything," Ian replied.

"Well, we need to decide something," Nathalie replied, "and

soon." She turned to look at Angela. "You know this area better than anyone, any suggestions for hiding it?"

"Before anyone suggests it, I think burying him by the house is a bad idea," said Ian. "The lawn's too neat, we'd be left with a grave sized patch of bare earth."

"That's a bad idea," said Susan.

"The woods are the best place," said Angela. "There are miles of forest tracks and fire breaks everywhere. You can wander in there for days if you get lost."

"Does anyone go there?" asked Ian.

"It's a managed forest, but there are areas where the workers don't go for months on end," Angela replied.

"What about hikers?" asked Susan.

"The Alps are half an hour down the road," said Angela, "there'll be no hikers."

"So what do we do," said Nathalie, "drive into the woods and bury him?"

"We won't drive," said Angela, "we can go by foot. Put him in a wheelbarrow and we can wheel him through the woods, staying off the paths so the barrow doesn't leave any kind of trail. Twenty minutes of that and we'll be far from here."

"If we move him at night, no-one will see us at all," said Nathalie, "we'll dig up some ground, then sneak back after dark, with GPS it'll be easy to find the grave."

"I don't see what else we can do," said Susan, "except for the 'we' part of it, like I said, you're resting for the next few days."

Nathalie looked down at her feet and sighed before looking up again.

"I'm sorry I dragged you into this," she said to Susan. "I never warned you we might be risking anything like this." Susan sat down beside Nathalie.

"You think I didn't know the risks?" she said. "You think I didn't know this could happen? I've watched my husband over the past few years descend into utter misery, ever since he had his accident. You offered us a chance to live again, to try and find the answers we were all looking for. And do you know what? You did it."

"Did what?" said Nathalie. "I don't understand."

"How did you feel after your accident?" Susan asked.

"Alone," said Nathalie. "Miserable, confused, a whole bunch of other crap things to feel."

"And what happened to change that?"

"I met these two," she said, gesturing towards Angela and Ian. "And they changed everything."

"You love them very much, don't you?" asked Susan. Nathalie just nodded as a tear rolled down her cheek. "Then imagine what it was like for David. It was years before we met you. He went from being the most amazing, exciting man I'd ever met, to a withdrawn, isolated and fragile soul I barely recognised."

"And now?" Nathalie asked.

"Now he has the giddy excitement of the young man I remember," she replied, closing her eyes and smiling for a second before continuing, "and he's never been so happy. He was so excited about coming here and meeting you all. It's like he's been reborn."

"But you could go to jail," said Angela.

"Yes, I could," she replied, "but it's worth the risk. And I'm not going to stop. Even if you guys were to quit, back out and never do this again, I'm going forward with it."

"We're not quitting," said Angela, "not ever."

"How could we?" said Ian. "How could we not want to find out more?"

"And we will, together," said Susan. "One piece at a time we'll unlock its secrets and figure out everything we can."

"We need to pause," said Nathalie. "Susan, you need to go back to New Zealand and stay there for a couple of months."

"What if people come looking for Daryl?" she asked.

"Then you're safe," Nathalie replied. "You're on the other side of the world, you're someone who can continue with this if we all get locked up."

"And once I've done this a few more times, maybe I can start a little branch of the cult in New Zealand," said Susan.

"Cult?" said Ian.

"That's how we'd look to outsiders," she said, "touting this crazy religion about the afterlife. Hell, the three of you even all sleep together, all the best cults have crazy free sex going on at the top."

"It's not like that," said Nathalie.

"I know," said Susan. "It's something else, isn't it? Something beyond sex or even intimacy for that matter."

"Yes," said Nathalie, "I can't explain what though."

"Can't you?" said Susan. "You three, you were all alone, cut off from the rest of the world by what happened to you, then you find each other and suddenly you have a friend, you have companionship."

"That's certainly part of it," said Ian.

"Yes, but then you start killing and reviving each other," continued Susan, "trusting each other with not just your lives, but the safety of your eternal souls. Who else can understand it but us? Who else could you share this with?"

"No-one," said Nathalie, "not unless they understood it too."

"This is the most important thing you'll ever do, that anyone will ever do," said Susan, "and you can't share it with others. Of course you're going to turn inwards for companionship." She looked up at Angela. "Was Nathalie your first woman?" she asked.

"Yes," replied Angela, "I'd never even thought about going with another woman before."

"And Ian, what about the other one," said Susan, "the priest. How do you feel about him?"

"What do you mean?" he asked.

"What if he came back, asked to join you all again? Would you be happy to let him in?"

"I'd like to see him come back," said Ian. "He was a lot of help, and I can't help thinking about him sometimes, about how alone he must feel."

Susan reached out and held his hand. "It goes beyond everything, doesn't it?" she asked. "Beyond gender, beyond sexuality, beyond everything physical."

Ian nodded. "I can't deny that," he said. "It'd be good to have him back."

"I know how you feel," Susan said. "David and I are happy, so incredibly happy together, but I feel the same bond you all feel. If I was alone, if I didn't have David, well I wouldn't want to go home, I'd want to stay here with you all."

"You really feel that way?" asked Ian. "You'd stay here, with Nathalie and Angela?"

"It's us and them Ian," she replied. "Those who know and those who don't. Everyone out there will try and stop us. They'd charge us with murder, lock us away forever. They don't understand."

"We can't trust anyone," said Angela.

"Only those who know," added Nathalie.

Ian looked at each person in turn. "There's six of us altogether."

"But one of us is missing," said Nathalie with an empty sadness in her eyes.

Angela turned to look at Nathalie. "We should try and get Richard back," she said, smiling softly.

"Yes, you should," added Susan. "Our numbers are small, everyone's needed."

"We should make him feel wanted," said Ian, "let him know how we all feel."

"He won't come back in a hurry," Nathalie said as she shook her head. "He's far too committed to the people in his church. But I'll contact him again, try and get him to help us figure out about the Mormons and their role in all this. Maybe he'll start to consider it."

"Perhaps if you visit him, maybe remind him what he could be missing," said Ian with a suggestive glance at Nathalie. "Maybe that could tilt the balance."

"You mean seduce him?" Nathalie asked.

Ian smiled and nodded.

"Whatever you do, we need him," said Susan. "We need all the help we can get."

"But he can't help us with our immediate problem, can he?" said Angela, nodding her head towards Daryl's corpse.

"No, so let's not linger," said Ian. "It'll be a few hours before it gets dark, why don't we get started? We can find our spot, maybe even start to dig a bit."

Angela stood up. "Yes," she said, "No point waiting, come on." She stood up and walked out the room, followed by Ian and Susan.

"Do you have any shovels?" asked Susan.

"There's a couple in the tool shed," said Ian, I'll get them and we can head out."

The woods were exactly as Angela had described them, and the group had no problem finding a suitable spot. Overgrown with shrubs and bushes and far from any firebreak or road they found the perfect place. Armed with shovels, buckets and rope, they could work without being seen and Ian and Angela worked quickly, digging down deep.

"We're not going to make this a shallow grave, are we?" said Susan. "The last thing you need is for dogs or something to smell it and start digging."

"Then we dig until we can only just climb out," said Ian.

They dug deep, pushing aside tree roots and rocks, delving ever deeper. Ian broke the ground and Angela shovelled it into buckets while Susan kept watch, pulling the buckets out the grave and piling it up by the hole.

"So that's us at head height," said Ian after several hours work. "Do we go any deeper?"

"Make a smaller hole in the bottom," said Susan. "If we break his bones we can get Daryl curled up into a small space."

Ian shivered at the macabre thought of mutilating the corpse but continued digging, this time for another metre but with a much smaller width to the hole. When he finished he was left with a hole almost a metre on either side. It looked to Ian like he could maybe just squeeze into it himself, and that was enough for him.

With the rope secured to a tree, he followed Angela as she climbed out. It was by now getting dark.

"Perfect timing," Susan said.

"Well, let's finish this," said Angela and the three walked back to the house in silence.

"I didn't know bones made that kind of noise when you snapped them," said Ian as he sat in Angela's living room. Still dirty from filling in the hole, he had a look of shell shock to him, aware of his surroundings yet somehow detached and living in another moment. He was in the darkness of the woods, his mind replaying when he had taken the shovel to Daryl's corpse, smashing the ribs and arm bones to compress the body into the hole.

"You'll get over it," said Nathalie who sat beside him. "And don't forget, you're not alone."

"We're here," said Angela, "we'll always be here."

"Have you thought about a cover story?" asked David.

"Not really," said Nathalie.

"It needs to be consistent, and as close to the truth as possible," David replied.

"We can't tell anyone the truth," said Angela, "certainly not the police."

"Why not?" asked David. "You don't say the whole truth, but it's on record in enough places we've all had near death experiences. You guys are all over the internet with it, so we could easily make them think we're some sort of support group."

"So if the police come looking, what do we say?" Ian asked.

"The truth, except for the obvious" David said. "That we get together to discuss what happened to us. And that tonight was the last time we saw Daryl."

"Would you be able to take his clothes back with you?" Angela asked. "That gets some evidence away from here and on the other side of the world."

"Yes," said Susan, "we can do that. We'll give them to a charity or something, lose them that way. Should be easy enough."

"Can we really get away with this?" asked Ian.

"Only if we stick together," said Susan. "That's the key to everything now. We stick together."

Chapter 16

The warm, dry summer of Munich seemed a million miles away from the dull, windswept coastline of Montrose. Staring out of the church window, Richard found himself cursing the weather and hoping some of the Bavarian sunshine he remembered would visit Scotland. A greater part of him wished Nathalie would visit as well.

When her number appeared on his ringing phone, he was overjoyed.

"Nathalie, how are you?" he said enthusiastically.

"I'm good, how are you?" she replied.

"Oh, you know, the usual, working hard, tending my flock, dealing with the worse crisis of faith anyone's ever had." He meant the last comment to be a joke, but as he said it, he realised he sounded bitter.

"Are you okay?" she asked.

"Don't worry, I'm fine," he replied. "How is it going at your end? Any progress?"

"We lost someone," she replied.

"Oh no," he replied. "Who was it?"

"A new arrival, not someone you met," she replied.

"What happened?"

"He attacked an angel, they killed him."

"You mean we're mortal in the afterlife?" he asked.

"We're human in the afterlife," she replied, "when it happened I went straight back in and did a quick autopsy."

"Interesting," replied Richard. "But what happened in this world? Did you tell the police?"

"No, we buried him in the woods. There's miles of it around Angela's house. It's managed land and the trees won't be felled for years."

"Bloody hell," replied Richard, "you left him in a shallow grave in the woods."

"Shallow? No chance," replied Nathalie. "We've all seen enough films not to make that mistake. He's buried in a hole ten feet deep."

"Would you have done that if I had died?" Richard asked. Nathalie decided not to answer.

"I need your help with something."

"Anything," Richard replied.

"Tell me everything you know about Mormons."

"Mormons?" asked Richard. "Why do you want to know about them?"

"I'll tell you in a minute," she replied.

"Well, they're a lovely bunch. Very friendly, kind, caring, always reliable, but completely bat shit crazy."

"Crazy by your standards or by mine?" she asked.

"Even by mine," he replied. "They think the Garden of Eden was in America and that the Native Americans were descended from ancient Jews."

"Oh, okay," she replied.

"They were founded a couple of centuries ago by an American called Joseph Smith who claimed to be a prophet. He wrote a third book of the Bible, to go with the Old and New Testaments, they pretty much proclaimed America as the Promised Land. He saw himself as a Moses figure I think, trying to lead people to a new home."

"So what else do they believe?"

"They believe God was once mortal and lived on a planet that had its own god. They deny the Trinity, so they believe God, Jesus and the Holy Spirit are three separate entities."

"That doesn't sound too crazy, not as religions go," Nathalie commented.

"But they also believe that all humans are capable of ascending, of undergoing deification if they are worthy."

"Interesting," said Nathalie, "but why would God consider them dangerous?"

"What do you mean dangerous?" Richard asked.

"Mormons are killed on sight in the afterlife," Nathalie said.

"What?" exclaimed Richard.

"They get stabbed to death as soon as they arrive. The angels seem to hate them."

"But that makes no sense," said Richard. "Muslims and Jews get into Heaven, even atheists aren't killed on sight."

"So what makes Mormons different?" asked Nathalie. "There must be something."

"I can't think what makes them so different from atheists or Muslims," replied Richard. "Their beliefs are pretty odd, even ridiculous, but nothing that would be dangerous."

"What's so ridiculous?" asked Nathalie, "I mean compared to Christianity."

"Well, for example, they used to have segregation, treating black people as second class citizens. In the seventies they suddenly announced God has changed his mind on the subject and made everyone equal. That seems pretty ridiculous."

"A bit like the way the old rules, about stoning people to death for the slightest thing, or cutting a woman's hand off suddenly changed?"

"Touch," replied Richard.

"So not really that ridiculous," said Nathalie.

"No, they are," insisted Richard. "No matter what the context, all they are is a bunch of very nice people who happen to think America is the Promised Land and invent any old crap to justify it. It's like some kind of Republican fantasy. Like I say, nice people, utter fruit loops."

"Yet they seem to be the greatest threat there can be to God," said Nathalie. "It makes no sense."

"Listen, let me do some more research, there's quite a few Mormon churches in Scotland, I'll approach them, spin them some rubbish about community relations or something, and find out what I can, okay."

"That sounds great, thanks for that."

"Anything for you Nathalie," Richard replied, "you just have to ask." There was a pause in the conversation, a brief awkward silence before Richard continued. "So how are you guys doing?"

"We're together," Nathalie replied.

"The three of you," asked Richard, "as in a relationship together?"

"Yes."

"And how does that feel?"

"Perfect, I've never been in so much love in all my life."

"Polygamy," said Richard with a laugh, "is an old Mormon tradition."

"Oh well, at least I know I'm not a complete heathen," she

replied, laughing. Her voice turned serious as she continued. "Do you ever regret turning me down that night?"

"All the time," he replied. Nathalie couldn't be sure if he was joking or not. "But it was the right thing to do. And it looks like I missed my chance."

"No you haven't," she replied. There was another awkward pause.

"Goodbye," said Richard, "and I'll speak to you soon."

"Bye," said Nathalie, and hung up.

"You know, I wouldn't mind," came a voice from behind Nathalie. She turned round to see Angela standing behind her.

"Wouldn't mind what?" asked Nathalie.

"Richard," she replied. "I know you like him, if you were to visit him, well if something happened, it'd be okay. Like Ian said, show him what he's missing." Angela sat down beside Nathalie and held her hand.

"I couldn't do that," said Nathalie, "I'd feel like I was betraying you two."

"Be happy," said Angela. "The thing about the three of us is that if one is all alone, the other two aren't. If you were to do something, I couldn't object, especially if it's with Richard, or even someone else who got involved."

"Don't worry...," said Nathalie, but Angela cut her off in mid sentence.

"Never say never," she said, placing a finger on Nathalie's lips to silence her. "And never be alone when you don't have to be, especially if I'm with Ian. Besides, Richard is one of us, and anything that brings him back makes me happy."

"One of us? I didn't realise you felt this way."

"I've been thinking this for a while. We're doing something extraordinary here, we're changing everything we think we know about the universe. The world is divided into two groups now. Those that know the truth, and those that don't. And I don't want anyone who does to be alone. I want them to be part of us."

"You make it sound like a cult, just like Susan said."

"Maybe it is, maybe this is how cults get started. Someone thinks they know something no one else does and wants to share it with the world. We're doing it one person at a time, but it's spreading."

"I never thought of it like that," replied Nathalie. "I'm used to thinking like a scientist."

"Well I'm not. I'm used to selling and marketing and making people think the way I want them to. And if we're going to spread the word about this, we need people like Richard."

"I want him back here too," Nathalie replied, "I feel calmer around him."

"Me too," said Angela, nodding and giving Nathalie a soft smile. "He's the final person we need to complete the team. The four of us along with Susan and David have all we need to take this wherever it goes."

"I don't think he'll join us, not completely, not unless something drastic happens," said Nathalie shaking her head. "But we've shared something special. There's something there between us, a bond, and he knows that too."

"Maybe you should visit him sometime?"

"He said he was going to research Mormonism for us."

"Then when he's got information, go and visit him," said Angela, "make him know he's part of our group, and that we love him."

"You love him?" said Nathalie, surprised to hear Angela's choice of words.

"Yes," she replied. "Like you say, he's one of us." Nathalie moved her mouth as if to say something, but words failed her. Angela's words had made her feel somehow warm inside, giving her an inner glow she felt words couldn't express. "Now come to bed, Ian's waiting for us," Angela continued, taking Nathalie by the hand and leading her to the bedroom.

"So what do we want from our next visit?" Angela asked the group as they sat round the dinner table.

"Well, I want to go back one more time before we leave," said David. "I have a lot to cross examine them about, especially about the Mormons."

"Agreed," said Ian. "If you tackle the issue from that direction, it's probably our best chance to get a few answers."

"Maybe Angela should go back at the same time," said Susan. "Despite your initial concern Nathalie, her heart's strong and healthy enough, so she could maybe try a good cop, bad cop type thing with David."

"Oh, just let me at them," said Angela, "I'll drag the truth out of them."

"Well, you should..." began Nathalie, but she was cut off when her phone beeped. She picked it up and read the message. "Nothing, just a news alert," she said, but the news quickly got her attention as she read more details. "There's been an earthquake, in Seattle," she said. "Scientists are saying it's one of the biggest ones ever recorded and the whole city may have been destroyed."

"Jesus," said Ian, "the death toll will be huge."

Angela immediately stood up and began to unbutton her blouse.

"David, let's go," she said.

"What?" replied David.

"Let's go there, to the Gates," she said.

"What, now?" he replied.

"The place will never be busier," continued Angela, "the angels will be overworked and confused, this could be our best chance yet." She turned and ran out the door, discarding her clothes in a trail behind her. Without another word, everyone followed.

Nathalie caught up with Angela in the treatment room and she was already stripped and searching through the sets of clothes with Velcro seams for quick removal.

"Where's the tracker? Make sure David has the receiver," said Angela as she began to pull clothes on. Nathalie disappeared out of the room to check that David had the receiver and returned quickly with the tracker. Angela took it and put it in her pocket.

"Just remember," said Nathalie as Angela emptied the ice machine's contents into the vat, "let David do some talking, don't hog all the time yourself."

"Me, do all the talking?" asked Angela, feigning innocence. "But push the limits with this one Nathalie, you and Susan said you can prolong the experience, so leave us there as long as you dare."

"I love you," said Nathalie as she finished strapping Angela down.

"I love you too," said Angela. The women shared a final kiss.

"David's all ready," came a voice from the door. Nathalie looked up to see Ian standing there.

"Tell Susan to do it," replied Nathalie as she placed the mask over Angela's face and hit the button to send her crashing into the ice cold water.

Angela sprang to her feet and looked around. Through the haze she could see dozens of people, milling about, looking confused without guidance. Angels seemed few and far between and the crowds seemed to grow by the second, with people rising out of the fog every few seconds. The normal serenity of the Gates had been swept away by a sea of humanity, instead replaced with screams of terror and panic as thousands arrived. The angels, under staffed and overwhelmed by the masses, simply did what they could, shouting out orders to groups and telling them where to move.

"Hello Angela," came a familiar voice from behind her. She turned round to find David standing behind her.

"You found me," she replied, "that was quick."

"We seem to be out on the edge here, but people are pouring in every second," he replied. "And if a tsunami follows, there'll be a hell of a lot more."

"Then let's get to work," Angela replied. She turned and began to move through the crowds, looking for an angel that might be worth a try.

"It's a little bit different this time, isn't it?" David said as they moved through the crowds. "Look at the angels, they're not greeting people, just shouting directions, ushering people through towards the evaluation area."

"They seem a little distracted, don't they?" said Angela. They looked around at the angels who were by now standing by the sidelines, herding people like sheep to the evaluation area. It wasn't long before they noticed that a few were standing by the sidelines, watching without acting.

"That one might be worth a try," said David, pointing to an angel at the side who seemed to be doing nothing more than observing.

"Then follow me," said Angela as she darted from the crowd and rushed towards him. David followed closely behind as she approached him.

"I think I just saw a Mormon!" she exclaimed as she rushed up to the angel. She turned, pointing randomly into the crowd, all the time with an expression of near panic on her face. "I saw him, over there, do something, do something!"

"Calm down," said the angel, "and don't worry, even in these crowds we will find the Mormons."

"Don't let the little bastard get away," Angela replied. "Oh, I hate them, with their silly little shirt and tie, knocking on my doors, spouting their blasphemy."

The angel smiled at Angela's last word.

"I can see you will do well here," he replied, "you seem pure in your love of God."

"Oh, of course, who wouldn't be?" she said, "Apart from these damn Mormons of course."

"Of course," replied the angel.

"And the Jews," added David.

"And those bloody Muslims as well," Angela said.

"Now, now," said the angel, "they are true in their love of God, they will be admitted to Heaven."

"But they blaspheme," Angela replied, faking outrage. "They deny the truth of our Lord Jesus Christ. Does that not make them worse than Mormons?" The angel looked at her angrily.

"No, it does not," he replied, his eyes narrowed with wrath. "Mormons tell evil filthy lies, spread their poison and deserve all the wrath they will receive."

"That's what I thought," said David, pushing Angela out of the way. "I always thought they were as bad as atheists."

"They are worse than atheists," replied the angel. "Their stories are offensive to the Lord, even dangerous."

"So they burn in Hell then," David asked.

"No, even Hell is too good for them," the angel said. "They are destroyed from existence itself, their souls reduced to nothingness."

"Why are the Mormons so dangerous?" said Angela. The angel looked at them suspiciously.

"I think it's time you were moving on," he said to them.

"Look, I know God would rather we didn't pursue knowledge," David said, "but I'd like to know why Mormons are so hated."

"It would seem you already know the answer," said the angel.

"So what they know is dangerous?" said Angela. "Do they know something they shouldn't, something that could hurt God?"

The change in the angel's demeanour was both sudden and extreme. He pulled a knife from his gown and leapt at Angela but she dodged him and struck him hard as he lurched past her, sending him to the ground.

"Time to go," said David as he took Angela's hand. They both ran from the angel in an attempt to lose themselves in the crowd.

But they began to stumble over bodies. A sudden surge of arrivals meant that people were falling over new arrivals lying in the fog almost as soon as they started walking. With every step Angela and David risked tripping over a new arrival.

"Looks like the tsunami just hit," said Angela.

"This is fucking horrible," said David, "all these people dead."

"Death is such a relative concept these days," said Angela as they continued through the crowd. "Anyway, I think we've lost him."

David turned around to see nothing but an ever thickening crowd, now with people pushing and shoving each other.

"Dammit, this is getting dangerous," said Angela as they began to hear screams of people being crushed or trampled underfoot.

"It's one thing dying, but to wake up in the afterlife and get trampled to death," added David, "it almost makes you think God doesn't know what the hell he is doing."

"That angel certainly didn't," Angela said, "he pretty much told us that Mormons have something in their belief God doesn't want known about here. Something beyond blasphemy, beyond a lack of belief."

"He certainly slipped up with that one, didn't he?" David replied.

The pair continued moving through the crowd, but the screams became more frequent and louder as time moved on. More and more arrivals thickened the crowd, and nothing seemed to be reducing the numbers.

"Shit, there are dead bodies here," said David as he stumbled over a corpse.

"Is this how God runs the place?" said Angela. "This is chaos."

"Omnipotence and competence don't always go hand in hand it seems."

"Now, while we're still here, we need to find another angel, let's try this way." Angela took David by the hand and led him through the ever thickening crowd to the edges where angels continued to usher them towards the evaluation area. They were on the edge of it now, approaching it from the side, and the front of the queues were no less chaotic than the rest of the place.

Angela and David watched as people were pulled forward by the evaluators, brought out one by one. Held by the evaluator's gaze for a moment they were immediately consumed, either by fire and flame, or by a radiant white light.

But in the chaos the fire and light consumed more than they should. The evaluators who normally had neat, orderly lines to deal with now had a mob, and the lights seemed unable to discriminate when they emerged. Centred around those that had been judged, the light would consume anyone beside them, damning the true believers to Hell and the unworthy to Heaven without discrimination. Who you were crushed up against mattered more than your own beliefs in the mayhem that the Gates had become.

"This is bloody chaos," said David to an angel that stood in the sidelines.

"It is a great tragedy that has occurred," the angel replied. "Many souls require to find their way."

"No, really, this is bloody chaos," David persisted. "Can't God make the room bigger? Or slow down time to make it all work properly?"

Screams turned Angela and David's heads to a man just a few feet away. Another Mormon was being stabbed.

"This is how it works," said the angel who looked at the dead Mormon's body, seemingly with glee. "It is not our place to question his plan."

"Well I know that, but is this really part of his plan? People being trampled to death, people dragged to Heaven or Hell just because of who they're standing beside. Is this really the work of an omnipotent being?"

"Why do you question the Lord when your judgement is at hand?" asked the angel. "Do you know how dangerous that can be, what it may mean for your soul?"

"Why is that so dangerous?" asked David who was now almost shouting his questions with anger. "Why does a little bit of doubt put my soul in peril?"

"You must love God with your heart."

"Look around you!" exclaimed David. "All this chaos and you expect people not to have just a little bit of doubt? What's so dangerous about doubt, anyway? Why does God need us to love him and not doubt him?"

"Be careful," said the angel, his tone changing to the now-familiar menace that accompanied any questioning of them. "Your immortal soul is at risk of being damned."

"Immortal soul?" snapped back David without a moment's hesitation. "Is that the same immortal soul those Mormon corpses had, or the same immortal soul of all the people that are being killed, here, again, in this stupid bloody crush?"

Angela immediately noticed a change in the angel's body language. She knew it was time to move along again.

"Let's go," she said, grabbing David's hand and leading him off, moving now behind the line of evaluators.

"God and the angels seem to be lying bastards," said David, his voice dripping with anger and contempt as they made their way through the by now thinning crowds.

"What is it about the Mormons though?" Angela asked.

"It must be something in their teachings," replied David.

In their conversation they hadn't looked where they were going, and without realising it, they stumbled right into an evaluator. He turned to face them, towering almost three meters high above them, a height they hadn't really appreciated until now.

"Blimey, you're tall," said David.

"Are you ready to be judged?" asked the evaluator.

"Oh, bollocks," said David, "can't it wait a minute?"

"No, it is your time," he replied.

But Angela didn't want either of them to be judged. She threw herself at the evaluator's legs, twisting them and knocking him off balance. The evaluator fell to the ground, screaming in anger.

"Run!" said Angela, but as they took off into the crowd they were separated. Angela desperately looked around trying to find David, but all she saw was the back of his head as he seemed to wink out of existence. He had returned to life, leaving her alone.

She felt two arms grab her from behind and she tried to turn round, but the arms held her firm.

"That was a mistake," a voice said from behind her. She was thrown to the ground and she looked up to see the evaluator standing over her, while flanked by two angels.

"You could have had immortal life," said the evaluator, "but you're too dangerous. You've been running round, causing trouble for my people. There's a price to pay for that."

"So you're going to kill me?" said Angela. She was beginning to regret telling Nathalie to keep her in the afterlife as long as possible, but she felt a slight dizziness come over her, not so strong as on previous occasions, but she hoped this meant it was ending and that all she had to do was stall for time.

"Yes, I regret you have left me with no choice." the evaluator said.

"Before I die, answer one question for me," she said.

"And what is that?" asked the evaluator.

"Why Mormons? Why kill them?" she said. "They're no different to plenty others who believe in and love God, yet they're singled out. Why?"

"They are too much of a risk," was the evaluator's answer.

"Why are they a risk?" Angela persisted, feeling the dizziness start to increase. "There's something in their faith that's a threat, isn't there?"

"You seem rather smart," said the evaluator, "to have figured that out."

"What is it, what's the danger from them?" Angela barked, now fighting to stop from passing out.

"Specifically? I do not know. God does not share that with us," he replied. "But I know it is a serious threat, a threat that could harm the very Heavens themselves."

"Thank you," said Angela, who gave into the dizziness, disappearing in an instant from before the evaluator's eyes.

Chapter 17

Nathalie stood braced against the lashing rain at the solid oak door of the Montrose church, her mind in turmoil. She was here to face Richard for the first time since their moment at the airport and she had been rehearsing what to say to him for days. Now she stood there, about to speak to him, and she found she had no idea of what to say.

With a deep breath she pushed the door open and walked in. The modest and intimate setting of the small church seemed more engaging to Nathalie than the great opulent cathedrals of the cities, a far more fitting and relevant arena for a man like Richard.

She turned the key that was in the door and closed the latch. She hoped they might not want to be disturbed later.

Her eyes scanned the room, and she found her target almost instantly. Standing by the altar, sorting through a collection of books, was Richard. He stood with his back to her but his head rose from his work the moment she began to walk down the aisle.

"Hello Richard," she said.

Richard turned round, his face breaking into a huge smile. "Nathalie!" he exclaimed. "I had no idea you were coming."

"I needed to get away," she replied, "and I thought coming to see you was the best thing I could do." The two of them met in front of the altar and exchanged an embrace.

"It's good to see you again," he said. "How is everyone?"

"Oh, the usual," she replied, "Angela still drives us forward, Ian still figures everything out."

"And how are you?"

"I'm good," she replied. "I'm really good. And even better for seeing you."

"Why are you here?" he asked.

"I need to know about the Mormons."

"I could have phoned you," he replied.

"I wanted to see you," she replied. "I miss you."

"I have to admit, this place has seemed a little emptier since I came back," he said, looking up and around the walls. "I'm glad you came."

"So what can you tell me?" Nathalie asked.

"Not so fast," said Richard, noticing her wet clothes and hair, "you're soaking wet, do you want a towel, or tea or something?"

"Tea would be nice," she replied. Richard ran off to the kitchen, returning with two mugs and a towel. As Nathalie sat on a front row pew and dried her hair, he looked at her, trying to dismiss the thoughts he was having about her from his head.

"Can I take your jacket?" he asked.

"No thanks, I'm dressed for a Munich summer, not a Scottish one," she replied, laughing. "I forgot how windy it gets in Britain." Richard passed her the tea and sat down beside her.

"So, Mormons," he said.

"Last time we sent Angela back she got someone to admit there was something about their faith that was a threat to Heaven itself."

"Well by that I think we can say against God," said Richard.

"Yes, probably," said Nathalie. "So what could it be?"

"Mormons have a lot of odd beliefs," said Richard, "at least by normal Christian standards, but a lot of them are no threat to anyone."

"Such as?"

"They have their own alternative history of America, about the origins of the original native inhabitants that's clearly all nonsense as genetics has proved they were Asian in origin, not Jewish as the Mormons claim."

"It's hard to see how that's a threat."

"They also believe we are all eternal, that we have always existed as some undefined intelligence before being born."

"That seems too vague to be a threat."

"They don't seem to say it out loud, but they seem to value

feelings over facts for determining truth," Richard said, his face barely hiding his dismay at the concept. "And they have their own cosmology too."

"Cosmology?" asked Nathalie. "You mean stars and planets?"

"Yes, they have this belief that the throne of God is on another planet, called Kolob."

"Another planet?" asked an incredulous Nathalie.

"And that he lives with other gods and that those gods may have their own planets as well."

"Not that crazy, I quite like the sound of this one," said Nathalie with a smile that suggested she was teasing him.

"Well, if you like that, you might like this. Remember I said that people can become gods themselves?"

"Yes," she replied.

"Well, if you become a god, you get a planet to rule as well. They even say God was once a mortal man who was deified."

"So I get to be a goddess?" Nathalie said, with a mock seductive smile. "Even if all that's true, how can knowing that be a threat?"

"If that's what it is. There's an awful lot more to pick from that's unique to the Mormon faith."

"What else?" Nathalie asked.

"Well here's a good one. They seem to think that even if they are wrong about the specifics they'll be rewarded with eternity in Heaven, because they believe in God and Jesus."

"That's a familiar line," said Nathalie, "that's the rules for getting into Heaven. That makes even less sense, it's openly admitted by the angels."

"Then there's the magic underwear."

"Tell me you're kidding," said Nathalie.

"Oh, I wish I could."

"What do they mean by magic?" Nathalie asked, "I have lingerie that could fit that description, I take it you don't mean that."

"Er, no," was Richard's awkward reply. "It's supposed to remind them of assorted rules they're supposed to obey."

Nathalie stared at him blankly, not sure if she should believe him or not.

"Oh, then there's the polygamy."

"Now you're talking," she replied.

"They believe God literally slept with Mary while married to Joseph, so multiple partners must be allowed."

"That's the reason? Really?"

"Well, they believe God has a physical body, so it's a bit of an unavoidable issue for them."

"You know, this is all quite different from the normal Christian beliefs," said Nathalie. "Where the hell did it all come from?"

"From Joseph Smith, an American who said he found ancient records of the Jews in America when an angel showed them to him."

"So he basically made this all up then?"

"Normally I would say yes," Richard said, "but from what you said you saw, it seems if he did make it up, then he invented something that just happened to be extremely dangerous to God."

"It can't be a coincidence, can it?" asked Nathalie.

"I don't know," Richard replied.

"How the hell do I find out?" Nathalie asked.

"Maybe you should go directly to the horse's mouth."

"If you mean God, I had been thinking about that, but it wouldn't work."

"Why not?"

"If I'm judged, I'll get sent straight to Hell. Think of all the things I've seen. I'm not exactly in love with God right now."

"Well, if you'll pardon the expression," said Richard, now with a wry smile forming across his face, "maybe you should go to Hell."

"Hi Satan, I'm Nathalie, can you explain the nature of the universe to me?" she said. "Yes, I can see that one working out well."

"What do you have to lose?"

"Just my eternal soul."

"Last year you probably thought you never had one," he replied. Nathalie nodded.

"So I have nothing to lose," she replied. "Just the prospect of an eternity in Hell."

"Nathalie, I'm not sure we can trust our perceptions of Heaven and Hell," said Richard. "Even the angels have admitted they've never seen Hell themselves."

Nathalie leaned back on the pew and sighed. "How did I get into this?" she asked. "Life used to be so simple."

"You wanted answers," replied Richard, "to questions everyone asks. You were just the first person to be able to answer them."

"I wish you'd come back to us," Nathalie said, leaning her head right back and turning to face him.

"I have commitments here," he replied.

"I know, but I still wish you were back with us." Nathalie paused for a second. "I wish you were a lot of things."

"I took an oath."

"To who?"

"To God," he replied.

"And has he lived up to his side of the bargain?" she said. "Has he shown himself to be the god of love and compassion you thought he was?" Richard didn't answer. "You know you're here for the people, not the church. You can't believe you owe the church and God anything."

"Nathalie, please."

"There are people who love you Richard," she continued. "We don't want to take you away from this, we know what it means to you, but we don't want you to feel alone, like you're carrying the secret."

"It is difficult, knowing this is all a lie," he replied, gesturing to the cross that hung above the altar.

"Please let me love you," she said, placing a hand on his cheek and drawing his face towards hers.

"Don't think it's that I don't want to," he said, his body now noticeably trembling, "it's just..."

"Just what?" she replied. "Do you really owe it to your God to deny yourself this?" She leant over and softly kissed his lips. He stifled a moan as their lips met, struggling with all his will to resist her.

"What do you want from me?" he asked as her lips lingered against his.

"I just want you," she said, slipping off her jacket. Underneath she wore a flimsy yellow summer dress that left little to the imagination.

"Nathalie, I've never done this," he said, but Nathalie just placed a finger on his lips, gesturing for him to be quiet.

She began to slowly unbutton his shirt, gently kissing his chest as her fingers undid the buttons, moving further and further down with each lingering caress of her lips against his skin.

As the last button went she pulled his shirt open before pulling her summer dress over her head. She reached out to take his hands and pulled him to his feet, crushing her body against his bare torso with her embrace and kissing him again.

"What should I do?" he asked with the nervous tremor in his voice of a teenage boy losing his virginity.

"Just enjoy it," said Nathalie as she unclipped and removed her bra. He stared hypnotically at her breasts as she took his hand and held it against one. "Is this nice?" she asked. He nodded and she slipped his shirt off. She smiled at him and looked down before her eyes came up to meet his, her tongue gently licking her lips. She held his gaze as she began to kiss his chest again, moving lower and lower before undoing his trousers and pulling them down along with his underwear.

Slipping off her own underwear she took his hand and led him to the altar. She stared at the assortment of books, silverware and the large wooden crucifix on it and with a sweep of her hand threw all of it onto the ground, where it landed with a crash.

"Are we really going to do this?" Richard asked, his chest heaving with excitement.

"Do you want to?" asked Nathalie.

"Oh yes," he said, "very much." Nathalie took his hand and turned him, backing him against the altar as she kissed him slowly.

"Lie down," she said, wearing a mischievous grin on her face.

"On the altar?" he asked.

"Give yourself to me," she said. "Give yourself to me on it."

He pulled himself up onto the altar and lay back and watched as she crawled slinkily onto it, moving like a wild cat on all fours stalking its prey.

"You ready?" she asked. He nodded and she knelt astride his waist and slowly lowered herself onto him.

Richard moaned softly as he entered her, his eyes glazing over with the pleasure that was overwhelming him.

Nathalie began to gently move, rocking back and forth slightly as Richard lay there, helpless before her. She began to look around at her surroundings and her heart trembled with excitement. For a moment she imagined the pews were full of people, watching them as they desecrated the altar and the thought excited her. Religious imagery surrounded her, images of crucifixions and rebirth, of sin, of submission and of redemption.

Then it came to her. The thought that had been lingering in her mind for months, the thought she had suppressed, the thought that was almost too terrible to contemplate, too enormous to even comprehend.

The seduction of Richard was an attack against God himself, a first strike in the war that she would inevitably find herself in.

Richard moaned underneath her, and she felt a wave of pleasure run through her. Excitement coursed through her veins as terrible and daunting thoughts rushed through her mind.

Richard was one of God's people, a foot soldier for the almighty, and here she was, turning him to her side and strengthening her own forces at the expense of God's.

She felt him begin to spasm underneath her with pleasure. Her own body shuddered in response as another wave of pleasure ran through her.

With a single act of carnal lust she felt she was throwing down the gauntlet to God, firing a shot across his bows inside his own domain that told him to watch out, that she was coming for him. There was no rational thought, no great plan, just the overwhelming acceptance that confrontation was inevitable, that perhaps she even held mankind's future in her hand, and that this moment was the start.

Richard shook more and more. Nathalie knew both their orgasms were imminent. Slowing down slightly she took his hands and held them against her breasts. His touch felt electric on her skin.

"You're mine now, aren't you?" she said between moans of

pleasure.

"Oh yes, yes, I am," he shouted before his body collapsed into a shuddering, screaming incoherent mess. Nathalie's eyes closed and she smiled at his words, savouring her success before she joined him, exploding in victorious orgasm and collapsing on top of him.

The sun streaming through the windows woke Nathalie early. She sat up and looked around her. She was in Richard's small single bed, her clothes scattered across the floor. Sounds from the kitchen downstairs told her where Richard was.

She cast her mind back to the previous night and smiled broadly. Her time with Richard had been every bit as wonderful as she had hoped it would be and her mind lingered on the detail. Of how they made love on the altar, of how they ran naked across the churchyard in the rain and pitch blackness of the night, clutching their clothes to get to his apartment.

But most of all she remembered her victory.

She swung her legs out of bed and stood up, stretching as the sunlight hit her body and luxuriating for a few seconds in its warmth. She turned and headed out the door, briefly looking at her clothes in a pile on the floor before walking downstairs to the kitchen.

Richard sat at his kitchen table, already dressed in clerical clothing and seemingly showered judging by his wet hair. His face went from surprise to shock to delight as Nathalie walked in and he saw her naked body before him.

"Good morning," he said. Nathalie sat down on his lap, wrapped her arms around his neck and kissed him.

"Good morning," she replied, taking the half eaten piece of toast from his hand and biting off a mouthful.

"Are you staying until later?" he asked. "I have people to see this morning."

"Oh, that's a shame," she replied. "I was hoping we could have a few more hours this morning. My plane leaves again tonight."

"So what now?"

"I'm not asking you to leave your people," she said, "I wouldn't want you to, not until you're ready to."

"Until I'm ready to?" said Richard. "Do you think I will be one day?"

"You have friends back in Munich," she replied, "and we want you back. But we're prepared to wait."

"You and Angela? What about Ian?"

Nathalie smiled and kissed him again. "Oh, I wouldn't worry about Ian, not unless he's a problem for you." She paused for a second. "Is he a problem for you?"

"Let's not rush anything," said Richard, "I only just broke my vows. I'm not sure I'm ready for all three of you, not yet."

"No pressure," said Nathalie.

"When will you be back?"

"Next time I make a trip to the afterlife," she replied, "hopefully in a few weeks."

"Are you going to try to visit Hell?"

Nathalie nodded.

When Nathalie returned to Munich, there was an unmistakeable spring in her step and she was more focused and single minded than ever before. The hugs and kisses she shared with Angela and Ian at the airport quickly led to conversations about the Mormons and Nathalie's further plans.

"This all makes no sense," said Ian. "We have this weird little cult from America that preaches something a bit odd and it costs them their lives?"

"There's a secret there, something we're missing," Nathalie replied. "And neither evaluators nor angels know what it is."

"Do you think you can go over their heads?" asked Angela.

"Exactly," Nathalie replied. "Someone must be in charge of Hell, every legend says that. Maybe he can help me."

"You know, the guardian of Hell, whatever legend you go to, tends not to be known for being helpful," said Ian.

"We only have God's word for that," Nathalie replied, "and that hasn't exactly been correct about anything else, has it?"

"Still, it's a hell of a risk," said Ian, "what if you get trapped there?"

"I don't think that'll happen," Angela said. "There's nothing special about the afterlife, it all seems to be in this universe, and

Hell and Heaven are probably the same. If we can come back from the Gates, we can probably come back from Hell."

"I hope you're right," said Ian.

"Either way, I'm taking precautions," Nathalie said.

"Precautions? What precautions?" asked Angela.

"I need you to get me a handgun," was Nathalie's reply. The suggestion came as a shock to both Ian and Angela.

"You want to go there armed?" asked Ian.

"I think it should be standard procedure," said Nathalie. "The angels are dangerous, we've already had a few close encounters, maybe it's time we stopped taking risks."

"Are you sure?" asked Ian.

"Yes, I am." Nathalie turned to Angels. "Can you get me one?"

"Well, this isn't America," she replied, "but it isn't Britain either. It'll take some time."

"How long?"

"I have a few contacts that'll help me sort out the permits, so give me a couple of weeks," Angela replied.

"In time for Susan and David's next visit?" Nathalie asked.

"Less than four weeks," Angela replied. "Yes, I should manage that."

"Look, are we sure this is what we want to do?" asked Ian. "It seems like a bloody big risk to take."

"I know what you mean," said Nathalie, "but we need the protection. Besides, plenty of people must die with a gun in their hand, so it won't exactly mark us out as anything unusual."

"And what do you think will happen if we go in shooting?" Ian asked.

"I'll go in and see," said Angela, "and I'll take David. If we're both armed, we'll be able to cover each other's backs."

"What the hell," said Ian, "are we planning on going to war?"

"If need be," said Nathalie. "Let's not kid ourselves here, when our death comes we're going to Hell, and that's me being optimistic. I don't intend to just stand around and let it happen."

"So we go in and kill angels?" said Ian. "We saw where that got Daryl."

"Daryl was crazy," said Angela, "but you may be right. For now let's just carry weapons for protection."

"Ian, I understand your objections," said Nathalie, "but we have to be together in this. If you disagree, I'll go unarmed." Ian sat back in his seat, thinking through what they were discussing. Eventually he reached the same inescapable conclusion.

"Okay, we carry weapons," he said, "but I don't like it."

"So how was Richard," Angela asked.

"More agreeable than last time," Nathalie answered as a smile crept across her face at the memory.

"So did you...?" asked Ian.

"Yes," she replied, "on the altar."

Angela and Ian let out an audible sound of surprise.

"Well, I guess that means he's not to loyal to the church anymore," said Ian.

"He's still loyal to his congregation," said Nathalie. "I think he feels he can help save them."

"Can we persuade him otherwise?" Ian asked.

"Let's see what I find out in Hell," she replied. "If things are drastically different from what we're expecting, then maybe saving them won't be so important."

"How so?" Ian asked.

"Well, if Hell isn't all damnation and torture, or Heaven isn't paradise, maybe saving them won't be so important," Nathalie replied.

"Well, that's what we find out next," said Angela.

Lying in bed, sandwiched between the arms of Ian and Angela, Nathalie struggled to sleep. Sex with the two had been magical that night, but her thoughts lingered on her conversations with Richard and her imminent return to the Gates. It was all she could think of now.

She shivered slightly as Angela moved in her sleep, brushing her hand against Nathalie's shoulder. Angela looked peaceful and beautiful in her sleep to Nathalie, but everything felt like a distraction now. She needed her familiar spot, her old haunt where she used to sit and contemplate everything.

Slowly she eased herself out of bed, moving cautiously and slowly, avoiding wakening her two sleeping lovers. The bedroom door opened with only the gentlest of creaks, and Nathalie snuck out of it, leaving Angela and Ian alone. She silently walked up the stairs, heading for her old apartment, and the balcony she had lingered on so many times before.

Stepping onto the balcony brought back so many recent memories. The glow of Munich on the horizon, the warm autumnal air on her body, all of it reminded her of the times she had stood here and pondered everything that they were doing. Now she found herself thinking about her next step and the danger they were all in.

First her mind was drawn to the wider picture. By starting on this route, there was no doubt in Nathalie's mind she had condemned them all. Angela, Ian, Richard, everyone who joined them faced a bleak future. An unknown damnation was one thing but she knew they now faced apparent oblivion. Did she have the right to take others down this path?

Once she may have had doubts, but no more. She had always believed truth was preferable to ignorance, no matter how painful, and she knew the others felt the same. Besides, as a former atheist, she had never feared the presumed non-existence that followed death, how was this any different?

She now saw God as a tyrant, as no better than a petty dictator, ruling those weaker than him with an iron grip. And she knew such men had to be fought, sometimes at a perilous price.

She sighed as a gentle wind swept over her. The thought that had been eating away at her since the death of Daryl was no longer avoided in her mind. Fighting God, taking arms against the almighty himself could be an inevitable path they would all have to take. But how could she fight God without knowing what he was?

She heard a noise from downstairs and her thoughts changed.

Ian. Richard. Angela. Who did she love? And how did she love them? She longed to be in Richard's bed right now, but the touch of Angela and Ian had been delightful tonight. Could it be that Susan was right, that she loved all three of them equally, even if not in quite the same way?

She heard a footstep behind her. She knew right away it was Ian and her heart skipped a beat. Richard evaporated from her thoughts in an instant.

"Nathalie," came Ian's voice from behind her. "Are you okay?"

"I'm fine," she replied as he wrapped his arms around her from behind. His very touch made her shiver.

"We missed you when you were away," he replied, "it's never the same when you're not here."

"I know what you mean," she replied as she turned to face him in their embrace. "I had Richard for company, but I so wanted you two there as well."

"I wish we could have been with you too," he replied.

"You? With Richard?" replied Nathalie.

"Yes" he replied. "In fact, I have a little confession to make in that regard." He smiled as he said it, raising his eyebrows slightly.

"Oh? What?" replied Nathalie, returning his smile.

"I find myself thinking about him," he replied. "Remember what Susan said after Daryl died, about how this goes beyond any normal relationship?"

Nathalie nodded.

"Well it's taken a long time to admit it to myself," he continued, "but I can't deny it. I've even fantasised about it."

"About the two of you, you and Richard?"

Ian nodded and smiled.

"What's brought this on?" asked Nathalie. "You never seemed into that kind of thing before."

"I guess I just needed time. And then when you went away to see him, I found myself hoping he'd come back, that maybe the three of us could take him to bed and give him a special welcome, if you know what I mean."

"Mmm..." replied Nathalie, "that does sound fun. Although I rather like the idea of watching the two of you together." He smiled broadly at the suggestion and she pushed him back gently onto the bench that sat on the balcony. He dropped down onto it and she knelt astride him and lowered herself onto him. Ian moaned gently as he felt himself enter her. Both wrapped their arms around each other tightly as they sat there, gently rocking back and forth.

"Now tell me what else you want to do," she whispered in his ear, "and with who." Ian didn't answer. Instead he breathed heavily, panting with each gentle rock of Nathalie's body against his.

"I think he likes you too," she whispered in his ear, gently nibbling it as she did so. "At least enough that he didn't dismiss the suggestion." She felt a spasm through her from Ian's body.

"I thought so," he replied, "I hoped so anyway. I'm a bit nervous at the idea though."

"That's okay," Nathalie replied, "there's no pressure, only do what you want."

"Thanks," he replied, his voice now trembling with pleasure. "I have a few decades to fight against of everyone telling me how bad men like that are."

"We'll help you get over it," said Nathalie. She embraced him tightly and began to rock back and forth a little faster. She heard Ian pant as she increased the speed of their lovemaking.

"How about if we watch you too, and maybe help a little," said Nathalie softly into his ear. As she said it, their eyes met, and Ian reached orgasm in an instant, the mental image of what Nathalie had suggested too overpowering for him. Crushing his face into her breasts with her embrace, she couldn't help but giggle slightly.

As a few moments passed, Ian collapsed on the bench, lying back with Nathalie still on top of him. She watched him as he lay there, breathing heavily, seemingly oblivious to the world.

"So then, you, me, Angela and Richard," she said. "How about it?"

"We belong together," he replied, "we're all in this as one." Nathalie smiled and leaned forward to kiss him.

"Then let's go back to Angela."

Chapter 18

Ian, Nathalie and Angela all stared at the box on the table with nervousness. None of them had ever held a gun before and now there was one right in front of them, and no one wanted to be the first to pick it up.

For once it was not Angela who would show leadership as Nathalie stepped forward and opened the box. Sitting inside the foam interior sat an automatic handgun, with two magazines packed beside it and she immediately reached in to remove it.

She felt the weight of it in her hand, then picked up a magazine and slammed it in.

"It's light, feels okay in the hand," she said as she released the slide stop with a loud click, trying to sound like she knew what she was talking about.

"Well, let's go try it out," said Angela as she turned towards the door. The other two followed her as she walked down the stairs to the basement, into a room Ian had prepared with padded walls.

"This should be safe enough for practise," said Ian, "although I've never used a gun, so I don't really know for sure." Angela and Nathalie gave each other a cautious glance. "However, everything's pretty soft," he continued. "There's padding over soft wood, so there shouldn't be any ricochets."

"Go on, take a shot," said Angela as she moved to stand behind Nathalie.

"Just remember to be really careful," said Ian. "Always point it either up or down, unless you're firing it at the target."

"You mean like this?" said Nathalie as she pointed it at the wall and emptied the magazine.

"Fuck me," said Ian as he held his hands against his ears. "That's bloody loud." Nathalie hit the magazine release button and it fell to the ground. She felt empowered by the gun, her confidence boosted by the strength it gave her.

"Well, we don't need to fear the angels again," Angela said as she stared at the smoking hole in the wall opposite her.

"David and Susan arrive in three days," Nathalie replied. "I'll be ready to go to Hell when they get here."

"Are you sure you're ready for it?" asked Ian.

"As long as I have this," said Nathalie, indicating the gun, "then I'm not scared of Satan."

"Just don't get carried away," said Angela.

"Don't worry, I won't," she replied as she left the room with her head held that little bit higher. Ian and Angela exchanged a nervous look as they followed her out.

That night it was Ian who couldn't sleep, and like Nathalie he found himself standing on the balcony, staring out at the glow of the lights of Munich. Nathalie's new found confidence and drive troubled him, and he found himself worried about her safety.

He wasn't alone.

"You too?" came Angela's voice from behind him as she stepped up beside him, placing a hand by his on the balcony's hand rail.

"Richard seems to have given her confidence," he replied. "I don't know what they talked about, but it changed her."

"For the better or worse?"

"I don't know," was his answer. "I mean I know we have to take this next step, but carrying a gun? Fine, she wants it for protection, but if it gives her too much confidence, she might do something stupid."

"We have to trust her. She's never done anything rash before."

"Yes she has, remember Daryl's death?"

Angela nodded.

"She went straight in and bloody dissected him in front of everyone."

"We learnt a lot from that," Angela said. "It was the right thing to do."

"No, it wasn't. We might have gotten away with it, but it was a hell of a risk drawing attention to ourselves like that. If we go one time too many, they might start to recognise us."

"We're not going to do this by hiding," Angela replied, "Nathalie saw an opportunity and took it."

"I know, I know, it's just she seems different. More focused."

"None of this would have been possible without her," said Angela, "I trust her completely."

"Or you," Ian replied, "you funded it all."

"And who had all the ideas for experiments? Who persuaded Richard to come over? It's taken the three of us to get this far. We're a team, an unbreakable partnership."

"I just don't want something else to break the partnership." Angela smiled and put her arm around him.

"I'm worried about her too," she said. "I love her as well. But getting ourselves judged is the next logical step. We have to see what's on the other side of the Gates."

"I just don't want to lose her."

"We won't," Angela replied, holding him slightly tighter, "she's a tough one. I pity the angel that tries to stand in her way."

"She'll blow his brains out then dissect him," he replied, laughing, but the laughter tailed off to a moment of awkward silence.

"She probably would, wouldn't she" replied Angela. Ian didn't reply. He didn't have to. They both knew it was true.

Three days later Nathalie lay on the board in the departure lounge, the gun in a holster beneath her left armpit. She steadied her nerves and Ian and Angela did up the straps while Susan inserted the line into her hand, ready to administer the anaesthetic.

"Now Nathalie," said Susan as she worked on Nathalie's hand, "as we discussed, I'll be giving you a lighter sedative this time, it'll prevent you feeling any pain, but it might not put you completely under." Nathalie nodded in response. "And it should help you recover more quickly than if you're all doped up," Susan added.

"Then let's go," said Nathalie.

"All ready here," said Ian as he finished the final strap. He turned and nodded to David, who stood by the main switch, ready to drop Nathalie into the tank.

"You ready for your drugs?" said Susan.

"Yes, do it," came Nathalie's reply.

"Okay, here we go then." Susan pushed the plunger down on the syringe in Nathalie's hand, and everything went blank.

Nathalie's eyes opened after what seemed like an instant and she felt the now-familiar floating sensation as she arrived once again at the Gates. She quickly jumped to her feet and looked around. The new arrivals seemed few and far between this time. Her breath quickened slightly with excitement at the thought that this might work.

"Welcome Nathalie," said a familiar voice from behind her. She turned to see two angels, standing there with their usual bland smiles. She patted the underside of her jacket to check she had the gun before she went any further.

"Well, let's go," she said enthusiastically as she felt the shape of her gun in its holster. The angels looked at her in surprise. "It's this way, isn't it?" she said, pointing to the area a few others were walking to. The angels nodded, looking slightly confused.

She immediately set off, almost at a running pace for the evaluation lines. Not wanting to waste any time she pushed her way to the front of the shortest queue she could find before the angels could even catch up with her.

"Just send me to Hell now," she said to the angel at the head of the queue. "I've never loved any god, so I'm screwed, just send me down now."

"Are you sure?" asked the angel, now with a puzzled look on his face.

"Absolutely, I always hated the bastard," was her reply. The angel's eyes narrowed coldly and with a gesture of his hand she felt herself consumed by fire and darkness took her. The ground seemed to fall away underneath her and she felt herself plummet down, alone and in complete darkness.

How long she fell she did not know, but the end of it came not with a hard impact but a slow deceleration to a stop that left her standing on solid ground. The darkness and fire that enveloped her cleared in an instant and a dull light filled her eyes.

Before her stretched a seemingly endless mountain range, with sharp, jagged peaks extending as far as the eye could see. Dark clouds seemed to fill the sky above her, extending almost all the way to the horizon, where the golden glow of what seemed like a setting sun silhouetted the mountains and brought the only light to her surroundings. She seemed to be standing on the side of one of the mountains, surrounded by this barren landscape.

"Hello Nathalie," came a voice from behind her. She spun round to see who had spoken and before her stood what she assumed was another angel. He was tall, she would have guessed almost three metres, and he had a hardened look to him, quite different to the effeminate smiling faces of the angels at the Gates.

"Who are you?" she shouted as her hand reached inside her jacket.

"My name is Lucifer," he replied. Nathalie pulled the gun and pointed it straight at him.

"Don't fucking think of anything," she snarled, "I've been dead a few times now and I know you people can die." Lucifer slowly dropped to one knee and held out his open palms.

"Do you think I would hurt you?" he asked.

"Isn't that what you do?" she said. "Torture the damned." Lucifer smiled a sad smile.

"No, it is not," he replied, "but I know that's what they say about me, Nathalie."

"How do you know my name?" she asked.

"I know everything about you," he replied.

"How?"

"When you were judged, the angel absorbed all your knowledge, and all the angels absorbed it as well. I must admit though, you seemed keen to come down here, most people would do anything to avoid it."

"Is that why you've come to meet me?"

"Yes. Attitudes like yours are rare to say the least."

"And now you know everything about me?" she said nervously. "And the angels do as well?"

"Yes, but it takes time to process. Is this a problem for you?"

"You tell me," she replied, "once you realise how I died and what I've been doing for the last year." Lucifer gave her a strange glance then seemed to stare into space for a few seconds. A look of stunned horror crossed his face.

"I see what you mean," he said. "How much time do you have?"

"Minutes usually. Why?"

"Listen very carefully to me Nathalie," he said. "Almost everything you think you know about God and the universe is not true. Let me try and explain."

"Better make it quick," she replied as she cautiously lowered the gun.

"This world is the third stage of human development," he began. "You spend nine months in the womb, then a number of years on Earth before you die and come here. Think of the Earth as God's womb, but God is only one of billions of other people, and each person has their own star and planetary system to gestate their young."

"So there's life on other planets?" she asked.

"Yes, on billions of them," he replied.

"So where is this? Are we in the same universe?"

"It would be more accurate to say that your universe exists within this one. We're governed by the same laws of physics here, although your people won't have discovered the physics surrounding the form of energy that binds you and other objects to the Earth until you die."

"So what happens when you die here?" she asked.

"You die," he replied, "and beyond that we know nothing, like you used to know nothing of here."

"So is God a person like us? What does he look like?"

"God looks like us, has two arms, two legs, a head. You are all made in God's image."

"Wait, you mean we didn't evolve over billions of years?"

"Oh no," he replied, "God's only been procreating for around ten thousand years."

"You mean Creationists are right?" exclaimed Nathalie. "The Earth is that young?"

"Yes, they are quite correct."

"But...but, what about geology, and fossils, and evolution?" said a confused Nathalie.

"Oh them," he said, rolling his eyes. "God wanted to screen out the thinkers and intellectuals from the blindly devoted, and so spent a long time setting up the planet so it looked old and that you had evolved from other creatures. God put a lot of work into it creating this illusion, it almost took a whole week."

"Are you saying he made the Earth in six days?" she asked.

"Well, all of the geology and fossils were faked in six days."

"So there was an Adam and Eve in the Garden of Eden?"

"There were many 'Gardens of Eden'," Lucifer replied, "all across the Earth. There was one in what you now call Lebanon, another in America, in Missouri, another on the plateau of Rannoch Moor in Scotland and others across the world."

"So God planted different races of humans across the globe about ten thousand years ago?"

"Correct."

"And the universe? How old's that?"

"Oh, that's much older," Lucifer replied, "billions of years old."

Nathalie breathed a sigh of relief.

"Well I'm glad that science got something right," she replied. "But none of this is in the Bible."

"I know," replied Lucifer, "God does not want you to know these things. However, I did explain it once to someone like yourself."

"Like myself, you mean they went back?"

"Yes, many years ago, when people being revived from death was much less common than now," he replied, "a man came here who began to quiz me, much like you did. He was curious about the universe and I began to explain it to him, but he returned before I finished."

"Do you know what happened to him?" Nathalie asked.

"I had hoped he would tell the world, and in a manner of speaking, he did."

"He can't have been successful," she replied.

"He took the information and based a religion on it, but he did not quite get it all right."

"Wait a minute," said Nathalie as something clicked in her brain, "this man, was his name Joseph Smith?"

"Yes, that was him."

"He founded the Mormons, an offshoot of Christianity," Nathalie replied. "They're generally considered to be a bit crazy, although most people also think they're harmless."

"God does not agree," said Lucifer.

"Of course, they're killed on sight aren't they?" said Nathalie. "I've seen it happen."

"Their knowledge is incomplete, but dangerous to God," said Lucifer.

"Tell me more about God," she said, changing the subject. Lucifer shook his head sadly, giving Nathalie a sinking feeling in her stomach.

"When you arrive here, you should be taken out into the world, to the place where your new life begins. There should be no selection, no demands of proof of belief in or love of God. But God is a truly disturbed individual. God wants to lock all you children away, to demand their worship and do God's every bidding. If God can turn your mind while you're growing on Earth, then it's obvious you can be kept as a slave here as well. Those who don't worship God get thrown down here to rot."

"So who are you?" she asked.

"I was," said Lucifer before he paused for a second, "a friend, a long time ago, since long before all this started," he replied, "but I discovered what was really going on I tried to put a stop to it. When I threatened to inform the authorities about what was happening I woke up one day and found myself down here. Somehow God had trapped me in my sleep."

"Where is here?"

"It's difficult to describe," he said, "but I guess it's analogous to being thrown in a dungeon in your world."

"So God is actually my parent and he's one of those nutters that lock their kids in the basement for years."

Lucifer looked at her with a blank look for a few seconds as his mind filtered through her memories. "Yes, that would be an accurate analogy," he replied, "well almost."

"So those who do worship, they get to leave I take it?"

"I cannot say for sure, but I doubt it. I do not know what God does with them."

"Is there any way to escape from here?"

"Not once you're completely dead and sent down here," he replied. "But that is not what you should be worried about right now."

"Oh no?" she replied.

"No, your biggest problem right now is that God will soon know what you're doing, and it'll be obvious that's a threat."

"I'm a threat?" she asked incredulously.

"Yes. You've learnt how to travel at will between your world and this one. And you know the truth about God. You've also probably realised that if you can avoid judgement then there's no way you can be forcibly removed from the Gates."

"The thought had occurred to me, in fact we've actively avoided being judged until now," she replied. Nathalie pondered his words for a few seconds. "If knowing this is a threat, does it mean we can achieve something by fighting back at the Gates?"

"Exactly," replied Lucifer, "The Gates are the doorway from your world to this one, and the buffer between Heaven and Hell. If you were to take control of the Gates, you could strike a serious blow. God will want to do something about that threat."

"What can he do?" she replied. "I'm assuming he's not as omnipotent as people claim."

"God's influence on the Earth is minimal, but very blunt. The power to shape your world, to cause earthquakes, maybe even to hurl things at it still exists, but nothing precise."

"He causes earthquakes?"

"God has wiped out entire regions with earthquakes if they don't measure up, such as the ancient Minoans who cast aside any belief in deities, but it's a power that must be used sparingly. The Earth is a fragile place given all the changes that've been made to it."

"How ironic," she replied. "The old clich is that why do earthquakes happen if God exists, and it turns out they're his way of performing abortions."

"Nathalie, I don't think you realise the danger you are in," he said gravely. "Within a few moments angels will realise what you've been doing. They'll know where you're based and who is involved. Your life is in immediate danger. Expect a massive earthquake where you are within minutes of waking up."

"Why am I a threat?" she asked. "How is it possible to fight back?"

"As long as you don't let yourself be judged and sent down here you can fight. Once in here, you're locked away until you return to Earth. You must avoid this at all cost."

"Is there any way to escape, or to free the people here?" she asked.

"The door to Hell is the Gates, and just like a door in your world it could be broken down if you had enough power."

"Power, what do you mean power?" asked Nathalie.

"There is a physical barrier that separates what you call the Gates from Heaven and Hell. Do not be deceived by the flames and lights when someone is judged, that is just there for effect. If you have the means you can break them down, and you could free anyone from either place."

"Means?" said Nathalie. "Do you mean we can physically blow the doorway to Heaven and Hell open?"

"It's possible, but it will take a powerful explosion," he replied. "But if you can do it, we have many people here who would like revenge on God."

"How many do you have in here?" she asked.

"Nathalie, in this world, barring accidents, you can live forever. Your body does not age here."

"That would mean you have a few billion people," she replied.

"And so does God."

"So I need an army," she said. Lucifer smiled.

"Nathalie, we have an army. There are billions of people here, willing to fight, angry at thousands of years of captivity. But yes, first you need your own army to break open the door to Hell. If many people came at once with the same purpose you could be a formidable threat." Nathalie's mind began to race with thoughts and possibilities she had been pondering for weeks. Could she form an army? Was it actually possible to fight God?

"Is there any way you can help me?" she asked. Lucifer nodded and stepped closer to her, holding his hand out.

"Nathalie, I can share some knowledge with you," he said, "information that will make things easier for you."

"Information?" she replied, "What do you mean?"

"We haven't been idle down here," he replied, "and we have some of the best scientific minds from your history down here that have been working on ideas to help someone like you."

"Ideas? Such as?"

"Such as this," he said and touched Nathalie's forehead. Nathalie winced as what felt like a bright light burnt its way through her head. After a few seconds had passed it ended and Nathalie found her brain was suddenly full of information. It overwhelmed her and she fought to put it aside until she had more time to consider it.

"Can I find you again if I have more questions?" she asked.

"They'll be waiting for you now they know you," he said, "so if you need to contact me, you need to send someone else, someone you haven't met yet, your other people will now be known to them as well. They'll kill you all on sight now."

"So what....," began Nathalie, but she felt dizziness began to take her. She knew it was time to return.

"Remember Nathalie," said Lucifer, "God wants you dead. An earthquake is the most likely form of attack, and it is coming, perhaps in a minute, perhaps in an hour. Be ready for it if you can. What I just did to you means you should wake up faster because I've stimulated your brain, perhaps you might even wake up almost immediately despite any drugs you've been given, but once you're awake you have to move quickly"

And with those words in her ears, she returned to the darkness.

She woke up screaming. Susan leapt back in surprise as Nathalie jumped up, panting and sweating. Nathalie turned to Angela and Ian with a look of terror in her eyes.

"He knows. He's coming for us," said Nathalie as she began to climb out of the bed. Susan moved to try and restrain her, but Nathalie was not going to be held down without a fight.

"Who?" asked Angela.

"God is, he's sending an earthquake for us," she said as she pulled the leads from her chest. Everyone else looked at each other in confusion. Nathalie staggered dizzily across the room, reaching out to Ian who caught her in his arms as Angela wrapped a blanket around her naked body.

"Get me out of here, out of the building right now," she said as she grasped his lapels. He nodded in reply and scooped her up in his arms. He turned and headed for the door with her while Angela followed close behind.

"Get David!" Nathalie shouted to Susan as she was carried away, "and get out of here."

Almost immediately they felt the ground begin to shake. The walls around them crumbled and the sound of falling debris could be heard from outside.

"Hurry!" screamed Angela as the two of them ran for the door while Nathalie, still weak and fragile from her near death experience, continued to huddle in Ian's arms.

As they cleared the door the intensity of the shaking seemed to increase. Ian and Angela were thrown to the ground and Nathalie fell from Ian's arms and rolled down the grassy slope by the house towards the swimming pool. As her tumble came to a rest she turned to look back at the house. She could see Ian and Angela were clear of the building, but there was no sign of Susan or David. Discarding the blanket she pulled herself to her feet and began to walk back, somehow hoping she'd be able to see that they'd escaped the building. Each step was a struggle with the shuddering earth, each movement closer to the house a sheer force of Nathalie's will to help her friends.

All hopes were dashed as the front wall of the building collapsed. She caught a last glimpse of Susan running for the door as falling masonry from the corridor collapsed, hitting Susan on the back and knocking her to the ground. Susan raised her hand as if to beg for help but a concrete block toppled and landed on her head. Nathalie fell to her knees in horror. It was clear to her that Susan was dead.

Then the whole building went. It crumpled on the inside first as the core of the building gave way, pulling the walls down around it. She thought she briefly saw what she assumed was David's arm as the last of the floors collapsed, but then he was gone, buried in the rubble.

She fell to the ground, weak, shivering and naked on the wet grass. She closed her eyes and wanted it all to end, but almost immediately she realised that death no longer had the finality she once thought it had. Weakness gave way to anger. Cold gave way to courage. She pulled herself to her feet and stared at the sky.

"You motherfucker!" she screamed with all her strength. "You think you can get me! I'm fucking coming for you! I'll kill you, you and all your followers!" She felt her knees start to buckle but she held herself firm, refusing to show weakness. "I'm fucking coming back, and I'm coming back for you!"

She could only resist weakness for so long, and again she fell to her knees. As she sat there fighting for breath on all fours she saw the figures of Ian and Angela run towards her, staggering slightly on the still shaking ground. Ian went to put the blanket around her but she cast it off in anger. She looked up at them, her eyes ablaze with a fire they had never seen before.

"We have an army to build," said Nathalie, "and a god to destroy. Are you with me?" Ian and Angela glanced at each other first, then down at Nathalie.

"Yes," they said in unison. Nathalie pulled herself to her feet and turned to look north. In the distance, beyond the trees, they could see smoke rising from Munich. The whole city seemed to have been consumed by the earthquake.

"How many people just died," she said as she stared into the distance. "All because of me?"

"Because of you?" asked Ian.

"When I was judged, God learnt everything about us. This was the only thing he could do to try and stop us."

"He'd kill thousands to stop us?" Ian asked.

"We're a threat," she said, "but that bastard doesn't know how big a threat he's just unleashed." Nathalie closed her eyes as her brain began to process the knowledge Lucifer had given her. She could see mathematical equations, physical concepts, all kinds of information flashing through her mind. She did not yet realise it, but if she was to turn from her course, she would be the equal of any Nobel Prize winning physicist, such was the information in her mind. She understood complicated mathematical techniques, and the physics of the whole universe opened up to her, physics that went beyond anything measurable in this world.

Then she saw what Lucifer had given her, what she could now do and how dangerous she now was to God.

"We have to split up," she said as she turned and began walking towards the garage. It had survived the earthquake unscathed, and she pulled the doors open and strode in.

"Split up, why?" asked Angela as she followed Nathalie.

"I have something to do," Nathalie replied as she opened the boot of Angela's car. She began to rummage around in the suitcase, looking for clothes. She quickly found them and pulled them on.

"What is it, can't we help you?" said Ian.

"No, you need to get as far away from me as you can, at least until I can set up a new base," Nathalie replied. "Take your car Ian, and the two of you should head to Richard. Stay there and stay hidden, he'll look after you until I'm ready to contact you."

"You're making no sense," said Ian.

"I've been given information," she replied, "information that makes me dangerous. I need to disappear, if anyone recognises me and dies, God knows where I am. Until I'm ready to fight back, we need to be separate, so if he kills me, you can both continue." Nathalie, now dressed, turned to the safe on the wall. She opened it and took her passport, a handful of cash and several credit cards.

"Where are you going?" asked Angela.

"I won't say for now," she replied, "but I have something to do, something that could cost a lot of money." Nathalie's eyes fixed on Angela. The cold stare of determination convinced Angela to follow Nathalie's lead, and to trust her. Angela stepped forward and embraced Nathalie, kissing her and holding her tightly.

"I love you," Angela said, "and I'll do what you say, wherever this leads." Both women turned to Ian, who joined the embrace.

"Now listen to me very carefully," said Nathalie. "If anything happens to me, you must continue this. Find another doctor and someone else willing to make the trip and get them judged and sent to Hell. Lucifer will give you what you need to carry on the fight. Do not go yourself. They'll be waiting for you."

"I don't understand," said Ian.

"Neither do I, at least not yet," said Nathalie, "but I'm figuring it out, and there's somewhere I need to go, something I need to do, and until I do it, it's not safe to be near me." Ian and Angela glanced at each other nervously, each looking for comfort in the others face but finding none. "I'll take your car," said Nathalie, indicating Angela's car. "We should both head south first to avoid the earthquake, Munich looks in ruins." Ian and Angela nodded. "But we split up as soon as possible," Nathalie continued. "You head west along the front of the Alps, I'll head elsewhere."

Nathalie exchanged one more lingering kiss and embrace with Ian and Angela before she turned away and into the car. Leaving them was as painful as anything she had ever done in her life, but she had a purpose now in her life, one she would not turn from.

She gave a last wave to her two lovers as she drove the car towards the forest road, and then she was gone.

Chapter 19

Sitting at the back of the plane Nathalie looked out of the window as it climbed away from Salzburg Airport. Far on the horizon she could see the smoke rising from the remains of Munich and she closed her eyes and tried not to think of her friends, down there somewhere, trying to get to safety.

Images slowly came to her head as her mind settled. The true nature of reality, of physics beyond anything comprehended in this world, had been revealed to her and step by step her brain was putting it together. The information given to her by Lucifer was going to change everything.

She smiled as another piece of the puzzle fell into place. The old way of freezing and reviving someone seemed as old fashioned to her as the methods of a medieval doctor who used leeches and drained blood. She had a new way of doing it now thanks to her new knowledge. It would not be easy or cheap, not using the resources of this world, but she could see how it could be done.

I have a lot of work to do, she thought as more images flashed through her head, images that revealed more and more detail of the laws controlling this world and the next, and of how they could be merged together.

She opened her eyes and looked out the window again. Munich seemed to be receding into the distance. She was leaving it behind, leaving all of Europe behind for her new destination. She needed an army, and there was only one place she could get it.

She closed her eyes again and thought back to the events of the past year. She had no more questions. She knew almost everything she wanted to know about the next world, and those answers had set her on a new path.

The time of exploration was over. Now there would come a time of war.

Also available:

Promoted Beyond Glory (series) by Stuart Pitsligo

and

The World Naked Bike Ride by Richard Foley

Naturist Red in Tooth and Claw by Stuart Pitsligo

One, Two, Free! by Anita and Wolfgang Gramer

Why Nude? by Howard Anderson

Romance Scam by Brigitte Schmid

for these and other interesting books connect with us online:

http://pub.rfi.net

Made in the USA
Monee, IL
28 April 2026